A WOMAN OF INDEPENDENT MEANS

*A Woman*

VIKING

ELIZABETH FORSYTHE HAILEY

*of Independent Means*

VIKING
Published by the Penguin Group
Penguin Books USA Inc., 375 Hudson Street, New York, New York 10014, U.S.A.
Penguin Books Ltd, 27 Wrights Lane, London W8 5TZ, England
Penguin Books Australia Ltd, Ringwood, Victoria, Australia
Penguin Books Canada Ltd, 10 Alcorn Avenue, Toronto, Ontario, Canada M4V 3B2
Penguin Books (N.Z.) Ltd, 182–190 Wairau Road, Auckland 10, New Zealand

Penguin Books Ltd, Registered Offices: Harmondsworth, Middlesex, England

This edition first published in 1995 by
Viking Penguin, a division of Penguin Books USA Inc.

1 3 5 7 9 10 8 6 4 2

PUBLISHER'S NOTE
This is a work of fiction. Names, characters, places, and incidents either are the product
of the author's imagination or are used fictitiously, and any resemblance to actual persons,
living or dead, events, or locales is entirely coincidental.

ISBN 0-670-86604-0

LIBRARY OF CONGRESS CATALOGING IN PUBLICATION DATA AVAILABLE

This book is printed on acid-free paper.
∞
Printed in the United States of America
Set in Videocomp Garamond

*for my grandmother*
*whose life inspired these letters*
*and for my husband*
*who inspired me*

Dear Reader,

When I started writing *A Women of Independent Means* in the mid-seventies, I was a young wife and mother, happily married but caught up in the ferment of feminine unrest. The year my younger daughter Brooke started nursery school, I began to feel that everyone in the family had somewhere to go each day, their own work, their own friends. Everyone but me.

One day I announced to my husband that I was going to write a novel, my first novel, and I was calling it "Letters from a Runaway Wife." He was not amused—and assured me runaway wives were a passing fad and would be history before I had time to finish a first draft. "Why don't you write about a woman who didn't have to leave home to be liberated?" he suggested. "A woman like your grandmother."

I thought about it overnight and decided he was right. The only part of my original idea I kept was the letter form, which seemed perfectly suited to my character. Letters are a very dramatic device, spanning time, eliminating the need for narrative description, and, most important, enlisting the imagination of the reader to supply the offstage action. I also wanted to write a novel my playwright husband would read. Like most dramatists who are challenged by the strict economy of the stage, he was impatient with prose.

Though not a heroine by any historical standards, my grandmother had challenged the conventions of her time, and her saga was a portrait in miniature of the broad changes in American life over the twentieth century. Using the large events of her life as a framework, I tried to imagine the letters she might have written from childhood to old age and to show how full of drama even a seemingly ordinary life can be.

There were no real letters. The only written records she ever kept of her day-to-day activities were her travel diaries; she clearly felt her life was not worth recording unless she was on the move. My best review, however, came from one of her friends, who wrote me shortly after the book was published to say, "How like your grandmother to have kept carbon copies of all her letters!"

At the time I wrote the book, I felt I had been relatively untested by life. The letter describing the train passing through the forest fire and emerging unscathed from the flames reflected my own feelings. My grandmother had survived more tragedies than I would have dared invent for a fictional heroine, and yet her zest for life continued unabated into old age. I hoped that by putting myself through her ordeals, at least in my imagination, I could discover the sources of her strength.

Four years after the book was published my husband was diagnosed with Parkinson's disease, a degenerative illness attacking the nervous system for which there is still no cure. He had struggled with it for ten years when he was told he had inoperable cancer. Less than a year after his death, my mother suffered a massive stroke and remained in a coma from which doctors doubted she would ever emerge. This was a vibrant, well-traveled woman who for her eightieth birthday the year before had bought for herself (and *read*) the new translation of Proust's masterpiece, now retitled in English "In Search of Lost Time." I went home to Dallas, to my first family, embarked on my own search for lost time—and rejoiced in my mother's miraculous return to consciousness.

My sense of renewal was reinforced by the second life my book was experiencing as a television miniseries. I witnessed part of the filming on location in Texas, feeling for the first time rather like a grandmother myself—I could share in the fun without being expected to do any of the work. The climax came when I watched my daughter Brooke—whose attendance at nursery school had started me on the road to writing the book—play me, the oldest grandchild, as a bride. I realized at that moment that my first novel had become a road map into my own future, and the words that echoed in my heart were the ones I had chosen for my fictional heroine as her epitaph: To Be Continued.

*Elizabeth Forsythe Hailey*

A WOMAN OF INDEPENDENT MEANS

December 10, 1899
Honey Grove, Texas

Dear Rob,

I just asked Miss Appleton to put us on the same team for the spelling bee. Since we're the only two people in the fourth grade who can spell "perspicacious," our team is sure to win.

Can you come over after school? The gardener is clearing the hollyhock bed so there will be more room to play tag. It was my idea.

Bess


January 2, 1900
Honey Grove

Dear Rob,

Happy New Century! I wish I could live to see a new millennium (if you don't know what that means, I'll tell you after school).

Can you come over today? I'll show you everything I got for Christmas. I got everything I asked for, but I always do.

Bess


May 30, 1902
Honey Grove

Dear Rob,

Good news! Papa rented his downtown lot to a merry-go-round for the summer. I talked him into taking half the rent in tickets. I'll split my share with you, and we'll ride round and round till time to go back to school.

Bess

February 8, 1906<br>Honey Grove

Dear Rob,

This has been the longest winter of my life. I wish my parents would let you come up to my room when you bring my schoolwork, but everyone knows tuberculosis is contagious.

I am sad to think you will be a grade ahead of me in September. To think I am just fifteen and I have already lost a year of my life! Somehow I will make up for it and then I will never lose another day.

Your Bess

May 1, 1909<br>Mary Baldwin College<br>Staunton, Virginia

Dear Rob,

I have seen enough of the world—or at least the world without you. College is fine but just the beginning of all I want to know. I can continue on my own. Next month I am coming home to stay.

I will be in the front row for your graduation. Please don't accept any job offers until I get there.

Ever your<br>Bess

May 5, 1909<br>Staunton

Dearest Mama,

I will be home in a month, and Rob and I will be married this summer. Please don't say anything to him as I want to be the first to tell him.

I would like to be married in our front parlor. It is more splendid than any church in Honey Grove and I have been happier there. I imagine it will be many years before Rob and I can afford a house as fine, but I want him to know what is expected of him

Your loving daughter,

Bess


May 20, 1909
Staunton

Dearest Papa,

Rest assured my education means even more to me than it does to you. I fully intend to *continue* it but since I never expect to *complete* it, why should I spend any more time at college?

I love Rob and I want to live my life at his side. I know his family has no money and he cannot afford to be married now, but my family does and I can. In the next few years he will be making decisions that will shape the rest of his life. If I plan to share that life—and I do—then I must share those decisions.

Your obedient daughter,

Bess


November 10, 1909
Dallas, Texas

Dearest Mama and Papa,

I miss you very much but even Rob now admits I was right in urging him to move here and go into real estate instead of following in his father's footsteps and teaching in Honey Grove.

Last week Rob sold a big block of property downtown and bought me a horse and surrey to celebrate. Sunday we are joining St. Matthew's Episcopal Cathedral. Please do not consider this decision any reflection on you. I enjoyed being a Methodist in Honey Grove but Dallas offers a wider choice in everything—even churches.

Your devoted daughter,

Bess

April 2, 1910
Dallas

Dearest Mama,

Please forgive this scribble but my hand is still shaking from a dream that seems more real than the daylight which has displaced it.

I was dead and had been for three days, but Rob continued to sit across from me at dinner, sleep beside me through the night, and kiss me good-bye in the morning—without even noticing I had ceased to breathe.

His indifference in the dream so paralyzed me that I pretended to be asleep when he left for the office this morning. He has begun encouraging me to sleep late—I suspect because he prefers breakfast alone with his newspaper. And the dream suggests that in my heart I suspect even more.

Dearest Mama, you asked me the night before my wedding if I had any questions. I didn't then. But now I am filled with them. I won't embarrass you with questions of a physical nature. In that area Rob has provided answers to questions I didn't even know enough to ask. Indeed nothing I had read or imagined prepared me for the physical passion marriage vows can unloose in previously chaste childhood sweethearts. Alone in the dark Rob and I are one—complete and perfect and inseparable—two equal halves of a whole.

It is daylight which disrupts the balance. My bad dreams begin at dawn when he arises for work, leaving me to sleep through the day if I choose. He asks nothing more of me than that I be waiting for his return each night. And I sometimes suspect he would not object if he found me still in bed. He is my whole life day and night, yet by day I become but a fraction of his.

Am I the only wife to feel so wasted, so unused, so alone? I would not put this question to anyone but you, dearest Mama. And indeed I would feel I were betraying Rob by even thinking it if my dreams had not already betrayed my doubts.

Please do not attempt to answer me on paper. I have decided to come for a visit next week so that we can talk at length—and in private. I cannot risk having Rob find out that, far from awakening Sleeping Beauty with his kiss, Prince Charming has put her back to sleep.

I love you and need you,

Bess

April 8, 1910
Honey Grove

Dear Heart,

I am sleeping in my old room where every night I dream you are with me and every morning I wake up alone, aching for you. But even though we are apart, there is a new heartbeat just below my own that joins me to you forever.

I pray my mother will live to see her first grandchild, but she seems to get weaker every day. She has not regained consciousness since I arrived. I must go to her now. If only I could make her understand how much I still need her.

Ever your
Bess


November 15, 1910
Dallas

Dearest Papa,

I just received your letter explaining the terms of Mama's will. I never realized she was a woman of independent means. I always attributed her sense of dignity and self-esteem to a more spiritual source.

Please do not give further thought to how I will handle such a large sum of money. My interest in the subject will compensate for my limited experience.

Please know that I share your loneliness and grief every hour of the day, even though I am busy with my own family. We are looking forward to having you with us next week to share your first grandson's first Thanksgiving.

Your loving daughter,
Bess

January 10, 1911
TO WHOM IT MAY CONCERN:
On this date a loan of $20,000 (twenty thousand dollars) was made to Robert Randolph Steed by his wife, Elizabeth Alcott Steed. To be repaid at the rate of $1,000 (one thousand dollars) a year for twenty years.

Elizabeth Alcott Steed

WITNESSED BY:   Annie Hoffmeyer, housekeeper
Hans Hoffmeyer, gardener

---

*The firm of Florence and Field,*
*Real Estate Investors,*
*takes great pleasure*
*in announcing the partnership of*
*Robert Randolph Steed*
*A reception in his honor*
*will be held at the Dallas Country Club*
*on Sunday, the second of April*
*from three until five in the afternoon*

R.S.V.P.

---

May 1, 1911
Dallas

Board of Directors
Dallas Country Club
Dallas, Texas

Dear Sirs:

Thank you for your prompt attention to our application for membership. Enclosed please find a check covering our initiation fee and the first month's dues.

Sincerely,

Mrs. Robert Randolph Steed

June 10, 1911
Received of Robert Randolph Steed the sum of $1,000 (one thousand dollars). Balance due: $19,000 (nineteen thousand dollars).

Elizabeth Alcott Steed

WITNESSED BY: Annie Hoffmeyer
Hans Hoffmeyer


August 8, 1911
Dallas

Dear Father Steed,

I am sorry to learn of your illness, and I hope you will soon be well enough to resume your place on the school board.

Please allow us to help you and Mother Steed in any way we can. A life devoted to public service has its own rewards, I am sure, but freedom from financial worry is not one of them.

In the two years since we have been married Rob has made a substantial place for himself in the real estate profession. I know you are disappointed he did not follow in your footsteps but had he chosen the field of education, he would have always lived in the shadow of your success and now he enjoys the sunlight of his own.

I trust you are as proud of him as I am—and will tell him so when you see him.

Rob brings with him my love and heartfelt wishes for your recovery.

Bess


September 10, 1911
Dallas

Dear Heart,

How sad to be spending nights in this house without you. I am overwhelmed by its loneliness. However, I realize that your father's estate makes demands that need more immediate attention than mine.

Now that I am again so visibly with child, I am trying to abide by convention and confine my daily circuit to our property. However, it was so beautiful this morning I could not resist taking Robin out in the surrey for a drive along Rawlins Street. To my delight there was a "For Sale" sign on the corner lot we have so often admired. In your absence I felt I had no choice but to make an immediate offer. Fortunately propriety does not prevent a woman in my condition from spending money.

Hurry home, dear heart—to reclaim the legacy of my love.

Ever your

Bess


December 20, 1911
Dallas

Dearest Papa,

We are so pleased you will be spending Christmas with us and bringing Miss Bromley with you. She sounds like a lady of admirable qualities. I visited in Mineola several times as a schoolgirl but the only Bromleys I remember were girls my age. Perhaps your Miss Bromley is an older relative.

Your namesake is doing fine. Even at the age of six weeks he has your dignified manner. He never cries, but his very presence is a command for our total attention. His older brother does not seem the least bit jealous but treats the baby as just one more curiosity in a world which has suddenly become accessible now that he is walking.

I have been meeting almost daily with the architect who is drawing plans for our new house. Building will begin as soon as he agrees with me on the plans—early in the new year, I trust.

A kiss until I see you.

Your devoted daughter,

Bess


January 2, 1912
Dallas

Dear Mavis,

Imagine my surprise when the Miss Bromley my father was escorting turned out to be my croquet partner of so many summers ago.

Watching my father with you, I began to think of him as a contemporary—an unsettling but ultimately rewarding experience. I have never seen him in better spirits and I am convinced the credit goes to you.

I can imagine the talk your friendship is causing in towns the size of Honey Grove and Mineola. To be frank, the disparity in your ages did not go without comment even in a city as large as Dallas, but perhaps that was my fault for planning an evening at the country club. Next time you visit, I expect we would all be more comfortable dining at home.

It was a joy to see you again—and to see my father so happy in your company.

Affectionately,

Bess

January 10, 1912
Received of Robert Randolph Steed the sum of $5,000 (five thousand dollars). Balance due: $14,000 (fourteen thousand dollars).

Elizabeth Alcott Steed

WITNESSED BY:  Annie Hoffmeyer
Hans Hoffmeyer

July 18, 1912
Dallas

Dear Mother Steed,

Our new house is nearly completed, and we hope you will share it. It is larger than the house where I spent my girlhood, but then Dallas is larger than Honey Grove so more is expected of us.

My father's marriage to Mavis Bromley has left me feeling somewhat bereft. I was still very dependent on my mother at the time of her death, and now in a strange way I feel I have lost my father too. This is no reflection on Mavis. I delight in her quick wit and unfailing good humor but there are times when I long for the advice and guidance of an older generation.

We will furnish the guest room to your taste if you will agree to occupy it on a regular basis. You are now the only mother I have left in this world.

Your loving daughter-in-law,

Bess

August 19, 1912
Dallas

Dear Lydia,

Your mother has become a valued member of our household, and we hope she will live here permanently. You have been a devoted daughter but it is the responsibility of a son to care for his parents in their old age, and your Manning should not be thrust into this role by marriage.

How is business at his store? He is such an intelligent, well-spoken man, but accounting cannot come easily to a man with his literary outlook on life. Fortunately, figures have always held a poetic fascination for me.

I hope you and Manning will visit us soon in our splendid new setting.

Fondly,
Bess

October 2, 1912
St. Louis, Missouri

Dear Papa and Mavis,

We have only traveled to St. Louis but I feel I am seeing the world for the first time. I will never be content to stay at home again—at least not for very long at a time. I am twenty-one. A third of my life is over (or maybe just a quarter—I am looking forward to a very long old age), and I am just discovering what a small part of the world Texas is, though you would never know it from living there.

I hope this will be the first of many trips Rob and I make together. I will go with him anywhere—for business or pleasure, though to him business is pleasure, a feeling I am beginning to share.

My love to you both,
Bess

October 3, 1912
St. Louis

Darling Robin and Drew,

Daddy and I miss you so much. We spent this afternoon walking through a beautiful park full of exotic plants and animals. The plants are in a building called the Jewel Box and the animals are in the best zoo I have ever seen. If I were a lion or tiger, I would rather live in the St. Louis Zoo than in the wilds of Africa.

Daddy is doing lots of business here, so we will come again soon and bring you with us. Remember, Robin, you are the man of the house while your father is away, so take good care of your grandmother and your baby brother until we return.

Hugs and kisses,<br>Mummy

October 10, 1912<br>St. Louis

Dear Mother Steed,

You would be so proud to see what a grand impression your son is making on all the important people of this city. He is the kind of man whose business will take him to the ends of the earth before he is through and I ask nothing more of life than to travel there with him.

I have decided to celebrate our return with a formal dinner party at home. Would you please take the enclosed sample to the printer and order fifty engraved invitations. I have left the date blank until you check with the caterer to see if she is available on either October 29 or 30.

Tell Annie not to be nervous at the prospect of a formal dinner party. I will hire someone to serve. And I give her my word she will not have to leave the kitchen, so she will not need a new uniform.

We long to see the children—and I suspect you long just as fervently to have them out of your sight for a while.

Fondly,<br>Bess

October 20, 1912<br>Dallas, Texas

Dear Lydia,

Your letter was waiting on our return from a glorious three weeks in St. Louis. We are anxious to see you and Manning but we have a social commitment we cannot cancel on October 29. Would the following weekend be equally convenient? We will plan a family picnic at Exall Lake so there will be no danger of interruption from well-meaning friends. We look forward to seeing you.

Love from us both,

Bess

January 10, 1913
Received of Robert Randolph Steed on this date the sum of $14,000 (fourteen thousand dollars), repaying in full the loan of $20,000 (twenty thousand dollars) contracted on January 10, 1911.

Elizabeth Alcott Steed

WITNESSED BY:   Annie Hoffmeyer
Hans Hoffmeyer

February 28, 1913
Dallas

Dear Papa and Mavis,

My life as a Dallas matron is proving very conducive to my continuing education.

I take French lessons two afternoons a week from a lovely Parisienne whose family owns a millinery shop on Oak Lawn. We redo my spring hats while we conjugate verbs.

Yesterday I read my first paper before the Shakespeare Club. The most prominent women in the city comprise its membership, so I was extremely nervous when I stood to address them. However, my first attempt at literary scholarship was received with great enthusiasm. Apparently I am not alone in my admiration of Lady Macbeth.

Devotedly,

Bess

March 18, 1913
Dallas

Dear Lydia,

Congratulations to you and Manning on the birth of your daughter. Robin and Drew are very excited about the arrival of their first first cousin—and the first girl in the family, though I trust not the last. I am expecting our third child—and praying for a girl. The experience of pregnancy is much too familiar not to hope for a conclusion of a different gender.

I dread the long summer ahead—no dinner parties, no dances at the country club, no evenings at the theater. How shall I pass the time until my due date of September 10? I so wish I could spend the summer in a place where pregnancy is a source of pride rather than embarrassment.

Please give Mother Steed our love. We miss her but understand your need comes first for now. Kiss the baby for me and tell her a new cousin will join her as soon as her impatient aunt can arrange it. Her uncle Rob adds his kiss to mine.

Love,

Bess

April 21, 1913

Dallas

Dear Mother Steed,

Ever since Annie described to me the freedom accorded expectant mothers in Europe, I have been hinting to Rob that I would be happier spending the summer abroad. Today he surprised me with steamship reservations for a transatlantic crossing, departing New York City May 30, arriving Southampton June 8. One of the reservations is for you, if you are willing.

When I spoke of traveling abroad, I of course hoped—and indeed assumed—Rob would be at my side, but unfortunately his business will keep him at home. He seems to have complete faith in my ability to manage without him. Why else would he encourage me to make this trip? I suppose I should be flattered. I've done everything in my power since the early months of our marriage to persuade him to treat me as a full and equal partner instead of a helpless wife who has to be protected by her husband from the outside world. But sometimes I wonder if I have not succeeded too well. I just hope he will miss me as much as I shall miss him.

However, I am thrilled at the thought of seeing Europe—with or without Rob. And we will not lack for male companionship since Robin and Drew will be with us—and of course our devoted Annie to look after them. Annie has not been home to Germany in ten years, so she is very excited about the trip. Hans will be staying here with Rob. Apparently he has no desire to see his homeland again.

I have traveled extensively in my mind since the year tuberculosis confined me to my room, but no mental journey can compare to the excitement of actually leaving home. I hope you will share my enthusiasm—and the trip.

Devotedly,

Bess

April 25, 1913

Dallas

Dear Lydia,

I know you were sorry to see Mother Steed depart, but now that the baby is six weeks old, you should be able to manage alone. We have so much to do here getting ready for the trip.

My friends are horrified at the thought of a woman in my condition undertaking such a voyage *without* her husband and *with* two small children, but none could suggest a more interesting way to spend the final months of pregnancy.

My only regret is that Rob will not be with me. We have shared every new adventure from the day we met in the fourth grade. It does not seem right for me to be seeing Europe for the first time without him. But the commitment that keeps him at home—his business—is the very one which enables all of us to go, so I must not complain.

Affectionately,

Bess

April 29, 1913

Dallas

Dear Papa and Mavis,

Thank you for your letters, both of which arrived this morning, but your fears are groundless, I assure you. No one could be more concerned about my condition than Rob—or more solicitous of my health and well-being. More than anything he wants me to be happy, and he knows how oppressed I would have felt at home this summer hiding behind shuttered windows. It is ironic that the Old World is more permissive concerning the conduct of pregnant women than the New World. We may have won our freedom as a country in 1776 but in the area of feminine rights the battle is still raging.

We will be traveling in complete comfort and style. Rob is making sure we have the best possible accommodations everywhere. We will return to Dallas in ample time for me to prepare for the birth of the baby in September and the start of the fall social season in October.

Devotedly,<br>Bess

May 28, 1913<br>en route to New York City

Dear Heart,

I know of no other husband in the world who could stand at the train station and wave his wife and family such a dear, brave good-bye. For one brief moment I wanted to pull the emergency cord and run back into your arms—but our reunion will be even sweeter in September.

The motion of the ship rocking on the ocean will be most welcome after two nights of grinding, jostling train travel along rocky roadbeds. I have read that the train tracks linking this country were laid by convicts and immigrants; with every rock they placed they must have sought revenge on the privileged classes who were to benefit from their labors.

I lay awake much of each night, with the window shade raised, watching the dark landscape rush past. Last night the train sped through the heart of a forest fire, and I watched with fascination as the flames encircled but could not touch us. Sometimes my life seems as safe and insulated to me as the compartment in which I was riding last night. I see the flames of death and deprivation outside, but they do not touch me.

All my love,<br>Bess

Dear Heart,

Flowers seemed to be growing from the walls of our stateroom when we arrived on board ship. How thoughtful and generous you are! We are surrounded on this voyage with evidence of your affection—the telegrams, the baskets of fruit, the champagne, the model ships for the boys. Thank you for everything—but especially for the flowers and the tender note that accompanied them. I fall asleep amid their scent each night, dreaming of your embrace.

Oh my love, how I cherish those blossoms around my solitary bed. When you are beside me, I am garden enough. I burst into bloom at your touch. Without you, I lie fallow, my only satisfaction watching a rose unfold. Why am I not content knowing I am nurturing a new bud of life inside me? Most of the women of my acquaintance find their husbands irrelevant during these months of impending motherhood, but the constant, tangible evidence of our love that I carry serves only to fan the flames of my desire.

Oh, my beloved missing half, how I yearn for your completion! I would surrender to you tonight more eagerly than I did on our wedding night. Then I only suspected the delights in store for me. Now I know what I am being denied by distance and circumstance —and every cell of my being cries out in protest.

Dearest, write as often as you can—and, please, no more letters dictated to your secretary. I know you think Miss Hopkins only types your letters but I suspect she also reads them. Take pen in hand late at night, my darling, the last thing before you fall asleep. Release me with words until I am back in your arms.

I am yours forever,

Bess

June 6, 1913
aboard the *Lusitania*

Dear Lydia,

I hope you will not find my handwriting illegible. For the past twenty-four hours we have been buffeted by high winds. All the furniture has been roped down, and the waves are so high no one is allowed to stroll on deck.

I spent most of the day in the stateroom, looking after Annie and Mother Steed, both of whom are suffering from severe cases of "mal de mer." The boys are fine. They put on their cowboy suits this morning and pretended that the raging sea was their bucking bronco. Each time the boat lurched, they howled with delight. And fortunately I too have survived the storm and stayed on my feet. Compared to the first few weeks of pregnancy, a storm at sea is a trifle.

I wish you could have seen Robin celebrating his third birthday. He was seated at the place of honor at the captain's table, wearing his starched white sailor suit—and there was not a man or woman on board who would not have liked to claim him. We were all given paper hats to wear and whistles to blow, and there was much merrymaking as a huge, three-tiered cake was wheeled into the room. The band played "Happy Birthday" and when it was over, Robin astonished us all by giving the captain a crisp salute.

Mother Steed says he won't remember anything about the occasion in another year but that seems of no importance to me. He understood everything that was happening as it happened. At that moment he was truly and completely happy and what more should any of us expect from life?

Tomorrow is our last day aboard and I am as excited about my first glimpse of the Old World as Columbus was when he sighted the New.

Love to Manning and the baby,

Bess

June 11, 1913<br>London

Dear Heart,

I am in London for the first time in my life but I cannot turn a corner without feeling I have been here before. I know now I have been a traveler all my life, but until this summer all my voyages took place within the covers of books. Today we visited the house where Charles Dickens wrote my beloved *David Copperfield*. I remember weeping as I read it, and today as I stood looking at his desk, I felt sure he wept writing it.

I go to the theater whenever I can arrange it. Yesterday Mother

Steed accompanied me to a brilliant production of Henrik Ibsen's *A Doll's House*. I am sure you would have found it as silly a play as your mother did. For the first time on the trip, I was grateful you were not with us.

I have not heard from you since we landed. I hope you are not too lonely without us. What have you been doing to amuse yourself? Please be specific when you reply as my imagination tends to run rampant at this distance. I trust Hans is taking good care of you. Annie assures me he is an excellent cook but I would like to hear it from you.

Annie is very homesick and cries herself to sleep every night. If it were not for the chance to visit her family in Germany, she would be on the next ship home. But I hold Hans responsible for her emotional state. She tells me he was very opposed to her making this trip and the day of her departure spoke of nothing but how lonely he would be without her, with no appreciation at all of the opportunities ahead of her. There are few men in the world as unselfish as you, my dearest, and Annie is certainly not married to one of them.

England abounds with evidence of the great love Queen Victoria bore her Albert and the overwhelming sense of loss she experienced at his death. At Windsor Castle she ordered the bells to toll continually for a *week* following his death. After a day the sound became unbearable to her, and she ordered the bell tower swathed in black woolen to muffle the mournful tones, but the tolling of the bells continued. She had all her fine clothes put away and wore black for the rest of her life. Our guide was quite offended when I dared question whether the Queen was truly honoring her consort's memory by ceasing to live her own life. If anything were to happen to me, I hope you would continue with unabated enthusiasm and determination in the direction you are now going, without guilt or grief, knowing that your life was the only life left to me.

Why is it that during even the shortest separation one's mind keeps returning to that ultimate separation?

I love you with all my heart,

Bess

July 3, 1913
Paris

Dear Papa and Mavis,

At last we are in Paris—"Cité de la Lumière" (Mavis, please translate for Papa). It is everything I imagined it would be. If only I had been born here! How I would love to claim this city for my own!

I am grateful for every hat Mademoiselle Girard and I made and for every verb we conjugated. Both have been put to frequent use since our arrival three days ago.

It is exhilarating to find that I can communicate in a foreign tongue, though my linguistic abilities are more appreciated by Frenchmen who cannot speak English themselves. In the hotel, though I always begin my questions in French, the concierge insists on answering in English, and rather than prolong the unspoken rivalry, I end by speaking English too. I have yet to meet a Frenchman who does not consider himself my superior.

Affectionately,
Bess

July 11, 1913
Munich

Dear Heart,

All of us are enchanted with Bavaria, and Annie is happier than I have ever seen her. In England she was homesick for Hans, in France she was openly hostile, but here she is genuinely happy.

She took us to meet her family and they received us with great warmth and courtesy. If it were not for Hans, she would be telling us good-bye here. I hope he understands how close he has come to losing her on this trip. Few husbands realize what a tenuous hold they have on their wives. Like magnets, they only attract within a limited range. But I have yet to travel beyond the powers of your love. Everything in me is drawn to you—no matter how far afield I roam.

I trust I have the same effect on you, though the language in your letters is so guarded I sometimes wonder. Why are men so shy about saying things that they are not the least bit shy about doing?

I appreciate your taking the time to write your letters in longhand, but are you sure your secretary is not still reading them? (Ha!) When I write to you, we are as alone as we are in our bed. But when I read your letters, I feel we are still being chaperoned—though by whom and for what reason I cannot fathom.

No, I am wrong and you are right. Words cannot take your place. I will not torment you further with my unappeased longing, but will suffer in silence until you are close enough to quiet the cries of which you are at once cause and cure.

You are my life,

Bess

July 25, 1913
Vienna

Dear Heart,

What I feared has come to pass. Annie did not leave Germany with us. She said she would think about rejoining us in Italy, but she could not promise.

When I mentioned Hans, she broke into tears and said she was convinced he was unfaithful. I asked what possible evidence she could have for such a statement, and she said the tone of his letters had changed drastically in the last few weeks. In the beginning he wrote only of his loneliness without her—but lately he has begun to urge her to enjoy herself and not think about him. To her this could only mean he had found someone to take her place in his affections.

I assured her she was being absurd. Not once have you lamented your loneliness, but only a fool would read into that any implication of infidelity. Why are women so afraid they are risking the affection of their husbands by asserting their independence?

I love you all the more for encouraging me to take this trip without you and to see for myself how much the world has to offer the solitary traveler.

All my love,

Bess

July 29, 1913
Vienna

Dear Papa and Mavis,

Vienna is like a city out of another century. People no longer live in this manner anywhere else in the world. The charm and courtesy of the people and their civilized life style are very attractive to me. I have found much to admire in every city we have visited but if I had to choose a place to live in Europe it would be Vienna.

Annie stayed in Germany with her family, so Mother Steed and I take the children wherever we go. Last night there was a special performance of Offenbach's *Tales of Hoffmann* at the theater in the Schönbrunn Palace in honor of Emperor Franz Josef, and I was fortunate enough to secure four tickets. Robin and Drew applauded for the Emperor with greater enthusiasm than anyone in the audience, though Robin was disappointed he was not wearing a crown and a velvet robe with an ermine collar, like the ones he saw in the Tower of London. I am sure many of those present wondered why anyone would bring children that age to such an adult event, but they may well be the only members of their generation in America to have applauded an emperor and whether they remember or not, it is a fact.

Affectionately,

Bess


AUGUST 5 1913
WIEN

ANNIE HOFFMEYER
6 MINDENSTRASSE
MÜNCHEN   DEUTSCHLAND
CHILDREN ILL   AM FIGHTING EXHAUSTION   DELAYING DEPAR-
TURE FOR ITALY   PLEASE COME AT ONCE

BESS STEED

Dear Heart,

Please do not worry when you read this. We are fine now, but I wanted you to know of the change in our itinerary.

Three days ago Drew became ill with the grippe, and by dawn the next day, after a sleepless night for all of us, Robin shared his symptoms. I wired Annie immediately and she arrived this afternoon. The first thing she did was put me to bed. I slept until dinner and am now feeling much better. Everyone else is asleep for the night. Just seeing Annie again is the best medicine the children could have.

I have wired the hotels in Italy to change our reservations. Mother Steed suggested we skip Venice and proceed directly to Florence, but I am unequivocally opposed to omitting anything from our itinerary. I hope and pray this is not my last trip to Europe, but I have no assurance of anything beyond tomorrow, and, providing of course that the children are well enough to travel, tomorrow will find us in Venice.

All my love,
Bess

August 9, 1913
Venice

Dear Heart,

We arrived yesterday just as the sun was setting into the Grand Canal, the perfect hour to see Venice for the first time—if indeed we have actually *seen* Venice. It is more like a dream to me.

The children seem to be completely recovered. However, except for a gondola ride this afternoon, they have stayed in the hotel with Annie all day.

Annie said my telegram was just what she needed to force her to a decision. Her brother had already urged her to sail home with us from Naples. He is convinced war is on the way and he told her if she didn't leave now, she might never see the United States or her husband again. A letter from Hans was waiting for Annie here. I have no idea what he said but fortunately Annie is now convinced he has remained faithful in her absence and anxiously awaits her return. As I trust you do mine.

Ever your

Bess

August 12, 1913
Florence

Dear Lydia,

Despite our truncated stay here, we have managed to see all the art masterpieces I had studied in school and quite a few I had not.

Mother Steed was somewhat shocked when she saw Michelangelo's *David* for the first time, and the size is indeed overwhelming. Though I myself am not shocked by anything I see in stone, I was not prepared for Italian men in the flesh. In every other country my very obvious condition has protected me from all the suggestions to which a woman traveling alone is prey. In Italy my condition, if noticed at all, appears only to enhance my attractiveness to the opposite sex. Even Mother Steed cannot walk down the street without comment. At home a forty-five-year-old widow is considered old; in Italy she is merely regarded as ripe. This is definitely the country to visit when your children are grown and you are beginning to feel your life is over—though, frankly, I cannot imagine ever feeling that way.

If we spoke Italian perhaps we could carry on an intelligent conversation with the men who follow us everywhere, but as it is we have to try to ignore the remarks they address to us and speak only to each other. Since arriving in Italy, we have gotten in the habit of eating dinner in our hotel rooms with the children, and we have given up our evening strolls after dinner. I bought an Italian-English dictionary and study it faithfully each evening but so far have not been able to find any of the words spoken to me by the men on the street.

I am delighted that Manning is joining Rob in business. When will you be moving to Dallas? I look forward to helping you find and furnish a house. Much is expected of the wife of a man going into business in a new city. I know Rob will give Manning the benefit of his experience and I will do no less for you.

Affectionately,

Bess

August 15, 1913

Rome

Beloved,

How I miss you! These warm Italian nights create such longings inside me. It is unbearable to be alone.

We went for a long carriage ride tonight and saw the ruins by moonlight. Time seems so fluid here. We step back and forth from past to present and I can even glimpse the future, imagining grand-children and great-grandchildren retracing our footsteps through the Forum.

You would enjoy this city more than any we have seen. That must be why I think I see you on every street corner—or perhaps it is simply our long separation that causes me to envision what I most long to see. Our unborn child is already demanding its right to a separate identity. I was almost asleep just now when the kicking woke me. Now all is still again but I cannot go back to sleep so I sit awake dreaming of once again lying in your arms.

All my love,

Bess

August 19, 1913

Naples

Dear Papa and Mavis,

This is the last letter you will receive with a foreign postmark.

Today we visited the ruins of Pompeii. Mother Steed says if she had a choice she would die like a citizen of Pompeii—caught without warning in the midst of life. Not I. I intend to give as much thought to my death as I have to my life. Nor do I want to be just another name in a long list of victims. I have no intention of being associated in death with people whose company I would not choose in life.

What is there about traveling in Europe that makes one view one's own life as part of history? It is an exhilarating feeling and one I never experienced living in Texas. But it is a perspective I plan to keep for the rest of my life.

All my love,

Bess

---

*Mr. and Mrs. Robert Randolph Steed*
*proudly announce the birth*
*of their first daughter*
*Eleanor Elizabeth*
*born August 25, 1913*
*aboard the "Nuovo Mondo"*
*en route from Naples, Italy, to Galveston, Texas*

---

October 12, 1914

Dallas

Frau Heinrich Mittler
6 Mindenstrasse
München, Deutschland

My dear Frau Mittler,

Annie has just told me of the sad loss of your son in the war. My deepest condolences. I am heartsick at what has befallen all the places and people we came to love just a summer ago. It is difficult for us to understand at this distance what is happening in Europe. No matter what official position our country takes, I will remain torn between the two sides, like my own great-grandmother, who had sons fighting against each other in our War Between the States.

You were so kind to us when we were in Germany, and Annie is like a member of our own family. You have my assurance that she will be always.

With deepest sympathy and abiding affection, I remain,

Yours truly,

Bess Steed

May 15, 1915
Dallas

Dear Papa and Mavis,

It breaks my heart to think of the fate that has befallen our lovely *Lusitania* since she carried us across the Atlantic two years ago. And though I pray we will return some day, we will never again see the Europe we saw in 1913.

We are all in good health, though Rob is working so hard I fear for his. Life insurance keeps him away from home more than I would like, but a new business is much like a new baby. It demands your total attention in the early years but soon grows quite independent. Eleanor no longer walks anywhere, she runs. None of us can keep up with her. I hope there is a special angel that looks out for small children because it is an impossible task for anyone without wings.

Annie has been in a state of great emotional stress ever since the war started, and I am afraid the job of caring for the children has become too much for her. So I have relieved her of that responsibility and her work is now confined to housekeeping. I have hired a lovely Scottish gentlewoman, the mother of the golf pro at the Dallas Country Club, to look after the children. Her name is Flora McCullough and her brogue is as pronounced as Annie's thick German accent but it is a more pleasing sound, especially in these troubled times. She is quite a bit older than Annie but the children are past the age of needing purely physical care; what they require now is someone from a background compatible to their own to give direction to their minds.

Much love,
Bess


AUGUST 5 1916
DALLAS

ROBERT STEED
JEFFERSON HOTEL
ST LOUIS   MISSOURI
ELEANOR STRUCK BY AUTO   IN COMA AT BAYLOR   COME HOME AT ONCE

BESS

Mr. Arthur Fineman
1300 N. Beckley
Oak Cliff, Texas

Dear Mr. Fineman,

Thank you for your letter of last week. I was not able to answer it until today when my child finally emerged from her coma. The multiple fractures she suffered left her immobile from head to toe. But this morning when she opened her eyes and smiled at me for the first time in a week, I felt as if she had leapt out of bed.

Thank you for your offers of assistance but we have the means of dealing with this emergency. Let me assure you again in writing that my husband and I have no intention of pressing any legal charges against you. My child stepped directly into the path of your car, and no driver could have humanly avoided the accident that followed.

I hold myself responsible. I had her hand in mine when she suddenly pulled free and ran to join her older brothers who had crossed the street ahead of us with their nurse. I ran after her and reached for her just as she stepped into the street—but too late. I have relived this scene continuously since it happened, as I am sure you have too. I cannot talk about it with anyone in my family; you are the only one who can share my guilt. Even my beloved husband appears to me now in the guise of grief-stricken father, and his usually comforting presence serves only as an unspoken reproach. I have never felt more alone in my life.

Life is so much more dangerous now than it was when I was growing up. I lived in a small town without sidewalks, and I remember skipping in the street alongside horses and carriages, with no thought that anything on wheels could ever hurt me or anything I loved. But that was before the automobile.

I must close now. Eleanor is waking up again.

Yours truly,

Bess Steed

August 15, 1916
The Clouds

Darling Eleanor,

You are the first mortal to receive a letter from the kingdom of the clouds, but all of us have been watching you in your bed in the hospital and we wanted to tell you how brave and strong we think you are.

The doll that brought this letter is the kind our children play with here in the clouds. Her eyes are as blue as the sky, her hair shines like the sun, and her dress is the color of sunset.

We know you have to lie very still all day, and all you can see from your window is the sky. But the sky is our world and more interesting than anyone on earth can imagine. Look closely and you will see us hiding among the stars and sleeping on the clouds. And we will look down at the earth and tell you all the funny things the other mortals are doing.

Love and kisses,
The Cloud Fairy


November 10, 1916
Dallas

Mrs. Martin Banks
Secretary
The Shakespeare Club
Dallas, Texas

Dear Exa,

It is with great regret that I am requesting an indefinite leave of absence, but since Eleanor's accident my life has been confined to my home and her hospital room. And will be for as far into the future as I dare look.

She is so brave it breaks my heart. Fortunately she is too young to have any real concept of time. Her calendar goes from Christmas to Easter to her birthday. The months between mean nothing to her, so when the doctor tells her she will be home by Easter and able to walk again by her birthday, that forecast does not fill her with the despair it does me.

Sitting here in the hospital room, I have reread all my favorite passages from Shakespeare but have found little to console me. Even Lear in his grief did not begin to express the emotions that have besieged me since the accident. I do not believe Shakespeare ever had the experience of seeing a child of his suffer as I have.

Please convey my appreciation to all those who approved my name for membership and my regret at having to relinquish temporarily one of the highest honors of my life, but my family has always held first claim on my time and now there is time for nothing else.

Sincerely,

Bess Steed

le 20 novembre 1916
Dallas

Mlle. Helene Girard
Paris Millinery
4608 Oak Lawn
Dallas, Texas

Ma chère Mademoiselle,

Je regrette beaucoup de ne pas continuer les après-midis français si agréables que nous avons passés les derniers trois ans, mais maintenant il faut que je sois à l'hôpital avec ma petite Eleanor tous les jours.

A ce moment-ci, je ne peux pas dire quand je pourrai les recommencer. Pour la première fois de ma vie, l'avenir m'effraye.

Je vous remercie encore des jolies fleurs que vous avez envoyées à l'hôpital. Depuis le 5 août, cette chambre est devenue le monde pour moi, et les fleurs sont des souvenirs d'un monde plus beau.

Avec mes sentiments les plus affectueux,

Bess Steed

December 30, 1916
Dallas

Dear Mr. Fineman,

It was very kind of you to remember us at this holiday season. The smoked turkey was enjoyed by everyone, as were the Corsicana fruitcakes.

Eleanor loved the basket of toy kittens. I hope they will assuage her disappointment when she comes home and finds her own kittens almost grown. Like all of us, she expects nothing to change in her absence.

I appreciate your tact in sending the gift instead of bringing it in person. No human being is associated with the accident in Eleanor's mind. The only culprit is a car, so she does not expect anyone to make amends. She considers the toy kittens simply a gift from a friend. As do I.

I was sorry to hear of your recent illness. Fortunately I have stayed in good health all fall—perhaps because I had no choice.

Eleanor has accepted her long convalescence with amazing cheerfulness. I read aloud to her for hours at a time, and together we retreat into a myriad of imagined worlds more pleasant than our own. Every morning when she wakes up, there is a letter from the Cloud Fairy on her pillow and a present beside it. I know now, looking back on the first frightening days following the accident, that I created a living kingdom in the clouds so she would know there were other worlds open to her if this one were suddenly closed. Or perhaps I was simply trying to sustain that illusion in my own heart.

Thank you again for your thoughtful gifts—and best wishes for the coming year.

Sincerely,

Bess Steed

February 16, 1917

Dallas

Dear Papa and Mavis,

The children were enchanted with the Valentine gifts you sent them. My Valentine present from Rob was waiting in the driveway when I woke up. An automobile of my own. A year ago I would have been thrilled, but today I was terrified at the prospect of driving such a dangerous machine. Ever since Eleanor's accident I have looked upon the invention with horror. But Rob says that is the proper attitude with which to approach an automobile. A year ago I would have treated it as an exciting toy. Now I know better.

Rob took me for my first driving lesson this afternoon. He says I did very well. However I felt the machine was my master instead of the other way around, a situation I plan to remedy by constant practice.

None of my friends knows how to drive and none of their husbands would allow them to try, much less buy them a car of their own and insist they learn to use it. But Rob is spending more and more of his time traveling, and he does not like to think of my sitting helplessly at home. I am constantly amazed at the independence he not only allows but encourages in me. We grew up as friends and equals and, unlike many other couples I know, marriage has not lessened our mutual respect.

Lovingly,

Bess


March 24, 1917
The Clouds

Darling Eleanor,

We all looked down and waved good-bye as you left the hospital today. What a brave soldier you have been these long months—as brave as the little tin soldier who brings you this note. Were you surprised to find a note from the Clouds waiting for you in your room at home? You will not be hearing from us as often as you did at the hospital. Soon you'll be up and about, running and playing, with no time for lying on your back and looking at the clouds, but we will always be here watching over you. And whenever the days on earth seem long and difficult, look up at the sky and think of the fun we're having here.

Love and kisses,

The Cloud Fairy


March 25, 1917
Dallas

Dear Mr. Fineman,

Eleanor had a joyous homecoming—and her happiness reached a peak when she saw the adorable Siamese kittens you sent to welcome her home. She still moves with great difficulty and pain, requiring several hours of rest for each hour of exertion, but when she lies down the kittens lie beside her and frolic on the bed, a source of endless delight and amusement to her. Anything that amuses her and keeps her still is a gift to me as well; my imagination has been severely depleted by the hours of storytelling at the hospital.

I am sorry your illness made it impossible for you to continue driving your car. But instead of selling it, why not encourage your wife to learn to drive? My husband bought me an automobile of my own last month and though I was terrified the first time I took the wheel, I now find the experience quite exhilarating. I of course proceed with the utmost caution and plan my routes carefully in advance to avoid left-hand turns. But as long as I am not in a hurry, I find I can reach any destination by turning right.

Best wishes to you and your wife for the holiday season ahead. I approach this Easter with a full heart. Having my daughter at home again, seeing her regain the use of her arms and legs, however slowly and painfully, I feel I have experienced the meaning of the Resurrection for the first time in my life. However, if I were of your faith, I would find equal significance in this Passover season, for truly the Angel of Death passed over our house this year. This Sunday I will sing "Hallelujah" with all my heart to the God of us all.

Sincerely,<br>Bess Steed

April 15, 1917<br>Dallas

Dear Papa and Mavis,

Today I brought my suitcases down from the attic where they have been stored for the last four years. When I returned from Europe, I thought travel had become part of the pattern of my life, but now I know there is no pattern to any of our lives—or if there is, it is much too terrifying to contemplate.

I am so excited at the prospect of a trip to New York City with Rob—and grateful that the two of you will be able to stay with the children. Of course Mother Steed is here and the children adore her, but the idea of accepting responsibility for any living thing overwhelms her. She even refuses to keep a plant in her room for fear it will die and be her fault.

Annie has now become an American citizen and therefore finds domestic service increasingly distasteful. She and Hans moved out of the servants' quarters over our garage last month and into a sweet little house of their own. Annie is having a baby in August—their first child—but has promised to work for us until midsummer.

Of course our dear Mrs. McCullough will be here with the children. She is devoted to them and they to her. They never tire of her Scottish tales and I must admit to occasional eavesdropping myself. Her son is doing very well at the country club. He has taught the game of golf to most of the prominent businessmen in the city. Rob took a few lessons but rarely has time to play. However my game continues to improve.

Lydia brings little Marian over every day for a visit. It is only in recent months that I have come to appreciate my sister-in-law. She plays the piano for the children and makes up little songs and dances to encourage Eleanor to do her exercises. Eleanor is moving much better now, but she has had to go through the experience of learning to walk all over again. It breaks my heart to see her fall, then bravely get up and begin again.

I must get back to my packing. I am using the guest room as a center of operations. There are clothes everywhere. What are women wearing in New York City this year? My head is in a whirl.

Love to you both,

Bess

April 20, 1917
Dallas

Mrs. Dwight Davis
33 Stonybrook
Westport, Connecticut

Dear Totsie,

How wonderful it will be to see you again—and to meet the man you talked about night and day the whole year we roomed together. Was it just eight years ago? I feel I have lived a lifetime since then. It is my conviction that the woman I am at twenty-six is the woman I will be for the rest of my life, but the girl I was at eighteen is gone forever. Or is she? I suppose I should leave it for you to decide.

I am anticipating this trip with such pleasure. Rob and I have had so little time together in recent years. It is ironic that the very ties that bind a husband and wife in theory—home and family—often serve to separate them in fact. Rob is no longer the man I married any more than I am the girl you remember, but I am not always sure who he has become.

When we were first married, I was perhaps more ambitious for him than he was for himself. But now he never stops looking for new opportunities for investment, and unfortunately they always seem to require large investments of time and energy as well as money. There are men in this part of the country building empires and I feel my husband will be one of them. There was a day when I could account for every penny he earned. Now, except for my household allowance, which has always been extravagant, I have no idea how much money he makes or where it goes.

I always thought marriage meant the merging of two lives into one —but the only mergers that really capture Rob's imagination are ones that show a growth and profit potential. Our bodies continue to share the same space, but our souls are becoming strangers.

I didn't know until I started writing this letter just how much I had missed you all these years. Remember how we used to fall asleep talking? Well, I am doing it again. It is 3 A.M. and I still have so much to tell you, but it will have to wait till I see you.

Je t'embrasse,

Bess

April 17, 1917
Dallas

Miss Josephine Farrow
2514 Elm Street
Syracuse, New York

Dear Cousin Josie,

Although we have never met, I have heard my father speak of you so often I trust it will not seem improper for me to address you as familiarly as he does.

My husband and I are traveling to New York City on May 4 for a two-week stay, and I would like very much to take a train to Syracuse one day to see you. My father has spoken so often of the kindness your mother and father showed him as a boy. I don't think he ever quite recovered from the loss of his mother at the age of eight, but his pain was eased by the loving way he was included in the life of your family.

Twice now my father has suffered the untimely loss of the most important woman in his life—first his mother, then his wife—which may explain why he chose someone so young when he remarried. Whatever else he expects from her, I feel certain he is counting on her to outlive him.

He has been very concerned about your recent illness. I have no wish to impose, but since I do not know when I will be coming east again, I would not want to miss the opportunity to meet you and get to know more about my father's side of the family.

Best regards,

Bess Steed

May 10, 1917

The Waldorf

New York City

Dear Papa and Mavis,

I spent yesterday with Cousin Josie at her home in Syracuse. She is very weak and coughs a great deal. She no longer receives any visitors but was kind enough to see me since I had come so far. I don't know how she would have managed without your support all these years, Papa. Her only other relative is a niece, who married and moved to another town. She writes occasionally but provides nothing in the way of financial aid.

I was distressed to learn that Cousin Josie has never made a will. She has no money, of course, but her home is filled with priceless antiques, which belonged to her parents and by rights should go to you when she dies. However, a court, unaware of your generous support, might designate her niece as legal heir.

Rob and I are thoroughly enjoying all that New York City has to offer. If it were not for the children, I could stay indefinitely.

The train trip was like a honeymoon for us—two days uninterrupted by business or family. I expect it will soon be feasible to cross the country by air, and, however happy a prospect that may be for some people, how sad it will be for women like me, married to men who will always choose the fastest means of transportation available.

Rob reserved a luxurious suite for us here. Unlike many of his associates, he enjoys spending money as much as making it, an attitude I share completely.

I have become completely stagestruck on this trip, seeing more plays in the past week than in my whole life until now. And what radiant performances! I will always treasure Ina Claire in *Polly with a Past* and Fay Bainter in *The Willow Tree*. I also love the way we live here—we go to the theater every night and dine afterward. There is nothing like champagne to ensure sweet dreams.

Rob is so quick to act on my slightest whim. I am as spoiled as a woman as I was as a child. And not only enjoy it but have come to expect it. There are those who would shake their heads in disapproval. But in my experience the most loving and generous people are those who have been loved. Having been given everything I wanted as a child and now as a wife, I live only to do the same for my family and friends. I am convinced that if every child in the world were spoiled, there would soon be an end to war and crime.

I hope you are enjoying your stay at our house and the children are not taxing your affection.

Much love,

Bess

May 12, 1917

The Waldorf

New York City

My precious angels,

Your father and I miss you very much and I hope the next time we come to New York City all of you will be with us. But we will be bringing quite a bit of the city home with us. Just wait till you see the treasures I have packed in my trunk. I spent all yesterday afternoon in the most wonderful toy store I have ever seen. I have heard people speak of the lack of manners in this part of the country, but I have been treated with the utmost courtesy everywhere I go. The clerk at the toy store in particular seemed to take a personal interest in all of you and gave me much good advice in making my selections.

How is your tunnel coming, Robin and Drew? Mother Steed is afraid you will be buried alive. She says she holds her breath from the time you disappear behind the rose bushes until you emerge again at the birdbath. Perhaps it would be best if you delayed further excavations until our return.

Eleanor, my dumpling, I am delighted to hear of your progress. I live for the day I hold open my arms and you come running into them.

A kiss and a hug for each of you,

Mummy

May 15, 1917<br>The Waldorf<br>New York City

Dear Lydia,

Rob and I have just returned from a weekend in Connecticut with my college roommate and her husband. As long as Totsie and I were just exchanging letters, we remained the best of friends. But our visit, instead of bringing us closer, has increased the distance between us.

Perhaps it was our husbands that made us seem like strangers. The two men come from such different worlds. Her husband was sent to boarding school at an early age and though deprived of his family's presence, their name was always ahead of him, opening every door. It incensed me to see that he considered himself superior to Rob, without having done anything to earn that distinction. I am determined to give my children all the advantages of wealth and position, if only to prove how meaningless they are. Then none of them will ever be made to feel as uncomfortable as Rob did all weekend.

We both miss Texas. We have decided to cut short our stay here and return home this weekend.

Love from us both,

Bess

May 15, 1917
New York City

Fifth Avenue Florists
New York City

Please deliver one dozen long-stemmed roses to Mr. and Mrs. Dwight Davis, 33 Stonybrook, Westport, Connecticut, with the following message: "Thank you for giving us our first taste of eastern hospitality. It was an unforgettable weekend. I hope you will come to Texas soon so we can reciprocate. Bess and Rob."

A check is enclosed.

Sincerely,
Mrs. Robert R. Steed


May 15, 1917
New York City

Director of Admissions
Choate School
Wallingford, Connecticut

Dear Sir:

My husband and I were driven through your impressive grounds this past weekend by our close friends Mr. and Mrs. Dwight Davis. Though we live at some distance—in Dallas, Texas—I am most anxious for my two sons, Robert and Andrew, to have the advantages of an eastern education.

I hope it is not too late to enroll them now for three years of preparatory school before college. Robert will be seven next month and Andrew will be six in November. Kindly reserve places for them in the appropriate classes.

Enclosed please find a check for $1,000 as a contribution to your current building campaign.

Sincerely,
Mrs. Robert Randolph Steed

May 15, 1917
New York City

Dear Totsie and Dwight,

It was kind of you to entertain us for the weekend—and quite an education to be exposed to a way of life that simply does not exist in Texas. I feel sure both Rob and I will profit from the experience.

Your home is lovely and I never tired of looking out our bedroom window into your exquisite English garden. There were flowers blooming I had never seen before but would like to try planting at home—if such aristocratic species can survive in Texas soil. I for one suspect they will do very well.

We are leaving for home tomorrow, several days earlier than we originally intended—a hotel and friends cannot replace home and family for very long.

Good luck to Dwight in his efforts as chairman of the Choate Building Campaign.

It was good to see you again. I'm glad I didn't seem like a stranger to you.

Affectionately,

Bess


July 5, 1917
Dallas

Dear Papa and Mavis,

The Liberty Loan Campaign was officially launched in Dallas yesterday with a huge picnic at White Rock Lake. Rob made a rousing speech.

I've never had political ambitions for him before, but yesterday, listening to the crowd cheer, I became convinced he could be elected to any office in the country. However, he is not interested in winning votes now—all his energies are directed toward winning the war. He will be selling war bonds over a five-state area, which means he will be traveling most of the time. I miss him so much more when I'm at home and he's away than when I was in Europe and he was here. I wish there were more I could do for the war effort. I've joined the Red Cross but it is difficult to bring much passion to bandage-rolling.

Robin and Drew are fascinated by all the war talk. They have dug a trench around the servants quarters and spend most of the day in it.

You would have rejoiced to see Eleanor playing with the other children at the picnic yesterday. At least that war is almost won!

Much love,

Bess

August 16, 1917
Dallas

Dear Heart,

I have now joined the ranks of those who also serve by only standing and waiting—but thank God your battlefield is a podium and your weapons war bonds. Even so, your absence makes my heart ache.

Our trip to New York last spring was like a honeymoon for me —but a honeymoon greatly enriched by all the experiences shared in the years preceding it. I am always amazed to hear people say the first weeks or months of marriage are the best and then, "the honeymoon is over." Of course I thought I loved you with all my heart when we were married, but it took marriage to teach me the outer limits of my anatomy, both physical and spiritual, and now I know that every moment we share further increases my capacity for love.

The only advantage of being apart is that we are forced to communicate by letter—and to express in words thoughts which might otherwise remain unspoken.

Goodnight, my love. Sleep well.

Bess

AUGUST 18 1917
DALLAS

ROBERT STEED
LIBERTY LOAN HEADQUARTERS
JEFFERSON HOTEL
ST LOUIS MISSOURI
HOUSE DESTROYED BY FIRE LAST NIGHT EVERYONE SAFE CHILDREN WITH LYDIA I AM IN BAYLOR WITH DISLOCATED VERTEBRAE

BESS

August 19, 1917
Baylor Hospital
Dallas

Dear Papa and Mavis,

Don't be alarmed when you read this letter. We are all safe now. Two nights ago our house burned to the ground. The children— thank God—escaped without physical injury, though we had to jump from a second-story window to avoid the flames.

Rob was in St. Louis so Mrs. McCullough and I were alone with the children (fortunately Mother Steed was spending the week with Lydia). Mrs. McCullough led the way out the window—followed by Robin and Drew, brave little soldiers that they are. They held hands as they jumped into a net held by firemen, but neither cried till they were safely on the ground. Eleanor was terrified so I held her in my arms and we jumped together. I was so filled with gratitude for our safe escape I didn't realize how much pain I was in until I was loaded onto a stretcher and taken to the hospital. I have several dislocated vertebrae so I will be here at least a week. Fortunately Rob is with us now. He and the children are staying with Lydia and Manning.

There is nothing for you to do—except not worry—but it is comforting to know you live so near. I cannot imagine children ever wanting to live at a distance from their parents, even when they are grown with children of their own. Life is too frightening to face without the support of a strong and loving family.

I will write again in a day or so. There is not much pain now— and my physical discomfort is so outweighed by my gratitude for the escape of my children, I hardly even notice it.

All my love,

Bess

August 21, 1917
Baylor Hospital
Dallas

Dear Mr. Fineman,

The basket of fruit and delicacies arrived this morning. What a thoughtful gift! Flowers always make me a little sad—their life span is so short. But I will be enjoying your gifts for weeks to come, at home as well as in the hospital. The basket looks like a beautiful bon voyage present, which allows me occasionally to forget my present circumstances and imagine I am in a cabin on a luxury liner, traveling to a new destination.

I was surprised at the full coverage our fire received in *The Dallas News*. It was kind of you to send me an extra clipping. I just wish they had included a picture of the house before the fire (I have several excellent ones—they had only to ask) to demonstrate the extent of our loss. Every inch of that house was built to our specifications. We will never find another as perfectly suited to our needs. And building a house is out of the question in wartime.

For the moment we are at the mercy of friends and family—a position that is new to me and rather uncomfortable. However, I suppose in a larger sense we are all helpless creatures at the mercy of one another, and fate is finally forcing me to accept this fact.

Whatever sadness I feel at the loss of our home loses significance beside my gratitude for the safe escape of my loved ones. As long as my husband and children are with me, I will have a home, no matter where I happen to be.

Sincerely,
Bess Steed

August 24, 1917
Baylor Hospital
Dallas

Dear Papa and Mavis,

I am much improved and the doctor says I may go home tomorrow. Home! What a habit that word is. Lydia has insisted we stay with her, at least now while Rob is doing so much traveling. And Rob agrees—he does not want me to be alone with the children.

Our devoted Annie entered the hospital last night and this morning she and Hans became the proud parents of a baby boy. They have named him Franz for her brother who was killed in the first year of the war. I went down to her floor to see her this afternoon and arranged for her to be moved to a private room.

It is sad for her not to be able to share this event with her family. She has not heard from them for many months, and now that our countries are officially at war, she does not dare write. She and Hans seem so alone in the world. Even though they have become American citizens, they will not truly trust our affection again until the war is over. Both have vowed never to return to domestic service. Hans is now working as a mechanic in a downtown garage, and Annie will be staying home with the baby.

Your letter was a great comfort to me. Lying helpless in a hospital turns an adult into a child again. Thank you for knowing how much I needed to hear from you.

Until recently, I inhabited a world that did not change from day to day, in spite of the larger events going on outside our lives. Eleanor's accident put my world in jeopardy for the first time and the fire confirmed my fear that nothing is given to us to keep. Our lives are all on loan and none of us knows when the mortgage will fall due. I sigh with relief that this time my house seemed to be sufficient payment, and I shudder to imagine what toll may be exacted next.

All my love,

Bess

August 24, 1917
Baylor Hospital
Dallas

Dear Cousin Josie,

I am enclosing a clipping from *The Dallas News* which will explain my delay in answering your last letter.

Our home and its contents were totally destroyed by fire, as you can see from the photograph. Each child escaped with a favorite toy, but all other artifacts of our life were lost. If it were not for my husband and children, I would still be in a state of shock, not knowing who I was.

Much as I look forward to leaving the hospital, I am heartsick at the prospect of being homeless. My sister-in-law and her husband have generously opened their doors to us for as long as we want to stay but it will be difficult for me to be a guest for very long in a home where someone else is giving the orders.

I am sorry to hear of your weakening condition, and I wonder if it is wise for you to continue living alone in that big house. Perhaps you should consider moving to a place where medical attention is available. For a woman in your position the upkeep of a large and fully furnished home is an unnecessary responsibility. Of course I know how much your home means to you. I felt the same way about mine. I am so grateful that so much of our family history is preserved within the walls of your home. Be assured that no matter what your circumstances are and where you decide to live, the contents of your home will be cared for and cherished by generations to come.

Your loving cousin,

Bess

September 10, 1917

Dallas

Dear Papa and Mavis,

The children and I are comfortably installed with Lydia and Manning. Little Marian is overjoyed at suddenly acquiring a large family and her parents have welcomed our invasion with good spirits.

Rob is in St. Louis this week at a meeting for war bond area chairmen. His campaign has been highly successful and his methods are being copied around the country. Nor have his patriotic efforts gone unnoticed in the business world. Life insurance sales have tripled in the last year and Midwestern Life has just opened a branch office in St. Louis.

Space is limited here so Mrs. McCullough has moved back with her son for a much-needed vacation. She will rejoin us when we move into our own home again. I have not had much time to look at houses, since Lydia and I share the care of the house and children. I offered to pay the full cost of a domestic but Lydia prides herself on taking care of the house without help. I am at a loss in the kitchen so she does all the cooking while I do my best to keep the house tidy. With four children around, it is work that never ends. For the first time I understand Annie's distaste for domestic service. It is difficult enough keeping your own house in order; doing it for someone else must be unpleasant indeed.

I just received a long letter from Cousin Josie, complaining again of ill health but refusing even to consider the possibility of moving into a nursing home. Her excuse is the expense; she says the amount you send her is not sufficient and she does not want to ask for more. However, I would be happy to furnish the difference so that she could be relieved of the tiresome burden of running a home. She is also concerned about the expense of storing her furniture, but I am sure that expense can be avoided.

Affectionately,
Bess


September 11, 1917
Dallas

Riverview Convalescent Home
Syracuse, New York

Dear Sirs:
I am interested in the facilities you might have available for an elderly female relative of mine who has been in ill health for some time. Kindly send me a brochure with a description of currently available accommodations. Please quote prices.

Sincerely,
Mrs. Robert R. Steed


SEPTEMBER 12 1917
DALLAS

ROBERT STEED
JEFFERSON HOTEL
ST LOUIS   MISSOURI
RESERVE ADJOINING SUITE   AM ARRIVING WITH CHILDREN TO-MORROW   HAVE DECIDED TO MOVE TO ST LOUIS

BESS


September 15, 1917
St. Louis, Missouri

Dearest Lydia,
I will always be grateful for the overwhelming kindness you showed us over the last few weeks. Thanks to you, the children do not look back upon the fire as a nightmare but rather as an adventure.

Who decided that permanence is a prerequisite for raising a family? Children thrive on change and indeed adjust to new surroundings with greater ease than their elders. I marvel as I watch my trio at play in our suite here, inventing games, making forts out of empty suitcases and tents out of sheets and blankets. I have had many moments of regret, thinking of all that was lost in the fire, but so far as I can see, the children have none. They speak often of the house and the things that were in it, but with no sense of loss. It is as if it still exists somewhere—in a distant place—waiting for us to come home when we tire of our travels.

I would like to do something tangible to thank you for making us feel so welcome in your home. I can already hear you saying no to anything I might suggest, so I have taken the liberty of going ahead without your consent. Our darling Mrs. McCullough refuses to leave her family in Dallas and join us here, but neither is she ready to retire. I have arranged to pay her a monthly pension (which I would feel obligated to do in any case, in return for her devoted attendance on us) and she has agreed to spend three afternoons a week at your house, doing anything you ask. She is delighted at the prospect, as I trust you will be. She is quite active for her age and adores the company of young children, though I expect a household with only one child will be a welcome change for her.

I know you take pride in managing your house without help and I admire you for it, though I frankly admit I could never do the same. So think of Mrs. McCullough more as a friend or relative and let her entertain little Marian on the afternoons she is there. Then maybe you will have an opportunity to get back to that novel about your childhood you started so long ago in Honey Grove. I have a great interest in seeing it completed since Rob and I figure in it so prominently.

Mrs. McCullough will be calling you later in the week so that the two of you can decide which days she should come. Please give her our love. And of course do the same for you and your family.

Bess

September 20, 1917
St. Louis

Dearest Papa and Mavis,

There is much to be said for being a transient—especially when one can afford to do it in style. Our accommodations are extremely comfortable and after the responsibility of running a house, hotel living seems quite carefree. This morning as we were strolling through the grounds, I noticed a periwinkle bed in need of thinning but how nice to know it was not my problem (though I did leave a short note for the head gardener).

I revel in the luxury of clean linens daily, and the children have grown so accustomed to room service they never want to eat in a dining room again. Everyone on the hotel staff greets the children by name. This has become our world and we all feel quite safe and at home here. There is always an off-duty maid to stay with the children when Rob and I want to go out, and indeed our social calendar has been crowded with invitations ever since I arrived.

Rob has been a prominent member of the business community for some years now, thanks to the astonishing growth of the life insurance company he started with Manning. And now we are assuming equally important standing in the social life of the city. And what an active social life exists here! Dallas would do well to take note of the imagination and energy that goes into entertaining. I sometimes feel I have moved from a frontier town into a cosmopolitan center.

I seem to be almost completely recovered from the back injuries I suffered in the fire but I am conscientious about doing all the exercises the doctor prescribed as therapy. The first ball of the season takes place in a month, and I want to be able to dance till dawn.

All my love,
Bess


October 1, 1917
St. Louis

Dear Cousin Josie,

Forgive my delay in answering your last letter, but, as you will see from the postmark, we are now living in St. Louis.

There is nothing like a change of setting to give one a fresh perspective on life. And as tragic as our loss was, I have found life in an impersonally furnished hotel strangely liberating. Like most people, I suppose, I enjoyed a sense of permanence and order living in a house built to my specifications and furnished to my taste. But the fire destroyed any illusion of permanence in this life as surely as the flames consumed the structure that sustained it. We are all transients on earth and the sooner we accept the impermanence of our condition, the more pleasure we can take in the unexpected freedom it provides.

With these thoughts in mind, I hope you will give a close reading to the enclosed brochure from the Riverview Convalescent Home. The accommodations appear quite comfortable and the dining and recreation areas most inviting. I could wish no better life for you than the security and convenience of a hotel, with all the details of daily life organized by other people.

My father is in full agreement with me, and though at first glance the cost seems greater than the monthly support he has been providing, we both feel confident that the proceeds from the sale of your house will come close to making up the difference.

Affectionately,

Bess

---

*Mr. and Mrs. Robert Randolph Steed*
*request the pleasure of your company*
*at a dinner dance*
*Saturday, November the fifth*
*at eight o'clock*
*in the Grand Ballroom of the Jefferson Hotel*

R.S.V.P.                            *Black tie*
*Suite 10D Jefferson Hotel*

---

November 10, 1917
St. Louis

Dear Lydia and Manning,

I am enclosing the front page of the society section from last Sunday's paper so you can see for yourself the full coverage our party received. It was *the* social event of the week (and indeed, in my opinion, of the season so far). I feel I can say without a doubt now that everyone in St. Louis who matters knows who we are.

The dance floor was filled with young men in uniform. A few years ago the sight would have thrilled me but now I could only think of the horrors ahead of them. Though not in uniform—thank God—

Rob has become a war hero here through his energetic leadership in the war bond campaign. It is even said that his efforts have not gone unnoticed in Washington.

Fondly,<br>Bess

January 8, 1918<br>St. Louis

Dear Papa and Mavis,

My first letter of the New Year! What would we do without a calendar to give our lives a sense of progression? Perhaps it is only an illusion but I look upon my life as a staircase, with each year taking me up another step toward some unknown but enticing destination.

Spending Christmas with you in Honey Grove left us full of longing for times and places now lost to us. I relived the happy holidays of my childhood, and the children finally understood the full loss of the fire, talking about the house and recalling for the first time, or at least the first time aloud, much-loved objects they will never see again.

I am meeting with a real-estate agent this afternoon to start my search for a new house. I realize now that we have all been acting like rejected lovers, protecting ourselves from future hurt by pretending we were happier without a home. As convenient as it would be to declare our independence of material possessions, we cannot escape the fact that we are body and soul, and both require shelter. Nor am I convinced that the two are at odds with each other and that to deny one is to satisfy the other. I find my spirit strangely appeased when my eye encounters beautiful forms, my nose discovers a familiar fragrance, my ear hears music, my tongue savors a new taste, and my fingers touch beloved objects.

I know now that to live in a hotel as we have done these past few months is to relinquish authority over the exterior of our lives. We all have the power—at least for a moment—to shape our environment, and how wrong of us to ignore this privilege just because it is fleeting. We must accept the fact that nothing we create belongs to us forever and let the act of creation be its own reward.

As you can see, I have had to travel a long path in my own mind to have the courage to buy another house and make it our own. I am still not strong enough to consider the possibility of building one; somehow I find comfort in the thought of occupying a house where strangers lived in safety.

All my love,

Bess


February 1, 1918

St. Louis

Miss Abigail Saunders
Director
Riverview Convalescent Home
Syracuse, New York

Dear Miss Saunders,

I would like to reserve a private room in the name of Josephine Farrow. Her arrival is contingent upon the sale of her home, which has just gone on the market, so it is impossible to set a definite date at this time. However, I am enclosing a substantial deposit, which I trust will compensate for any inconvenience the indefinite arrival date may cause you.

From the photographs in the brochure, I see that some of the rooms look out on the mountains. Does this add to the price of the room? I am sure my cousin would derive great pleasure from the view—but not if she knew she were paying for it.

I would appreciate a prompt reply from you, confirming this reservation.

Sincerely,

Mrs. Robert Randolph Steed


February 14, 1918

St. Louis

Dear Heart,

How sad to be apart on Valentine's Day! That must sound silly coming from a grown woman with three children, but to me it will always be the day on which you first declared yourself.

It was in the fourth grade, shortly after Miss Appleton taught us the meaning of circumnavigation and I decided to make my world in you. In those days there was no difference between us. We were not boy and girl but two creatures totally alike—and set apart from all the rest. Whatever games we played, we were always two of a kind—two explorers, two sailors, two cowboys, two swordsmen. In our Sherwood Forest there were even two Robin Hoods. No Maid Marian for me!

Then you gave me my first Valentine—a banner emblazoned with the crest of Richard the Lion-Hearted. I have never been prouder of any present until today—when I received the stock certificates registered in my name, making me a major stockholder and member of the board of the Midwestern Life Insurance Company. It was another kind of banner. We were equals when we met and it is nice to know marriage has not changed my standing—in your eyes at least.

In your absence I have been occupied looking at houses. I am seeing one this afternoon that sounds most promising. It was built a year ago by a prominent attorney and his wife, but they had only occupied it six months when he died. His widow plans to move to San Francisco. They had no children but many out-of-town visitors, so the house is large and comfortable.

The newspaper carries daily accounts of the war bond drive. It is thrilling to see how much money you are raising. How fortunate for the country that you are too old for the trenches! And how fortunate for me that I have only had to lend my husband to the war effort— and not to lose him. Even so, these long separations are becoming increasingly difficult for me. Are our lives ever to belong to us again? Come when you can, my dearest. The home front is here!

Ever your

Bess

FEBRUARY 15 1918
ST LOUIS

ROBERT STEED
BLACKSTONE HOTEL
CHICAGO ILLINOIS
MY BID ON HOUSE ACCEPTED    AM SIGNING PAPERS TOMORROW
IF YOU OBJECT PLEASE ADVISE IMMEDIATELY    OTHER BUYERS
WAITING

BESS

February 20, 1918
St. Louis

Dear Cousin Josie,

I was delighted to get your letter listing the offers for your house, but I am puzzled by your refusal to accept any of them. The last offer in particular came so close to your asking price I do not see how in good conscience you could reject it.

I know you find the idea of bargaining distasteful, but, believe me, it is in no way dishonest to ask a higher price than you expect to get—and in no way a defeat to accept a lower price than you ask. Besides, if you refuse to take a penny less than your asking price, you are depriving the buyer of an important sense of accomplishment. Having just been in this position, I know how essential it is to feel you have saved money when in fact you have just spent a great deal.

We have bought a spacious three-story home in the center of town and will be moving next month. By then I trust you will have sold your house. Fortunately you do not have to worry about what to do with your furniture. From the first minute I saw it, I felt it was part of my heritage, and I would certainly not want it sentenced to storage in a warehouse. I am convinced everything you own will look perfect in my new home.

I am sure your friends already in residence at the Riverview Home are looking forward to your arrival, and their company should provide a welcome change for you after so many years of living alone. Friends are a great blessing, especially in the absence of immediate family. However, you may count on the continuing affection of your devoted cousin,

Bess

February 28, 1918
St. Louis

Miss Abigail Saunders
Director
Riverview Convalescent Home
Syracuse, New York

My dear Miss Saunders,

This is to notify you that my cousin, Miss Josephine Farrow, has just sold her home and would like to assume occupancy of the private room reserved in her name in two weeks. Since she will only be in residence half the month of March, I assume the usual monthly rate will be prorated accordingly. Please send the bill to me at my new address.

Sincerely,
Mrs. Robert R. Steed

MARCH 12 1918
ST LOUIS

MISS JOSEPHINE FARROW
2514 ELM STREET
SYRACUSE NEW YORK
ADVISE AGAINST DELAYING CLOSE OF ESCROW AM ARRIVING THIS WEEKEND TO HELP YOU MOVE PACK ONLY WHAT YOU WILL TAKE WITH YOU

BESS

March 18, 1918
Syracuse, New York

Dear Papa and Mavis,

I am spending the night in the house where you spent so much of your childhood, Papa. Even here I cannot imagine you as a carefree little boy, but perhaps it is because you never were. I am filled with sadness imagining what it was like for you to lose your mother at the age of eight, and I understand fully for the first time the debt you feel to Cousin Josie and her family. But you have carried it long enough. Now it is my turn. Tomorrow I am accompanying Cousin Josie to the convalescent home where a very comfortable room awaits her. I was there today making the final arrangements.

She was extremely reluctant to put her house on the market and even as late as yesterday had to be coaxed like a child into signing the final papers. I feel she was very fortunate to find a buyer who would meet her price. The house is in need of extensive repairs (a fact I had to point out privately to Cousin Josie). She had always lived here like a tenant, leaving the responsibility and expense of maintaining the house to someone else: first her parents, then you. However, it is solidly built and, with a little work, should provide a splendid home for its new owners and their children, of whom there are five with another on the way.

The furniture is even more magnificent than I remembered. I am having it all shipped to St. Louis, where I trust it will help transform our new house into a home with a sense of family history.

Cousin Josie absolutely refuses to consider making a will. It is an admission of mortality she will not even discuss. However, it is no longer necessary, since, with the furniture, she is repaying all debts, past and future, to me and my family in advance of her death.

You must plan a visit to St. Louis soon to see us in our new home.

Much love,<br>Bess

March 20, 1918
TO WHOM IT MAY CONCERN:
On this date Josephine Farrow of Syracuse, New York, turns over all title to furnishings contained in her former residence to her cousin, Elizabeth Alcott Steed, in grateful acknowledgment of the continuous financial and emotional support provided her by the Alcott family.
SIGNED: Josephine Farrow
WITNESS: Abigail Saunders
            Director
            Riverview Convalescent Home

*Addendum:* The four-poster bed, which formerly occupied the master bedroom of the Farrow home, will be moved to the Riverview

Convalescent Home and remain in the possession of Miss Farrow for as long as she wishes, or until her death, at which time it will become the property of her cousin Elizabeth Alcott Steed.

March 20, 1918
Syracuse, New York

Dear Heart,

I have seen the future and it frightens me. Shakespeare was right about old age. Cousin Josie was as terrified as a child on her first day of school when I left her at the convalescent home this morning. Her room is sunny and comfortable, though not nearly as large as it looked in the brochure. But perhaps that is because it is so completely dominated by the four-poster bed she insisted on bringing with her. The bed has been in her family for generations. She was conceived in it, born in it, and intends to die in it. I would hate to think that my life ended in the same place where it began.

I know now one must plan one's old age as surely as one plans any other stage of life. The tragedy of Cousin Josie's life is that she never knew what she wanted at any age—only what she did not want. She never wanted to marry nor to pursue a career, and in life, unlike grammar, double negatives do not produce an affirmative.

I have never been more grateful for my family than I was this morning when I told Cousin Josie good-bye. I tried to convince her that I will always care about her but she just shook her head and continued calling me Mrs. Steed. She has never called me "Cousin" and now I suppose she never will.

I am spending the weekend with the Davises in Connecticut and then Totsie and I are going into New York City for a few days. We plan to share a hotel room, see plays, and pretend we are still schoolgirls with all the world ahead of us. Having begun this trip by facing old age, I shall end it by remembering my youth—an attempt to balance the future with the past before coming home to you, my beloved present.

All my love,
Bess

Dearest Totsie,

I came home last March and planted a garden as close to yours as I could manage in our Missouri climate. Everything is in bloom now and I can proclaim the effect a triumph. I became a member of the St. Louis Garden Club in April on the basis of my design for a new garden (though to be frank, membership is based more on social standing than on horticultural talent). I invited the entire membership to an outdoor tea last week, and as a result my social life is now in full flower also.

Rob still spends more time traveling with the war bond campaign than he does at home. Victory appears close but there are still battles to be fought—and financed—and Rob is finding it increasingly difficult to convince people to contribute to a cause that seems so nearly won.

We receive many invitations and I accept all of them, with the warning that my husband's acceptance is only conditional. If Rob is out of town when the day arrives, I go alone. Fortunately, with so many men away at war in one capacity or another, a woman alone is not the social anathema she once was, and I trust this attitude will not disappear when the war is over.

To be truthful, even when he is at home, Rob prefers to be closeted with a few associates, working for a good cause, than to lend his presence to any social event. Sometimes I wonder what our life will be like after the war. We have traveled in such different directions in the last few years.

Forgive the smudges on this page, but I have just bought myself a typewriter and I am teaching myself how to type. I began by typing only my business correspondence but I have grown very fond of the sound of the keys clacking to accompany my thoughts and now I even type my laundry list. I feel I am functioning as my own secretary and suddenly see my whole life very objectively as an ambitious and well-planned enterprise. I now make carbon copies of everything I write and last week I bought a filing cabinet so that I can keep a permanent record of all my correspondence. It may sound silly, but somehow as a result of my new typewriter, my life has acquired a sense of order and importance it never had before.

Darling Totsie, it is so good to feel as close to you again as I did at college. Since marriage, I have made very few friends purely on the basis of my own delight in them. We must try to see each other more often—and preferably without our husbands.

It is nearly 4 A.M. now. I must end this and try to sleep. With Rob away, there is never any immediate reason to turn out the light, and I have been surprised more than once in recent weeks by an early sunrise.

Je t'embrasse,<br><br>Bess

June 29, 1918<br>St. Louis

Mr. Marvin Hamilton
Vice-President
Midwestern Life Insurance Company
921 Olive Street
St. Louis, Missouri

Dear Marvin:

Rob will be out of town at the time the next stockholders' meeting is scheduled so I will be representing both of us.

Enclosed is the proposed agenda you sent me, with an addendum I drew up yesterday detailing some other matters which I feel should be discussed by the entire board. I have not had much to say at meetings since I became a major stockholder but I have listened—and learned. Now in Rob's absence, I feel I should speak out when the occasion demands and the fall dividend is a topic that greatly concerns me.

Best,<br><br>Bess

cc: Robert R. Steed

July 7, 1918<br>St. Louis

Dear Cousin Josie,

I am glad you liked the lap robe. But you should not have been surprised that I remembered your birthday. There is tangible evidence of you and your family throughout our home now. We eat at the table where you shared so many meals with your mother and father. I am writing this letter at the desk where you so often sat to write me. Our lives have blended now and I would like to think that we are as much a part of yours as you are of ours.

At my insistence my mother-in-law has moved to St. Louis to share our home. She keeps your old piano in her room and gives daily lessons to the children. Their love for her makes them more diligent pupils than they would be otherwise, I am sure, and even little Eleanor, who is not quite five, goes dutifully to her grandmother's room every morning to practice her scales. In the afternoon the boys practice and it is only in the evening, when their patient teacher sits down to play, that recognizable chords can be heard coming from the room.

I would love to have the house filled with music all day and once the children have acquired some small ability, we will move the piano downstairs into the central living area. But for now it is a blessing (for their parents, that is) to have their early efforts inaudible to all ears but those of their teacher. The proximity of the sounds of practice will no doubt inspire her to even greater efforts in furthering their musical education. No doubt there are often times when she would gladly exchange the noisy companionship to which her role as grandmother entitles her for the solitude you find so oppressive.

There must be many interesting lives gathered under the same roof with you. Sharing someone else's life—even for a few minutes a day—is not always easy but I feel sure you would find it worth the effort. I find it is that constant ebb and flow from solitude to society (in its broadest usage) that allows one to experience life in all its variety. Too much of either is unendurable—at least to me. Please write again soon. Though my own life is filled with activity, letters encourage momentary escape into other lives, and I come back to my own with greater contentment.

Affectionately,<br>Bess

July 10, 1918
St. Louis

Dear Papa and Mavis,

How I wish you could be with us this summer. The garden is in full bloom, as are the children. It has been almost two years since Eleanor's accident but my heart still turns over with joy every time I catch an unexpected glimpse of her running and playing with her brothers. As hard as they try to elude her, she is never far behind —and when she finally does catch up, she always greets them with a radiant smile, never guessing that they might not be as glad to see her as she is to see them. I know now good health is a gift and I will never again take it for granted.

I am so sorry, Papa, that your heart condition prevents you from planning a trip to St. Louis. I would like for you to see how well Cousin Josie's furniture fits into our new home. Since she insisted on taking the four-poster bed with her, I have furnished our master bedroom with the two twin beds from the guest room. However, it has occurred to me that the two of you might enjoy the comfort of twin beds, especially in view of Papa's present difficulty in breathing. Many married couples, as they grow older, change their furnishings to conform to their changing circumstances. Why don't I ship the beds on to you—and you can send me the double bed my mother brought with her as a bride to Honey Grove. I know she always intended for me to have it some day, and it would mean a great deal to me if that day could be now.

Lovingly,

Bess


August 10, 1918
St. Louis

Dear Papa and Mavis,

Not having had a reply to my last letter, I was astonished when the bed arrived yesterday without an accompanying word.

I hope my suggestion did not offend you, but please be assured your comfort was my prime consideration. I assume you do not want the twin beds I mentioned. They are in very good condition, and if you place them side by side, the effect is entirely one of shared repose. However, I will wait to hear from you before I send them in case I have misunderstood your intentions.

Rob knew nothing of my letter to you so was completely taken by surprise when he arrived home this weekend and found the double bed waiting in our room. We have been separated so much by recent events that when we are together we cherish our closeness. I could not bear the thought of buying a bed when I knew my mother had always intended for me to have hers, but thank you for allowing me an early inheritance.

My love,

Bess

September 16, 1918
St. Louis

Dear Mavis,

I was shocked to learn from your last letter how much Papa's health has failed in recent months. I am writing him separately so please do not share this letter with him as I want to be able to express my anxieties openly with you.

I understand now your delay in responding to my inquiry about the beds. Of course you will have no need for the matching twin beds now. I think your decision to occupy separate bedrooms is very wise and one which I frankly would have urged on you some time ago in view of Papa's advancing years had I not been afraid of intruding into the more private realms of marriage.

I can imagine the devoted care you have been giving Papa and I envy the nurse's training you received as part of your college education; however, I would feel so much better about both of you if there were a professional nurse in residence also. Heart patients require constant vigilance, and it is a physical impossibility for one person to be on guard around the clock. You must protect your own health —for Papa's sake as well as your own.

I don't think I have ever expressed to you how much your presence has meant to him—and to all of us who love him. He had very little desire to go on with his own life once Mama died and, unlike many parents, he was much too proud and independent to share mine. You have done for my father what no dutiful daughter is able to do, and I am so grateful for all that you have given him. I hope and pray there are still many years ahead for you both, and in that hope I urge you to conserve your energies by sharing your duties with a nurse.

I know my father's reluctance to spend money for anything he considers an extravagance, so I am writing to tell him the nurse is a gift from me. She will only be doing what I would be doing if I were there—but with a great deal more efficiency and skill. I will leave it to you to make the arrangements but I urge you to do so immediately. I am sure you are exhausted, and we cannot afford to have two patients.

Devotedly,
Bess

October 10, 1918
St. Louis

Dearest Papa and Mavis,

I was very distressed to learn there were no trained nurses in your area available for private employment. But I certainly do not consider the matter closed.

I am writing Lydia to make inquiries in Dallas. And Mother Steed remembers with great affection the nurse who took care of Father Steed during his last illness. She has since retired and now lives with her sister in Wichita Falls but she would undoubtedly welcome the chance to renew her friendships in Honey Grove and Papa might enjoy the company of someone his own age for a change. I will contact her immediately and let you know when I hear from her.

Devotedly,
Bess

November 5, 1918
St. Louis

Dear Papa and Mavis,

Peace at last! There is much joy in the streets here. Total strangers smile at one another and clasp hands.

I was in the garden working when I heard the news—from a delivery boy shouting at the top of his lungs as he drove his truck down the street. Our gardener was beside me on his knees, taking in bulbs for the winter. He sprang to his feet, threw his arms around me, and kissed me. I cried for joy and kissed him back and it was minutes later before either of us even seemed surprised at what we had done. Then tears began to roll down his cheeks and he said his son's life had been spared. He was too young for the last draft, but the next one would have taken him. I shared his joy. I have been terrified wondering how much longer Rob would be spared active service. I do not think I could be one of those wives who bravely send their husbands off to die. I am a good citizen but I am a better wife. My gardener now says that his son will never know what war is like. I pray he is right.

Miss Sarah Powell, the nurse who took care of Father Steed, will be arriving to help you next week. I have sent her first month's salary in advance. We had no difficulty agreeing on the amount but it is based on the assumption that she will do everything you ask of her. If you feel she is remiss in this regard, please let me know before I send next month's salary.

We think of you hourly, and our Thanksgiving prayers will begin with one for Papa's quick return to good health.

Lovingly,

Bess

December 5, 1918
St. Louis

Dearest Totsie,

The news that you and Dwight are adopting a baby is the most appropriate Christmas greeting you could have sent. What a joyous experience awaits you! You must not worry about Dwight's reluctant consent. I wonder how many men would freely elect fatherhood if the decision were left entirely to them. It is fortunate for the future of the race that it is almost never their decision.

No returning soldier could have received a more jubilant welcome home than Rob. His pace for the last year has been grueling, and I realize now he has kept himself going purely by an effort of will. I hope he will be able to rest now that he is home for good. However, he is concerned about the amount of time he has spent away from the business and anxious to move ahead with expansion plans designed to capitalize on the spirit of optimism already engendered by the Armistice.

The New Year will truly mark a new beginning for us all. And a new life will be joining you. Now that Eleanor is five and in many ways already an eccentric little adult, I am beginning to miss the presence of a baby in the house. But I suppose I must give Rob a few months to renew his acquaintance with the children he already has. However, next year at this time we may have a nativity of our own to celebrate.

Je t'embrasse—and Dwight too,

Bess

---

Deck the halls and forget the past
Our husbands and fathers are home at last!
So lift your glasses and give a cheer
For a joyous Christmas and a peaceful New Year.

Bess and Rob Steed
Robin, Drew, and Eleanor

---

January 3, 1919
St. Louis

Dear Lydia,

We loved having all of you here for Christmas. It was especially good to see Manning again. Your frequent letters keep us close to you, but Manning has become a stranger to us. I must admit Rob and I were quite unprepared for his decision to leave the insurance business and enter the academic world. But we admire your decision to take a teaching job to support the family while he completes his graduate studies. I trust this new field of endeavor will satisfy his interests as a person and at the same time enable him to fulfill his responsibilities to his family. I am fortunate to be married to a man who takes such joy in his business, quite apart from the financial rewards, but I must confess to an equal fascination with the world of high finance. I know Rob will miss having Manning as a partner but I hope he will compensate by confiding more often in me.

Thank God we have won the war and can start working toward goals of our own. How I look forward to the coming year!

I must close now. Rob has been in bed for hours. He comes home from the office so exhausted that he is often already asleep by the time I read the children their bedtime stories. While he was away, I came to look upon the late night hours as my own. With the children asleep and the house quiet, I could escape completely into my own thoughts. I thought this would change once Rob was home, but it's hard to break the habit—and many nights I don't even feel like trying. I suppose that is why I do most of my letter writing at night. With pen in hand I can carry on my end of a conversation even though the other party is asleep. Still, it will be morning soon so I must try to rest. What a waste of time spending so many hours unconscious, eyes and ears closed to the beauty of the world. If I live to be a hundred, the days will never be long enough for me.

Write soon. I love hearing from you.

Love to you all,

Bess

January 10, 1919
St. Louis

Dear Mavis,

I have been meaning to write since Christmas, but the holidays left us all exhausted, and I am afraid the children paid for their "visions of sugarplums" with aching tummies. At last I dare say that is all it was. With influenza running rampant, no mother dares dismiss even the most common childhood illness, and I was terrified when one child after another showed the same symptoms.

Eleanor was the first to complain of stomach pains and the next day Drew joined her. Sturdy little Robin was the last to succumb, but one afternoon when I had tucked the other two in bed for a nap, he crawled in beside them and that night none of us slept. But the worst is over now and tonight all three are curled up beside their father in my mother's big double bed reenacting the battles of the war with their toy soldiers.

Miss Powell wrote of Papa's improvement, but I was glad to have your letter confirming her report. I am so happy she has relieved you of your responsibilities in the kitchen. Now you have more time to spend with Papa. You mustn't worry that you are neglecting him by no longer cooking for him. Remember, he married you for your mind, not your lemon meringue pie.

Please encourage Papa to follow Miss Powell's advice about proper eating habits. If you need any help along this line, do not hesitate to let me know. My father would swear he never took an order from a woman in his life, but looking back, I realize now it was my mother who made most of the decisions that shaped our lives. I always envied her ability to insinuate her ideas into other people's minds while remaining docile and eager to please on the surface. I have never been patient enough to practice this subterfuge and fortunately with my own husband it has not been necessary. We grew up being outspoken with one another and marriage has mercifully failed to impose more conventional manners on our relationship. But I know from past experience the flattery required to get my father to change his mind about anything, and I will be happy to help in any way I can.

Fondly,

Bess

January 25, 1919

St. Louis

Dear Marvin,

Rob awoke in the night with severe chest pains. I was able to persuade him to stay in bed today by promising to drive down to your office personally and put these contracts on your desk so that you would find them waiting on your return from Kansas City. He is most anxious to talk to you about the trip and discuss your feelings about opening a branch office there, so please call immediately.

However, allow me to interject a wifely word of caution at this point. In the last year Rob spent all his reserves of energy on the war bond campaign. He is simply in no condition to oversee an ambitious expansion program at this time. If you could advise a delay as a result of your findings on this trip, it would allow him time to recover at least some of his former strength.

As a stockholder I know the importance of moving ahead when the time is right but not at the risk of ruining the health of the man who began the business in the first place. I cannot take care of him alone. I can stand between my children and anything that threatens their well-being, but I can only stand beside my husband. I need your help—and so does he.

Bess

Dear Lydia and Manning,

Thank you both for writing. Your letters were so full of love and support I broke into tears when I read them. I had to compose myself before I took them in to Rob. I wish I could tell you he was feeling better but since I wrote you his exhaustion has given way to influenza —not a severe case according to the doctor, which I suppose means he has seen worse, but I haven't.

Rob seems so weak and helpless—and for the first time in his life welcomes every suggestion I make. Though I have always prided myself on an independent spirit, I see now I have been like a child, stubbornly insisting I can do everything alone but secure in the knowledge that someone wiser and stronger was waiting in the background, ready to help at the first sign of trouble. Whenever I have attempted anything on my own, Rob has always been standing by—to be summoned at a single cry. In my vanity I have thought I stood beside him as an equal, but in the past few days, with our roles reversed, I have felt for the first time the weight of unspoken dependence on my shoulders. I am just beginning to understand what enormous demands a wife and children make on a man—even though they may never ask for anything.

How I wish the two of you were here with me. During the holidays, as we went from one party to another, I felt as if I had lived in St. Louis all my life. Now suddenly I am a stranger here. I am afraid Rob may not recover and I cannot imagine life without him. When Papa was so ill last fall, I was able to accept the possibility of his death. I was filled with sorrow and determined to do every-thing in my power to prevent it, but I was prepared to be told that nothing could save him. I thought at the time my attitude was mature and reasonable but now it seems callous and insensitive.

How dare we not be outraged by death, at whatever age it occurs!

Oh, my dears, keep your hearts close to mine. My own beats so loudly it obliterates the dreadful silence that surrounds me.

Bess

February 1, 1919<br>St. Louis

Dear Miss Powell,

This is an urgent appeal for your help. My husband is gravely ill and there is no one here I can trust as I do you. Please come to us.

My father is nearly recovered now and in my mind you are the reason. I have to believe you can accomplish the same miracle for my husband. Enclosed is a check to cover transportation costs and a month's salary. Please write me your arrival time and I will meet the train personally. I am desperate. The doctor says nothing can be done. Influenza must run its course. But I cannot stand by helplessly watching my husband suffer. You must come. You have my gratitude in advance—and forever.

Bess Alcott Steed

February 4, 1919<br>St. Louis

Dear Papa and Mavis,

Forgive me for taking Miss Powell away from you—and for not telling you sooner about Rob. It is difficult enough for someone in good health to bear the suffering of a loved one—I wanted to spare you as long as possible.

Rob is a victim of that terrible war as surely as any wounded soldier. This epidemic is thought to have originated in Europe and been conveyed across the ocean by returning soldiers. What grim irony that it was Rob's very effort on behalf of the war that left him exhausted and vulnerable to the new enemy brought home by the Armistice.

He is very weak but fights to remain conscious. It is an effort for him to speak but he manages a gallant smile every time he opens his eyes and sees me looking at him. It takes all my control not to kneel beside him and gather him into my arms but I must not let him see how frightened I am.

Pray for us both,

Bess


February 6, 1919

St. Louis

Mr. Joseph Darnell
Attorney at Law
The Wilson Building
Dallas, Texas

Dear Joe,

I am enclosing a codicil to Rob's will that he dictated to me this morning. The signature is very shaky but I can attest to its authenticity as I helped guide his hand. He has been bedridden with influenza for over a week now, and his condition grows more critical by the hour. The doctor says there is nothing more we can do—each body has to fight the disease in its own way. I am appalled at how helpless all the supposed advances of modern life have left us as individuals. Science may be the new religion, but I have yet to hear a minister say there is nothing more he can do. At least they pray with you to the end.

I remember how I had to urge Rob to make a will after our first child was born. We both felt we had our whole lives ahead of us, and he wanted no part in planning his death. But I had just seen my mother die at an early age, and I felt it was important to our child to plan our deaths as carefully as we were planning our lives. And of course you agreed with me.

Last night, as he dictated this, Rob forced me to face with him the terrifying possibility that his life may be coming to an end. But having faced it bravely, without flinching, as a soldier a firing squad, I must believe our courage will be rewarded and we will be allowed to return to battle side by side.

Thank you for all your help, dear Joe—for what you have done for us in the past as well as for what we may require of you in the future, though, God willing, it will be the distant future.

Devotedly,

Bess

February 8, 1919
St. Louis

Dear Papa and Mavis,

Miss Powell is truly an angel of mercy. She arrived two days ago and immediately took charge of the household. She never gives orders but conveys such an innate sense of authority everyone is anxious to accommodate her.

It is such a blessing that she knew Mother Steed when she was younger and stronger. I suppose any mother, seeing her child so perilously ill, would feel the whole balance of nature had been upset, but Rob's illness has shaken his mother to the core and she cannot even discuss it with the children without bursting into tears. But Miss Powell's presence seems to remind her of the strength she showed during her own husband's last illness and today she is much calmer.

Rob is a little better this morning—or am I just pretending that Miss Powell can work miracles? I know I am investing her with superhuman powers, but the doctor will not admit to any and God seems so far away. I have to believe that someone can help and aside from everything else she has done, Miss Powell has given me hope.

Your illness brought her into our lives, Papa, and so as terrible as it was for you and all of us who love you, it left at least one blessing in its wake. Now we must pray with clenched heart that these fierce waves will wash over us and leave us still clinging to the shore—spent and exhausted—but alive!

Your loving presence sustains me, even at a distance.

Lovingly,

Bess

FEBRUARY 10 1919
ST LOUIS

MR AND MRS MANNING SHEPHERD
2793 SWISS AVE
DALLAS   TEXAS
ALL HOPE GONE   COME AT ONCE   ROB IS ASKING FOR YOU

BESS

Dearest Papa and Mavis,

Forgive me for ending our conversation so abruptly this morning. My throat closes when I say "dead" as if my whole body were trying to strangle the grim fact before my lips announce it.

Rob faced his death more honestly than I did, never indulging any false hope toward the end, but calmly making changes in his will and charting future courses of action for me to follow. The love he felt for me in life was never better proved than by the concern he showed for me in death. He spent his final hours anticipating every decision that awaited me, and now as I go about carrying out his instructions, his presence is still part of me. He was more afraid of leaving me alone than he was of dying, and he did everything he could to spare me those lonely decisions that every new widow must face.

Widow! My hand suddenly cramps with pain. And my fingers rebel as my throat did earlier. I must go to the children for awhile.
8 P.M.

The children are finally asleep and I will be following their example soon. I have always hated to turn out the last light, but tonight I am eager for oblivion. You must not worry about me. I am surrounded by people who share my grief, and for the sake of Papa's health, you must stay where you are.

Lydia and Manning arrived yesterday morning and spent all day at Rob's bedside. I was so thankful they could come. There was not a chapter of his life Rob did not try to complete in the short time left to him. Manning promised to stay with the company indefinitely, even though his interests now lie elsewhere. This is a sacrifice on his part, but one which I have accepted with gratitude. Lydia was too overcome with emotion to tell Rob good-bye, and today she is filled with regret at all the things she failed to say. She told me today Rob was and will always be the finest man she has ever known. How sad for Lydia to bestow that superlative on her brother rather than her husband.

Mother Steed is not speaking to me. Yesterday, after she said her farewell to Rob, she went to the children and told them all good-bye. She said her life was over, and she prayed she would be

dead by morning. Then she announced she was going to bed—
although it was only three in the afternoon. Eleanor of course
broke into sobs. Drew was very brave and promised tenderly to
bury her in the back yard beside his pet turtle. And Robin ran to
me and asked solemnly if Daddy wanted all of us to die and go to
heaven with him.

When dinner was served and Mother Steed refused to emerge
from her bedroom, I took a tray up to her personally. I knocked but
when there was no answer, I marched into the room, set the tray
down on her bedside table, and announced that I would continue
bringing her meals to her room. I said I could not permit her to see
the children again until she could offer them some assurance that she
wanted to go on living. If she intended to die, I continued, then they
might as well get used to her absence now. She pretended to be
asleep while I was talking, but after I slammed the door, I heard the
rattling of silverware.

After putting the children to bed, I went back to Rob, relieving
Miss Powell, who had kept devoted watch since dawn. I promised
to wake her if there were any change. Then Rob and I were alone.
For a few moments the sheer pleasure of completely possessing each
other's attention allowed us to forget everything but the present. He
reached for my hand and held it through the night. Though he slept
for awhile, I could not bear to close my eyes, knowing he might soon
be gone from my sight forever. I was filled with a strange sense of
elation, and my tears seemed to spring more from a feeling of joy
at what we had been given than from sorrow at what we were about
to lose.

When morning came, Rob insisted I get the children ready for
school. I shook my head, I wanted them with me today but then he
reminded me it was Valentine's Day. On what other day does a
parent send his child into the world and know he will come home
feeling more loved than when he left? Rob kissed each of them
good-bye and though it was an unbearable moment for me, they
were so excited about the festivities awaiting them at school, they left
without a backward glance.

When I came back into the room, I thought Rob was asleep but
then he smiled and said for the first time since we met in the fourth
grade he didn't have a Valentine for me. The two of us have never
paid much attention to our birthdays. To me birthdays are a celebra-

tion between parent and child and Christmas is a birthday celebration for all children. But Valentine's Day belonged to the two of us, and Rob always prided himself on extravagant gestures on that occasion.

He asked me to lie down beside him and I did. He said I was his life and as long as I was alive, the best of him could not die. I clung to him and put my head against his chest. I could barely hear his heart beating and I was afraid I was making it more difficult for him to breathe, but when I raised my head, he pulled it back against his chest and said he thought he could sleep if I stayed with him. I fell asleep with his arms around me. A few hours later I was awakened by an awful silence. My head was still on his chest but his heart had stopped beating. At that moment I knew I had no right to be angry with Mother Steed. I wished with all my heart that I had never wakened from the last sleep we would ever share.

I stayed beside him till the pain of knowing he was dead was too great to be borne alone. Lydia and Manning were waiting in the next room, respecting my right to be alone with him at the last. I did not have to tell them. Though their loss is great, their first words were for me. Then they went into him and I went to Mother Steed. She knew from my face what had happened and before I could apologize for my burst of temper the night before she accused me of deliberately depriving her of a last word with her only son. She brought him into the world, she said, and had a right to be present when he left it.

I was dismayed and fled to my room. Somehow anger was able to dislodge the sobs buried deep inside me. I shrieked my rage and grief at the impassive ceiling that seemed to confine me in my room as cruelly as the sky prevented my soul from escaping this now alien earth.

I fell on my bed but lay awake for what seemed like hours. Finally Lydia came into the room and we shared our sorrow like sisters. Then I dressed and went downstairs to meet the doctor and the minister who had come to certify that the body was dead and the soul departed.

The funeral service will be held tomorrow in the cathedral. I have requested flags and trumpets to accompany the singing of "God of Our Fathers." Perhaps it is an illusion ever to regard a single death as part of a larger sacrifice, but it is a comforting one and I have as much right to indulge in it as the widow of any soldier killed on the field of battle.

I have decided that the burial will take place here. So even if Mother Steed were still speaking to me today, she would not be tomorrow. She of course has space reserved for both her children in the family plot in Honey Grove. But death is defeat enough. I will not retreat into the past. St. Louis is where the present came to an end for us, and here I will stay until the future forces me to move in a different direction.

I must try to sleep now. There is so much to do tomorrow—thank God! If I imagine the two of you holding me close, I may have the courage to turn out the light.

Please love me.

Bess

2 A.M.

I finally fell asleep but was awakened a few minutes ago by Eleanor crying and calling for me. I brought her into my bed and she immediately fell asleep again cradled in my arms. What a blessing to forget my own need for a few minutes! The children think of me as someone strong and brave, and so with them I become everything they imagine.

Rob had that kind of power over me from the day we met. But what will I be without him to tell me how beautiful and bright I am? Are other women as frightened as I am, wondering how much of what they are is merely a reflection of what others see in them? What am I when I am all alone? Am I strong and brave without the children to assure me I am, out of their own need? Will I ever believe I am beautiful and bright out of the sight of a man who loves me? I feel as if I have just been born—cut apart from the sustaining presence that made all my decisions for me and left helpless in the hands of strangers.

I have spent so many nights alone this past year. But none of them prepared me for tonight. How I dread tomorrow!

I wish you could talk to me for awhile. I am so weary of my own thoughts.

All my love,

Bess

Harold D. Perkins
Editor
*The Dallas Morning News*
Dallas, Texas

Dear Mr. Perkins,

Though we have never met, we have many mutual friends and I am sure you are aware of my husband, Robert Randolph Steed. He made quite a name for himself in real estate and insurance circles during the eight years we lived in Dallas.

I know you will be distressed to learn of his untimely death from influenza yesterday in St. Louis. We have many friends in Dallas who will mourn his passing so I am enclosing an obituary notice which I typed myself late last night. I am sending it directly to you because I do not know who is in charge of the obituaries of prominent men, and I would not want someone in a lesser position on the staff to overlook the story simply through ignorance of who my husband was.

I will be very grateful if you will give this matter your personal attention. I have continued to subscribe to *The Dallas Morning News* even though I now live in St. Louis. I noticed a few weeks ago when Mr. Clark of the Lone Star Bank died, in addition to a conventional portrait, the paper printed a picture of him at groundbreaking ceremonies for the new bank building. Therefore, I am including a photo of my husband at the formal opening of the St. Louis office of the Midwestern Life Insurance Company, which was the reason for our move here. (I am the lady on the left, holding the roses.) I am also enclosing a recent portrait (which I fortunately requested for an anniversary present last year). Both of these photographs are copies, so please feel free to keep them permanently in your files. You may have further need of them in years to come when reference is made to my husband and his many outstanding accomplishments.

Sincerely,
Elizabeth Alcott Steed

Enc.

ROBERT RANDOLPH STEED

Robert Randolph Steed, 29, prominent real-estate developer in Dallas and founder of the Midwestern Life Insurance Company, died last Thursday of influenza at his home in St. Louis.

He was born in 1890 in Honey Grove, Texas, the son of a prominent educator. In 1909 he married Elizabeth Alcott of Honey Grove and moved to Dallas. He made his name in real estate with the development of the Junius Heights area, and became a partner in the firm of Florence and Field.

In 1915 he was attracted to the growing field of life insurance and started his own company. His success in this new venture led to the opening of an office in St. Louis, and he moved there with his family in the fall of 1917.

He was area chairman of the Liberty Loan Campaign and traveled extensively over a five-state area on behalf of the war effort. He was personally commended by the Secretary of the Treasury for the success of his campaign.

He was a member of the Dallas Country Club and St. Matthew's Episcopal Cathedral in Dallas, and in St. Louis served on the board of directors of the Chamber of Commerce and belonged to Christ Church Cathedral.

Funeral services and burial took place in St. Louis last Friday. Mr. Steed is survived by his wife, Elizabeth Alcott Steed of St. Louis, and three children, Robert Randolph, 8; Andrew Alcott, 7; and Eleanor Elizabeth, 6; his mother, Jane Cantrice Steed, and a sister, Lydia Steed Shepherd of Dallas.


February 16, 1919
St. Louis

Dearest Papa and Mavis,

How I wish you were here with me, and yet what a comfort it is late at night to set down my thoughts in a letter to you.

The funeral service was magnificent and for a moment even I believed that death could be the triumphant conclusion to life. The cathedral was packed with people from all walks of life, many of whom were strangers to me. I suppose it comes as a shock to any wife to realize how little of her husband's life has actually been shared with her. He would have known everyone at my funeral. However, it was thrilling to see in what affection and respect he was held in this city. Though I am sure I would have loved him if all the world had been against him—and indeed at times might have welcomed the adversity that would have left us with only each other—I am grateful to know so many share my loss.

After the service friends came to our home to pay their respects. Lydia and Mother Steed stayed upstairs with the children, not wanting to share their grief with strangers. But Manning offered to stay with me and I accepted gratefully. I also felt it was important for him to meet some of the men who had been so helpful to Rob when he first decided to open an office here.

I have always found it difficult to express my sympathy to anyone who has suffered a loss and I was afraid I would find it even more difficult to accept such expressions. But the alchemy of grief transforms the most awkward phrases into sentiments of purest gold, and I treasured every word of comfort offered.

Many of our friends brought food to the house—and the dining table looked as if we were preparing for a banquet. It all seemed so festive I impulsively ordered the imported champagne we had been sent as a gift last Christmas by the Secretary of the Treasury to be put on ice and served to our guests. After all, the same efforts that earned the champagne had brought about this occasion. This was to be Rob's last party and I decided to make it one he would have enjoyed.

Manning was a little shocked but I insisted he make the first toast and he rose to the occasion with unexpected wit and style. He spoke eloquently about Rob and the boldness of his vision. Suddenly my own personal loss seemed insignificant compared to what the country had lost in the death of the man who was my husband. After Manning, others spoke and at the end of each speech we raised our glasses.

The other men present, including some of the most prominent businessmen in this part of the country, accepted Manning as one of them and their obvious regard, reinforced no doubt by champagne, seemed to transform my shy, scholarly brother-in-law into a figure of consequence in the world of finance. I am convinced he could have a splendid future here if he had someone who believed in him at his side. But the man I saw tonight is not the man Lydia loves, and her hopes for him are quite different than mine would be in her place. I see now how much of what a man becomes is due to the woman at his side. A life can go in so many different directions and though a man may be the captain of his soul, he needs a good navigator at his side if he dares sail into uncharted seas.

Lydia came down after all the guests had left. She declined our offer of champagne and said she was shocked by all the laughter she had heard. She announced that Mother Steed was returning to Dallas with her and she had spent the afternoon helping her pack. I said nothing, but if I had chosen to speak my thoughts aloud, I would have asked which of the three women who loved Rob—his wife, his mother, or his sister—had done more to honor his memory that day?

Manning, once again the docile husband, accompanied Lydia upstairs. I called for the children and they came running, eager to sample all the food. I poured ginger ale into champagne glasses for them and asked each of them to propose a toast to their father. I wish you could have heard them. They said what they felt so beautifully it brought tears to my eyes, and suddenly the control I had maintained so successfully since morning collapsed and I finally began to cry. Children are terrified of adult tears and the three of them clung to me, repeating every hollow word of consolation I had ever used on them. I struggled to regain my composure and nodded my head in agreement. "Yes, I know. Everything's going to be all right." How I wish I could believe those words.

The three children and I are like survivors of a terrible shipwreck. We crept into the big bed as if it were a life raft, and they went to sleep easily. I lay awake for a long time, taking comfort in the sounds of their breathing, then finally turned on a light at my desk and sat down to write. I am terrified of tomorrow—and all the tomorrows I must face alone.

I love you with all my heart,

Bess

February 25, 1919<br>St. Louis

Dear Mr. Fineman,

I was deeply touched to hear from you again and to know that in a sense we are sharing another time of tragedy. I am sorry I did not know of your wife's death last year. I still subscribe to *The Dallas News* but there are days when I fail to read it as closely as I should.

I derived great satisfaction from the account of my husband's death in the Dallas paper. Thank you for enclosing the clipping. People think they are sparing my feelings by keeping the tone of their letters abstract, but I take comfort in anything that offers tangible evidence of my husband's existence, and I was very pleased that both pictures were used.

I am stunned by the rage that has surfaced within me since my husband died. I have always thought of myself as a tolerant, broad-minded person who wished everyone well. But I see now I was that kind of person only because I had no reason not to be. Injustice makes villains of us all, and I am afraid I am going to lose more than my husband before I find enough charity in my heart to forgive those whose only sin is that they are still alive.

Forgive me for inflicting so many of my unspoken thoughts on you, but I sensed you would understand. Here at home and in my letters to friends and family, I have to maintain a calm façade that becomes more foreign to me by the hour. I hope you will permit me the luxury of exorcising a few more demons in yet another letter. You were so kind to write—and even kinder now to listen.

The children are all well. Eleanor is active and healthy and I suspect she has almost forgotten the tragic occasion that acquainted us with one another.

Sincerely,

Bess Steed

March 5, 1919
St. Louis

Dear Manning,

I have been with Marvin Hamilton all morning discussing the alarming deficit in the company's finances due to deaths from influenza. The cash flow from the sale of new policies has been diverted to pay all the claims made since Christmas.

Under no circumstances can we consider paying the stockholders a dividend this quarter. I am determined to meet all the claims as promptly as possible, though this may entail considerable personal sacrifice on the part of everyone involved in the company.

Rob of course carried a sizable policy on his own life but I am shelving my claim for the moment. I am also foregoing the benefits to which I am entitled as the widow of an executive, and I am asking everyone to continue working at his present salary in spite of the higher title he inherited at Rob's death.

I think it is important for you to attend the board meeting here next week. Some long-range decisions will be made and I want you to be part of them. I hope you will plan to stay with us. The children would be so happy to have you under our roof, however briefly.

My love to Lydia and Mother Steed,

Bess

May 14, 1919
St. Louis

Dearest Totsie,

Your letter brought me the first bright day I have known since Rob died. The thought of joining you in Vermont for the summer fills me with delight! What a reprieve from the terrible reality of my life just now!

Once we decided to close the St. Louis office of the company, I knew I had no choice but to sell my house here and move back to Dallas—but to return without a husband and with less money than when we left is an unbearable admission of defeat. And I will postpone it as long as possible.

Your invitation for the summer is such a tangible offer of comfort at a time when words of sympathy ring hollow in my ears. I am so weary of people asking if there is anything they can do for me. Of course I always answer with a polite no, and they go away satisfied at having done their duty. If only once I dared answer in the affirmative. But nothing frightens people more than undisguised need. I have kept all my old friends through this difficult time by never demanding the dues of friendship. Not that I doubt they would be paid—but only once. Friendship to me is like a capital reserve. It pays dividends only so long as the principal remains intact. Whatever personal sacrifice is required, I am determined to come through this experience without spending my principal—on any level.

The children are very excited at the thought of a trip east. We are all eager for the sight of a landscape without memories. How I look forward to holding the baby—and you. Please thank Dwight for his share in your kind invitation.

I love you dearly,
Bess

May 25, 1919
St. Louis

Dear Cousin Josie,

Forgive me for the long delay in replying to your letter of condolence, but I was in such disagreement with the sentiments expressed I could not bring myself to acknowledge them.

Of course I am outraged by the untimely death of my husband, but I am even more outraged by your willingness to have been taken in his place. I will not die willingly, even if I live to be a hundred, and your welcoming acceptance of the end of life seems to me an affront to all that has gone before. I realize now that when you sat down to write me, you imagined I was looking at you through your own self-denying eyes and thinking, "Why couldn't she have been the one to die?" You do me a great injustice by attributing such a thought to me—and you do an even greater injustice to yourself.

If you have read this far, please believe that if I did not love you, I would not have been so upset by your low estimate of your own life. Surely you are not surrounded by people who share your contempt for life. But do not count on others to convince you your life matters. All of us are finally alone with only a single opinion to sustain us—our own.

I hope you will write again. I would appreciate a letter, but I am offended by self-pity masquerading as sympathy. How can death be a loss to someone for whom life has no meaning? Forgive me the arrogance of being so outspokenly alive, but I am at war with death and all those who collaborate in its victory by their silent assent. I am determined to win you to my side—the least we can do is prolong the battle by making the enemy take us by force.

I have sold our house here and am putting your furniture in storage while I take the children to Vermont for the summer. Perhaps you will come visit us once we are settled. I will write you as soon as we arrive and have a better idea of the living arrangements.

I am, as always, your devoted cousin,

Bess

June 1, 1919
St. Louis

Mrs. Leonard Maxwell
President
St. Louis Garden Club
St. Louis, Missouri

Dear Lucy,

I am addressing this letter to you in your official capacity since it concerns a business proposal. But first let me thank you again for the impressive wreath the club sent to Rob's funeral, in addition to your own personal floral tribute. My garden has been a great source of strength and comfort to me this spring, and every flower that blooms is an affirmation. I am very sad at the thought of leaving our beautiful home here and with it all the friendships that have flowered in the past two years.

Beyond this summer my plans are indefinite, but I am afraid there is no possibility of staying in St. Louis. I am very concerned about the care of Rob's grave site in my absence. Of course I have paid the cemetery for perpetual maintenance, but I am enclosing herewith a donation to the St. Louis Garden Club in the hope that the membership will collectively assume the responsibility for the upkeep of the grave. My membership in the club has been a source of enormous pride to me, and I would like to think of the grave site as a small garden reflecting the same standards of taste and excellence that the club has always set for its members.

I do not know whether there is any precedent for such a project, but it would certainly fill an immediate personal need on my part. Indeed, I expect the idea would have strong appeal for the membership at large and in the future might even provide a lucrative source of revenue for the club.

I am leaving St. Louis at the end of the week and would very much appreciate an answer before I go. Thank you for your unfailing courtesy in this as in all matters which have come to your attention as club president.

Gratefully,

Bess Steed

June 15, 1919

Woodstock, Vermont

Dear Papa and Mavis,

I am like a child again, living in this old farmhouse, surrounded by stone-walled fields of daisies, with only my own children to remind me of the adult life I left behind in St. Louis.

The train trip to New York was an adventure for the children but I was too encumbered by the luggage of remembered landscapes to share their enthusiasm. I spent hours staring out the window but saw only the interior of my own mind.

We took a milk train from New York to Vermont, which seemed to stop at every populated crossing en route. But this part of the journey was new to me and I welcomed every chance for a closer look at the countryside. My friend Totsie was waiting for us at the station with a neighboring farmer and wagon she had hired to transport us to our summer home.

Totsie and her husband discovered the property on a trip through New England last fall. The farmer who owned it was very dubious about renting it as a vacation home, with no plans for cultivating anything but pleasure, but he finally consented to a short-term lease.

Dwight and Totsie worked on the house all spring, rebuilding the stone fireplace onto which all the rooms open. Only the two downstairs bedrooms are finished. Upstairs is an open sleeping loft which looks down on the living room. Totsie intended to keep the baby in the master bedroom with her since Dwight is not expected for several weeks and give me the other bedroom, but I elected to share the loft with the children. We fall asleep talking and telling stories as if we were all the same age. How I wish they could have known their father as a child. What fun the five of us would have had that summer you rented your downtown lot to a merry-go-round. Remember, Papa? I can just see us—Rob, Bess, Robin, Drew, and

Eleanor, all friends the same age—riding round and round together. Time is a cruel thief to rob us of our former selves. We lose as much to life as we do to death.

Here in this place Totsie and I have managed to repair some of the ravages time has worked upon our friendship. We squander our days like schoolgirls on holiday, interrupting our idleness only to feed and care for the children. But it is amazing how much they are able to do for themselves as long as we ignore those twin tyrants, propriety and punctuality.

Everyone retires and arises at any hour he likes, wears clothes of his own choosing, and eats when he is hungry. We buy fresh produce and dairy products from our landlord's nearby farm. Totsie has as little interest in the culinary arts as I do, so we never sit down to a formal dinner. The first one to become hungry at night gets out bread and cheese. We keep a soup kettle going on the stove at all times. Its outward appearance changes somewhat from day to day as new ingredients are added but its basic character remains sturdy and substantial. We have virtually become vegetarians because it is so much simpler. Also the children are on a first-name basis with every four-legged creature within walking distance, so I suspect any beef, pork, or fowl found on their plates would be instantly suspect.

I live immersed in the present. To avoid thinking about the past, I avoid planning for the future. For the moment we are all well, and who can ever say more than that?

All my love,
Bess

June 30, 1919
Woodstock

Dear Lydia and Manning,

Thank you for your kind letter of advice concerning my financial situation. Let me assure you that the profits I realized from the sale of my house are safe in a savings account. I agree that this may be the last large sum of money I will see for some time and I promise to consult you before acting on any opportunities for investment that may present themselves.

Perhaps this trip did sound extravagant, but the train tickets have been our only large expense. At my insistence I share the cost of food with Totsie but everything else has been provided for us. We lead a deliberately simple life. The children are thriving on it and knowledge of how little we need to survive is making me strong.

I do not know what we will do when summer ends. I have thought about staying on here. The children could walk to the village school and I would welcome the isolation of a New England winter. But there are two months between me and any decision—thank God!

Tell Mother Steed I inquired about her health and though she may prefer not to correspond with me, the children cannot understand why she no longer writes to them.

I hope you will write again soon. The arrival of the mail is a great event around here. Eleanor loved her letter from Marian and is hard at work on a reply.

Love,
Bess

July 3, 1919
Woodstock

Dear Mr. Fineman,

Your gracious letter was forwarded to me from St. Louis. How curious that you have just returned from Boston! Our travels have taken us in the same direction this summer without our knowing it.

I did not realize your work involved stocks and bonds. I am very interested in new opportunities for investment, having just sold my house in St. Louis, and I would welcome your advice in this area. My life is in such a state of flux just now I have decided not to reinvest in real estate. I will rent a place wherever I decide to spend the winter. I am primarily interested in investments with growth potential, since I have adequate income to see me through the coming year.

Forgive me for taking advantage of your brief mention of a business trip to apprise you so fully of my own financial situation but it is a great relief to discuss money matters with an objective outsider. All my other advisors are involved at least indirectly in my financial future, and as a result their sense of responsibility for my welfare exercises undue restraint upon their judgment.

I very much enjoyed your descriptions of the people you met and the places you visited on your trip. My life here is so removed from the world you describe I could be living in a foreign country. Our daily life is confined to the farm and the few neighbors within walking distance—so social exchange is kept at a minimum.

Yesterday the farmer's wife who sells us milk and eggs invited us into her home for the first time this summer, as we were caught in a cloudburst. She is always taciturn and rather sullen, even in the most pleasant weather, but yesterday she seemed especially gloomy. Once inside her house, I learned why. As I sat in the parlor and strained for a look through the window at the view outside, she burst out bitterly, "I know, I know. It's too high and you can't see out."

"What a shame," I murmured. "You have such a magnificent view. Can't your husband lower the windows?"

She shook her head sadly. "He says it's easy enough to go outside and look at the view if you want to see it."

As we left she took my hand in a surprising show of affection. "I hope you appreciated your husband while you had him. I didn't know how well off I was the first time. Mr. Stone is my second husband." She stood in the doorway until we were out of sight. At first I thought she was sorry to see us go, then I realized she was just admiring the view.

This was the first time I had confronted my own feelings about remarriage and I was surprised to realize how opposed to the idea I am. Life seems so short I cannot bear the idea of repeating any experience—even one that brought such happiness the first time.

I look forward to hearing from you again and would welcome your suggestions for a long-term investment.

Sincerely,

Bess Steed

July 10, 1919
Woodstock

Dear Cousin Josie,

The children and I seem to have adapted to New England faster than our Pilgrim forefathers did—but then our circumstances are a great deal more pleasant.

A lady from Chicago stopped by our farm this past weekend, hoping we might have some old family Bibles or records that would aid her search for ancestors in this area. Unfortunately we were unable to supply her with anything more helpful than our interest but we did accompany her to two nearby cemeteries.

I could not go into the first one I was so overcome by the memory of the grave I left behind in St. Louis, so I stayed outside and held the baby for my friend Totsie while she and the children helped our visitor search for clues. To the children it was like a game of hide and seek through history and they got very excited running from marker to marker, comparing names and dates, guessing at family relationships and sentiments from the size of the headstones and the words engraved on them.

By the time we got to the second cemetery, I was able to accompany them inside. By now the children were so carried away by their game they had grown rather unruly and our visitor wondered aloud if a cemetery were a proper place for children. I was stunned at the vehemence of my own response. I said I could not speak for all the dead, of course, but having lost my husband just five months ago, I could vouch for his delight in the sight and sound of children at play. We parted company soon after this. Our visitor climbed into her chauffeured car headed for her next destination, and we returned on foot to the farm.

The episode kindled a spark, however, and I have resolved to take advantage of this summer in the land of my ancestors to trace my own lineage. I remember my father talking about a family tree your mother kept in the living room. For years I imagined a huge tree growing in the center of the room, with members of the family comfortably ensconced among its branches. When I visited your house for the first time, even though I was an adult and knew better, I must admit to a small pang of disappointment upon entering a conventional parlor in place of the tree-sheltered room I had imagined as a child. But I cannot remember a family tree of any kind in evidence on either of my visits. Does one exist? If so, do you know where it is? I would be so grateful to have the chance to study it this summer. I am also interested in any written records or family histories you might have in your possession.

We would be delighted to have you visit us here. The change would be good for you and we would enjoy your company. Also, if you traveled here in person, you would not have to entrust the family records to the post office.

Please give serious thought to this invitation. The children love the idea of meeting a cousin who is older than their grandfather. With the hope of seeing you soon, I remain,

Your devoted cousin,

Bess

July 17, 1919
Woodstock

Dear Arthur,

It feels strange to address you by your first name but pleasant to regard you as a friend.

I am very interested in the brochures you sent me. Would I be imposing on our friendship to ask you to set up an account for me and buy five hundred shares each of the six stocks you recommend? I appreciate your note of caution, but I am not in the market for bonds at this point, nor do I require the quarterly arrival of a check to keep faith with a company.

I thought you might enjoy the enclosed photograph of the children on the seesaw they constructed from a barrel and a plank. They invent games by the hour—the limited supplies they have here seem to stir their imaginations more than the best-equipped playroom. We will be living on a much more modest scale from now on and it is reassuring to realize my precious children will not suffer.

Thank you for your interest and attention. I look forward to hearing from you again soon.

Gratefully,

Bess

August 1, 1919
Woodstock

Dear Lydia and Manning,

I was distressed to learn from your letter how poorly the life insurance business is faring in my absence. I had hoped that by closing the St. Louis office and consolidating its resources, the company could weather this crisis. I am so grateful you are there to deal with these problems, Manning—though I am sure there are times when you wish you were anywhere else. If we can just hold on to what we have, I know business will improve and our tenacity will be rewarded.

I have opened an account with the brokerage firm of Meyers, Miller, and Fineman and have decided to invest the proceeds from the sale of my house in the stock market. You may disagree, but at this time in my life I do not feel I can afford to be cautious. However, lest I appear reckless, be assured I am acting on the carefully considered advice of a close personal friend, Arthur Fineman, a senior partner in the firm.

Totsie's husband, Dwight, arrives tomorrow and we have spent all week getting everything in order. Today Totsie decided to have her hair done. There is no beauty parlor in town, but the wife of the local postmaster gives shampoos in her home, using soft rainwater collected in barrels and heated in kettles over the fire. I wasn't planning to go, but Totsie begged me to keep her company in case the woman turned out to be as reticent as most of her neighbors. Only in New England does one run the risk of encountering an inarticulate beautician!

We left the children with our neighbor, Mrs. Stone, who put them to work in the orchard picking cherries for her exquisite pies. She put the baby in a cradle in the kitchen and rocked it with her foot while she rolled out the pie crust. Mrs. Stone raised eight children of her own and I could not imagine how she managed so many until I saw how easily she fitted our four into her afternoon's activities.

It was the first time Totsie and I had been away from the children all summer, and we suddenly felt as unfettered as young foals. We tried to maintain a sedate appearance befitting our position as we walked through town, but we were practically dancing when Totsie arrived for her beauty appointment. In our lightheaded mood she had no trouble persuading me to join her in a shampoo and soon we were both snow-capped with lather.

There was such an air of expectation about us that the postmaster's wife overcame her native shyness to ask whom we were expecting. Totsie began to talk about Dwight while the woman rinsed her hair with lemon juice. Then, while Totsie sat outside in the sun letting her hair dry, the woman turned her attention to me. In what was for her, I am certain, an unusual display of interest, she asked if I were expecting anyone special this weekend.

She was rinsing my hair at the time and attributed my long pause before responding to the water cascading over my ears. But it was not rainwater that wet my cheeks and the bitter taste in my mouth was more than lemon. I could not speak but finally shook my head negatively.

"Oh, well," she said, trying for a light tone, "who needs a reason for looking pretty?" But we both knew the answer.

I have been so happy here this summer and I truly thought I had succeeded in eluding the sorrow that has pursued me so relentlessly since Rob died. But the prospect of Dwight's arrival has made my solitude unbearable. I do not know how I am going to get through the next two weeks. I feel more alone tonight than I have ever felt in my entire life.

I love you both for being part of my memory of Rob.

Bess

August 5, 1919
Woodstock

Dear Cousin Josie,

I am sorry you felt a train trip was too arduous for you. Personally, I have always found daily routine more tiring than travel. In fact, the very thought of seeing anything new invigorates me. However, it was kind of you to send the genealogy book in your place. I was thrilled to learn that a branch of my father's family can be traced to the American Revolution and am anxious to do research and discover the extent of their contribution to this chapter in history.

It was very generous of you to give me the family tree. I only wanted to study it, not rob you of your heritage. However, if you sincerely feel it is safer in my keeping, I will be honored to have it for future generations of our family. But I am puzzled by certain omissions on the tree. The genealogy book mentions a family living in Salem, Massachusetts, in the seventeenth century that I feel sure we have a right to claim but your mother did not include them when she had the tree drawn.

I have been anxious to explore New England on my own and so have decided to take the children on an excursion next week. Totsie's husband, Dwight, has kindly offered me the use of his car.

I plan to go first to Salem and check the local records to establish our connection with the family I mentioned earlier. It is thrilling to feel personally linked with the people who founded our country. I will let you know the results of my inquiries as soon as I learn anything definite. I know you must be as interested as I am in the missing chapters of our family history.

Much love,

Bess

August 15, 1919
Boston, Massachusetts

Dear Papa and Mavis,

The discovery of our family's role in the history of this country has left me in a state of shock.

In Salem I established beyond a doubt our descent from the family of the town crier in the seventeenth century but learned at the same time that his oldest daughter was an accuser in the first witch trial. I understand now why their name is deliberately deleted from the family tree, and I suspect Cousin Josie knew all along to what an ignoble end my search for illustrious ancestors would lead me.

In Boston I hoped to redeem the ignominy of our earliest known forebears with the brave acts of our revolutionary ancestors. What a blow to find our family's name on a list of Tory sympathizers.

We are returning to the farm tomorrow. I promised the children we would retrace Paul Revere's ride on our return route and I cannot disappoint them, but every historical mile we travel will drive another nail of disappointment into my already splintered heart.

I know now that history cannot be counted on to furnish us any reason for pride in who we are. We have to do that for ourselves. I guess I should be glad I learned the truth while I still have so much of my life ahead of me. What a year! I lost my husband in the spring and my heritage in the summer. I am truly on my own.

All my love,

Bess

August 20, 1919
Woodstock

Dear Cousin Josie,

I am returning herewith the genealogy book and family tree you were kind enough to lend me. I have no further need of them and no wish to own anything that more rightfully belongs with you. After all, it was your mother who ordered the family tree made and kept it hanging in her living room until someone (you perhaps?) discovered a reason for taking it down. I understand now why it was not on display when I visited your house for the first time, and only wish you had seen fit to spare me the trip that brought me face to face with facts I would rather never have known.

However, some good may have come from my experience ancestor hunting. Dwight Davis, my friend's husband, comes from an illustrious family, many of whose members served with distinction during the Revolution. But family history is an all-or-nothing proposition. There is no way to claim the good while denying the bad, and I have warned him of the betrayals lurking in any close examination of one's origins. His wife has implored him to remove the family tree hanging in his study before their adopted child is old enough to understand his omission from it, but so far Dwight has refused. However, I think I may have abetted her cause by hinting at the existence of a few skeletons among the branches of the family tree, and Totsie has privately predicted that the tree will be out of sight when she returns home at the end of the summer.

The end of summer—how sad that sounds to me. I must make plans—and yet it is so difficult to know where to start. There must be days when it is very reassuring to you to know where and how you will spend the rest of your life—and to have all your decisions made for you by someone with your best interests at heart. I wish I could be as decisive in my own interests right now as I have always been in the interests of others. I wish there were another "I" with an existence separate from my own who could tell me what to do. At this moment I would gladly take orders from anyone who spoke with authority.

Your devoted cousin,

Bess

August 21, 1919
Woodstock

Mrs. Annie Hoffmeyer
210 Gaston Avenue
Dallas, Texas

Dearest Annie,

I read your letter with tears of joy. I was not sure I would ever hear from you again. But what unexpected bereavement brings us together! I lost my husband to death and you lost yours to another way of life. I would not presume to say which is the harder loss to bear.

I find myself in much the same position you do as fall approaches —with small children dependent on me and no husband to provide for us. Perhaps our mutual need can serve us both. As much as I dislike the idea of retracing any of my steps, I must return to Dallas next month and try to save what remains of my husband's business. And as I feel certain you are anxious to leave the scene of marital discord, let me suggest that I rent a house large enough for both of us and our children. That is, of course, if you will assume the responsibility of running it. I cannot afford to pay you a salary at this point, any more than you can afford to pay me rent, but in return for your services, I will gladly provide food and shelter for our two families.

I know when you left my employ you were firmly resolved never to return to domestic service, and I respect your decision. However, in this case you would not be working for me, we would be helping each other through a difficult time in our lives. I hope you will agree to the arrangement, as I feel we could both profit from it.

I am sending by the same post a present for each of the children. They were hand-made by the wife of the mayor of our village here. The gingham snake is for little Franz and the knitted dress for your new daughter. How cruel of Hans to make her arrival the occasion of his abrupt departure from your life.

The children send you hugs and kisses—as do I. And we all eagerly await your reply to my proposal.

Your devoted friend,

Bess Alcott Steed

August 29, 1919
Woodstock

Dearest Annie,

Your prompt reply was cause for celebration! The children and I are thrilled at the prospect of seeing you again and sharing your life. The house you mentioned sounds perfectly suited for all our needs. I am enclosing a check to cover the first month's rent, effective at the earliest date you care to move.

We plan to stay here another ten days, through the Labor Day weekend. We are planning a large picnic for the friends we have made this summer. However, as people in this part of the country are not used to socializing (most of them have not set foot in a house other than their own in years), we are not sure how many will accept our invitation. The children are preparing a play to entertain the guests—if there are any. Most of them have had even less experience with plays than they have with parties, so this occasion will be an education for all of us.

We will be arriving in Dallas some time in mid-September. Suddenly I am not afraid of decisions, and I have you to thank. I have spent the summer scrupulously living a day at a time and refusing to face the future, because I could not bear to face it alone. I deeply regret the unhappy circumstances which have placed you in a position comparable to my own, but how grateful I am for the prospect of your company through the long winter ahead.

Kisses from all of us,

Bess


August 29, 1919
Woodstock

Miss Mabel Swift
Town and Country School
2316 Maple Lawn
Dallas, Texas

Dear Miss Swift,

My children and I are returning to Dallas this fall, after a two-year stay in St. Louis that was abruptly and tragically terminated by the death of my husband last spring.

I have spent the summer visiting a friend in New England, and my plans for the fall did not become definite until today. I know it is late to be asking you to reserve places for my three children in your fall classes but I trust that in considering this request you will not overlook the outstanding achievements of my two sons during their earlier time with you, and I can assure you that my daughter is in every way their equal.

In the hope that you will understand and allow for the tragic circumstances that prevented me from submitting this application any earlier, I am enclosing a check covering tuition for the first semester. I know only the first month's tuition is required in advance, but I trust the size of my deposit will be adequate proof of my intentions. I will be here for another two weeks and would appreciate a confirming letter from you before our departure.

Specifically, I am requesting space in the first grade for my daughter, Eleanor Elizabeth; in the second grade for my son, Andrew Alcott; and in the fourth grade for my older son, Robert Randolph. I have grown so used to thinking of him as the man of the family this summer, it comes as a shock to realize he is only in the fourth grade. He has assumed his new responsibility with solemn pride, but it will be good for him to be with children his own age again.

I look forward to hearing from you and to renewing our acquaintance, which I remember with great pleasure.

Sincerely,

Bess Alcott Steed

SEPTEMBER 1   1919
WOODSTOCK   VERMONT

MANNING SHEPHERD
2793 SWISS AVE
DALLAS   TEXAS
CHILDREN AND I EN ROUTE TO DALLAS   PLEASE DELAY BANKRUPTCY PROCEEDINGS PENDING MY ARRIVAL   I WILL ASSUME PERSONAL RESPONSIBILITY FOR COMPANY DEFICITS   WILL CALL ON ARRIVAL FRIDAY

BESS

ARTHUR FINEMAN
MEYERS MILLER AND FINEMAN
PRAETORIAN BUILDING
DALLAS TEXAS
PLEASE SELL ALL STOCK PURCHASED IN MY NAME AND DEPOSIT
PROCEEDS TO MY ACCOUNT   AM IN URGENT NEED OF CASH TO
KEEP MIDWESTERN LIFE INSURANCE COMPANY FROM DECLAR-
ING BANKRUPTCY   ARRIVING DALLAS FRIDAY

BESS

September 10, 1919
Dallas, Texas

Dearest Totsie,

Your long, wonderful letter made me forget for a few minutes our abrupt departure from the farm and even feel part of the Labor Day picnic. The turnout was certainly a tribute to you and the affection in which you are held by our friends and neighbors there. I suspect this is the first time any of them has ever admitted to friendship with one of the "summer people."

The children talk about the farm as if it were just across the street, but the events of the last ten days have made it seem sadly remote to me. Unfortunately, more than time and distance now separate me from the happiness of summer. Financial distress stands like a grim sentinel forbidding me entrance to the palace of peace and prosperity where I once lived. Russia is not the only scene of revolution these days. My life has been overthrown by the armies of death, and no provisional government seems possible. Every cent I have is committed to saving the company, but I am afraid all my efforts may be in vain.

Support has come from an unexpected source, however. The employees have rallied to the cause, giving up part of their salaries for the present in favor of stock options for the future. They announced their decision at a company-wide meeting last week after I made a short speech pledging all my personal assets against the mounting debt faced by the company if it continues to pay off all its claims. Perhaps if I had not just gone through the experience of widowhood, I would not feel so strongly about the responsibility of the company toward its policyholders, but I know too well the terror of being left alone in the world and I am determined that no survivor shall be denied the benefits to which his hard-earned monthly payments have entitled him.

Annie found a charming little house for us and we are all living together quite comfortably. The rooms are small but with no man in the house, privacy is a luxury we can ill afford. Fortunately a large, tree-sheltered vacant lot adjoins the house and I can escape there with a book whenever my desire for solitude threatens my good manners.

I will never be able to express adequately my gratitude to you for sharing your New England summer with four frightened refugees from St. Louis. Beyond the basic provision of food and shelter, you were unstinting in your supply of sympathy and kindness. Already I look back on my summer as an island of unexpected tranquillity in a relentlessly stormy sea. But like an explorer of long ago, I have set my course and I cannot turn back. I cling to my belief that the welcoming shores of a still uncharted continent await me—and sail on.

Je t'embrasse—comme toujours,

Bess

September 20, 1919

Dallas

Dearest Papa and Mavis,

Though we have still not greeted each other face to face, at least we are all living in the same state again. I hope to bring the children for a visit before the end of the month and hear your "welcome home" with my own ears.

Unfortunately, our return to Dallas has not been a homecoming in the true sense of the word. We have come back to a life very different from the one we left behind when we moved to St. Louis. Not many of our old friends even know I am here and I prefer it that way—at least for now.

I appreciate your offer of financial assistance but am determined to face this crisis as bravely as Rob would have done—and without falling back on friends and family.

Manning is still with the company—though openly opposed to the course I have taken. I suppose he looks at the figures more objectively than I do. To me they represent not only dollars but hours spent by Rob organizing the company and planning for its future. To Manning declaring bankruptcy is a means of erasing debt—to me it is a betrayal of everything Rob was trying to do. Manning and I stand divided on the issue and Mother Steed and Lydia understandably are on his side. They met us at the station when we arrived from Vermont, but it took only one brief conversation to establish our conflict over the fate of the company, and we have not seen them socially since.

The estrangement from their cousin's family and the fact that we are living in an unfamiliar part of town have led the children to believe that we did not move back to Dallas after all. I share their sense of dislocation. Everything is at once familiar yet at the same time strange and different, like a city seen in a dream. I live my days in a nightmare world from which there is no waking—and my nights are even worse. With no routine duties to keep terror at bay, I lie helpless in the dark, wishing only for oblivion.

Somehow I manage to maintain a cheerful façade in front of the children, at least for the hour it takes to get them dressed and ready for school in the morning. I am so grateful I paid their tuition for the first semester in advance. Now I would feel I could not afford it, but fortunately there is no way to reclaim it. And at least at school they have some sense of belonging. If only I had somewhere to go each day where kind people would look after me and tell me what to do. A widow seems to me like some parasitic plant still clinging tenaciously to the limbs of a fallen tree, ignoring the fact that the tree now lies lifeless on the ground.

Forgive me for inflicting my despair on you—but please understand how much better I feel for being able to express it.

All my love,

Bess


September 25, 1919
Dallas

Darling Totsie,

I cannot describe the joy that fills my heart when I see your exquisite penmanship on the outside of an envelope. I am more alive

---

97

in the presence of a letter from you than in the company of most of the people I encounter in my daily life.

I was amazed to discover that it was as difficult for you to face the responsibilities of fall as it has been for me. Our summer was like an oasis in a desert of never-ending duty. I even had the illusion I had learned to live with grief. But like a clever enemy, it only stayed hidden while I was strong—and waited till I was alone to attack again in full force.

I miss you so much. I have never shared my life so fully with anyone—not even my husband. We would meet in the night like two strangers, having traveled all day from different directions. We seldom knew the joy of watching a whole day unfold in each other's presence, each moment made richer by seeing it through the other's eyes.

Annie and I get along very well but it is hard for her to forget our former relationship. During the day while she is busy around the house she is happy and at ease, but once dinner is over, she seems quite uncomfortable sitting in the living room without anything to do.

It occurred to me we could put this awkward hour to good use if Annie would undertake our instruction in the German language. She was delighted and confessed how much she has missed the solace of her mother tongue—it seems Hans never allowed her to speak German around the house. He felt she should devote herself to improving her English so their children would grow up thinking of themselves as American citizens. Annie obeyed him in this as in everything but on the evenings when Hans was away, as he was more and more in the final months of their marriage, she would sing her children to sleep with German lullabies.

Our first language lesson last night was a great success. Annie could not stop laughing at our struggles with the guttural sounds which come so easily to her. It was good for her to be giving orders for a change, and she would not end the lesson until I had mastered the beginning rules of grammar. I hope, in the course of our instruction, to learn some of her self-discipline along with her language. I would undoubtedly be able to put the former to more immediate use than the latter.

When the lesson was over, Annie got out her wooden recorder, which she had brought with her to this country as a bride, and played folk songs for us, teaching us the words as we went along. To my amazement, the children learned the lyrics almost immediately. But I suppose the lyrics to many of our own songs are nothing more to them than a collection of sounds, and the German songs make just as much sense.

For the first time since we left the farm the children and I had the feeling of being a family again—or at least of being part of something larger than ourselves.

Please give my love to Dwight. I envy him for sharing so many hours of your life.

Je t'embrasse,

Bess

October 15, 1919

Dallas

Mr. Hans Hoffmeyer
7963 Alameda
Los Angeles, California

Dear Hans,

Annie received your letter but refuses to answer it, so, with her permission, I am taking the liberty of speaking for her. You are undoubtedly surprised to be hearing from me again after so many years, but events of the last few months have left Annie and me on a parallel course, and we decided to join forces in an effort to survive our mutual solitude.

When you abandoned home and family to try your luck in California, Annie wrote to me in the hope of returning to my employ, but the death of my husband last spring left me in severe financial straits and I am unfortunately in no position to hire anyone. So for the moment we are sharing a house and she is paying for room and board for herself and your two children with her services. But she has other expenses and cannot continue much longer without some form of financial assistance.

She was frankly dismayed to find your letter unaccompanied by any tangible evidence of concern for your children's welfare. At the very least you are responsible for half their support—a responsibility dating from the day of your departure, so your debt is already two months overdue. If your conscience does not hold you accountable, I can assure you that the courts will.

I look forward to hearing from you promptly—as do Annie and the children.

Sincerely,<br>Bess Alcott Steed

November 2, 1919<br>Dallas

Dearest Totsie,

I am hurrying to write this in the hope it will reach Westport before you and Dwight leave on your trip. How I would love to be with you, motoring through New England, stopping at old inns along the way.

Autumn does not arrive unnoticed in Texas—the oak trees are especially spectacular this year—but we do not enjoy it as you do. Sometimes I am filled with such longing for the part of the country my ancestors left behind. I wonder if I will ever feel as rooted to the land around me as you do. I have such a strange, unsettled feeling living in Texas again—as if I were only here because there was nowhere else to go.

Annie's husband, Hans, suddenly reappeared two nights ago. By a strange irony, it happened to be Halloween and when she opened the door, Annie shrieked as if she had seen a real ghost. If it had not been for me, I suspect she would have slammed the door in his face, but I insisted she invite him in for a cup of tea. Having failed to make his fortune—or even a living—in California, Hans has returned to Texas for the time being.

In spite of my letter describing my financial reverses, I think he fully expected me to give him a job, or at least to help him find one. I have no idea what to do for him, but I am determined to find a means of keeping him in town. Annie needs his help with the children and we can all profit from the occasional presence of a man in our lives—even an inadequate one.

The children were out trick-or-treating when Hans arrived and so when they returned home and saw him seated by the fireplace, they shrieked as loudly as Annie, but with joy, not terror. Children have no fear of ghosts—at least on Halloween night. I envy their ability to move so freely between the world they see and the one they only imagine. For them it is all one country which they can travel at will, whereas I am halted daily at the frontier of fantasy by the stern border guards of fact and logic who insist on reminding me that my husband has died and I am alone.

I am grateful that the children have been spared the sense of isolation that besets me. For them, their father is simply out of sight on some extended trip that could end any day. I doubt if they would be any more surprised to come home and find Rob sitting in our living room than they were to see Hans there. I went to early communion on All Souls' Day and prayed for the soul of my departed husband, but sometimes I feel the children are closer to him through fantasy than I am through faith.

Je t'embrasse,

Bess

November 20, 1919

Dallas

Dearest Papa and Mavis,

Since Halloween the children have talked of nothing but Thanksgiving. I don't know how they would measure time without holidays. We will be arriving Wednesday afternoon—by automobile!

Annie's husband, Hans, has moved back to town and gotten a job as a garage mechanic. In return for my continued support of his wife and two children, he is renovating a used car for me. He was able to acquire it at a very good price from a client who was upset by the constant service it required. I agreed to buy it on the condition that Hans would be responsible for its upkeep, so I trust I will be spared the problems that plagued its former owner.

Though Hans and Annie are still estranged, we have all come to depend on him in countless ways. Annie continues to punish him relentlessly for his ill-considered exit from her life last summer, but their small son welcomed him home instantly. The baby, of course, was too young to know she had been abandoned—even briefly—and will not hold him accountable until she is old enough to be told what happened by her mother.

My children have always adored Hans and his affection for them is uncomplicated by the guilt he feels toward his own offspring. I sometimes think men would make better fathers if they did not happen to be married to their children's mothers.

Annie will not allow Hans inside the house, so when he comes to see the children, he spends his time outdoors, and our small garden is thriving under his attentive eye. He is building a tree house on the branches of the only tree in our back yard large enough to support it and the children are already threatening to move in permanently.

We can hardly wait for next weekend. We'll start honking as soon as we cross Main Street.

Much love,
Bess


December 6, 1919
Dallas

Dearest Totsie,

Now that I have a car of my own, I am a new woman. I drove the children to Honey Grove for Thanksgiving, but once there I could hardly sit still long enough to pay homage to the obligatory turkey dinner. After the last piece of mincemeat pie had disappeared, I talked the family into leaving the table just as it was and going for a drive in the country.

The children were restless without a destination by which to measure our progress, but I was elated at the endless road ahead of us. I could have kept going far into the night if I had not had other passengers to consider. When it grew dark we headed reluctantly back into Honey Grove and found the dining table just as we had left it. We were all hungry again, so we merely exchanged used china and silverware for new and sat down to cold turkey and dressing.

Now that I am alone, my father and his wife have reasserted their parental role and I am astounded to admit how much I welcome their advice and concern. In the last few years I had begun to feel responsible for them, but my need seems to have made them strong again, and I am grateful for their renewed authority.

I had an unexpected phone call yesterday from the gentleman who has been handling my financial affairs since Rob's death. He has been away on business all fall and apologized for his neglect. Since I was forced to sell all the stocks he advised me to buy last summer and am in no position to reinvest, it had not occurred to me to feel neglected. Rather I felt in all fairness my financial position no longer merited his attention. However, he has invited me to have dinner with him next week at his downtown club to discuss my future. Since my financial future is nonexistent—at least for now—I cannot imagine what he has in mind. If common courtesy alone were not sufficient reason, curiosity would compel me to accept his invitation.

Je t'embrasse,<br>Bess

December 14, 1919<br>Dallas

Dearest Totsie,

Last night I dined with Arthur Fineman—and he gave me back my future. It seems he chose to ignore the telegram I sent him last summer from Vermont ordering him to sell the stocks he was holding in my name. He confessed to me last night that the check he sent me at that time was a personal loan, undertaken at his own risk and without my knowledge.

Last week he sold all the stock I still owned in a locally-based petroleum company—for four times the amount I paid. The difference was enough to repay my entire debt to him. And I still own the other stocks he advised me to buy. I was absolutely speechless on hearing the news last night—and still am today. Fortunately for my sanity, my pen continues to function even when my tongue fails me. However, there is no one within speaking distance who will rejoice at my good fortune as you will on reading this letter. You have always been close enough to hear a cry from the heart, whether the cause be pain or pleasure.

Until last night, I had no hope of being able to do more than go through the motions of Christmas merrymaking, and I was planning a multitude of holiday activities—stringing popcorn and cranberries, baking sugar cookies, making fudge and divinity—to compensate for the lack of presents under the tree on Christmas morning. Then Arthur Fineman appeared on my horizon, as welcome as a wise man from the east, bearing treasure greater than gold, frankincense, or myrrh. What irony that someone who does not believe in Christ has made it possible for us to celebrate Christmas this year.

When I tried to thank him, he said he had been in my debt for a long time now—and nothing he could do for me on a financial level would ever repay the kindness and consideration I had shown him after Eleanor's accident. He has not seen Eleanor since that fateful day, so I have invited him to come to tea next Sunday and meet the children.

He was rather hesitant about accepting the invitation. He has no children of his own, and suddenly I realized he was terrified at the thought of spending the afternoon with my trio. I suppose there are any number of men—and even unmarried women—who look upon children as an alien race, not seeing in them anything of themselves, but I never cease to be astonished by this reaction. I have never treated a child as anything less than my equal and I am invariably accorded the same consideration.

This letter will have to serve as my holiday greeting to you and Dwight and the baby—though now that he is walking, he can hardly be considered a baby any more. We wish you joy and prosperity for the coming year—and today for the first time dare hope it for ourselves.

Je t'embrasse,

Bess

December 18, 1919

Dallas

Dear Papa and Mavis,

The closer we get to Christmas, the harder it is for me to live in the present. I am besieged by memories of last Christmas. The war was over and Rob was home again. Never was a holiday so filled with joy. Though I will never know such happiness again, at least I knew it once, and only some mind-shattering illness can keep it from being mine forever. Children fortunately approach each holiday as if it were happening for the first time, and they are eagerly looking forward to all that Christmas will bring.

Annie's husband, Hans, has secured by means we decided not to question a pine tree from the woods of East Texas and we have decorated it with iced sugar cookies and candy canes (the advantage of edible ornaments is that they do not have to be stored).

Today Hans presented the children with a charming wooden

crèche he carved by hand, devoting every lonely hour to it since his return. Though he is too proud to admit it, he clearly regrets his impulsive departure last summer, and I am ready to forgive him even if Annie is not.

Annie and I are planning a traditional German dinner for Christmas Eve—roast goose, red cabbage, and an array of pastries that will take her a week to bake. The children are learning some Christmas carols in German. To hear them sing "Stille Nacht" is almost to forget that terrible war.

We hope you will join us for the holidays. I have invited Lydia and Manning and little Marian to come for Christmas Eve dinner and bring Mother Steed but so far they have not given me a definite answer.

My love to you both,

Bess

December 20, 1919

Dallas

Miss Abigail Saunders
Director
Riverview Convalescent Home
Syracuse, New York

Dear Miss Saunders,

Enclosed please find a check covering past-due charges for room and board for my cousin Josephine Farrow. I apologize for the delay in making the payment, but the death of my husband last February left me in difficult circumstances, which I have only recently begun to surmount.

I am very sorry to hear of my cousin's illness. I have not received a letter from her since last summer and I was beginning to wonder what reason I had given her for such a long silence. When she regains consciousness, please tell her I wrote to express my concern.

If she does not regain consciousness, may I remind you that I am the legal owner of the four-poster bed she now occupies, and in the event of her death, it is to be shipped C.O.D. to me here in Texas.

Cordially,

Bess Alcott Steed

Dearest Totsie,

It is New Year's Eve—and I bid 1919 adieu without regret. Last year at this time I was a child in my knowledge of the pain life is capable of inflicting upon us. In the space of a year I watched my life come to an end—and then slowly begin again.

I went out of my way to make sure we would have a large crowd on hand for the holidays. My father and his wife drove down from Honey Grove. They were only planning to stay overnight but the children clamored and cajoled until they finally agreed to spend the week with us.

Rob's sister, Lydia, along with her mother, her daughter, and her husband, joined us for a gala dinner on Christmas Eve. We have seen them only a few times since our return to Dallas so there were some awkward moments at first among the adults. The children of course were as comfortable with each other as if they had been living next door all this time. The tension caused by my estrangement from my husband's family was compounded by Annie's nervousness at appearing as an equal in front of people who had known her previously as my employee. She had prepared a superb dinner, but, instead of taking her place at the table, insisted on running back and forth to the kitchen to serve everybody. I finally resolved the problem by appointing Robin butler, a role he relished.

After dinner we gathered around the fire to sing Christmas carols. Suddenly to my amazement my stepmother pulled a harmonica from her pocket and began to play a rousing accompaniment to "Hark, the Herald Angels Sing." It was hardly heavenly music, but surely even the angels would have applauded our spirit. Tonight I am having dinner with my friend Arthur Fineman at his downtown club. He warned me that we would probably be the only ones there, but the thought of a quiet New Year's Eve appeals to both of us. It is a comment on our society that the only club a man of his faith is allowed to join is a downtown business club, where membership is based on earning power rather than religious affiliation. I suppose either criterion is equally discriminatory, but at least the former seems more in keeping with the spirit of free enterprise on which this country was founded.

Darling Totsie, your friendship was the greatest gift the old year had to offer—and I hope every New Year will reaffirm it.

Bonne Année,

Bess

January 10, 1920

To The Stockholders
Midwestern Life Insurance Company

A NEW YEAR'S GREETING

FROM THE CHAIRMAN OF THE BOARD

Last year we shared a tragedy in the death of my husband. My personal loss was great—but no greater than the loss to the company of a bold and imaginative president. The severe influenza epidemic which took the life of my husband threatened the existence of life insurance companies across the country, and there were many casualties. Fortunately Midwestern Life Insurance was not among them. Thanks to stringent economic measures and great personal sacrifice on the part of its employees, the company was able not only to survive the crisis but to emerge in a strong competitive position at the beginning of this New Year.

The Board of Directors hopes to show its faith in the future by reinstating dividends next quarter.

Happy New Year!

Sincerely,

Elizabeth Alcott Steed

February 14, 1920

Dallas

Darling Totsie,

It is 5 A.M. I have not been able to sleep all night.

It was a year ago this morning that I awoke for the last time in the arms of my beloved husband. At this moment, with the children still asleep, the emptiness of my life is almost unbearable. If it were not for them, I wonder how I would have survived. I am grateful every day for the unceasing demands they make upon my time and energy.

I know I should cherish their growing independence but every new step they take on their own seems to lead them further from my reach.

I had my heart set on having another child when Rob became ill last winter—another girl, I hoped. Sometimes in the still hours of the night just before I fall asleep, I can almost see her. Though never conceived in my womb, she is perfectly formed in my mind—an enchanting little creature, with a smile so radiant it could only exist in a dream. The dream is so real to me that I awake doubly deprived.

At times like this I take great comfort in the presence of Annie's two small children and sometimes in the early morning hours, when I am the only one in the house awake, I tiptoe into the nursery and take the baby in my arms. Her warm presence does more than any word of comfort to fill the aching void in my heart.

Yesterday my friend Arthur Fineman invited me to accompany him to a production of *Aïda* at the Opera House here. Impulsively I asked if I could buy three more tickets and take the children with us. The only available seats were in the balcony, so Arthur gallantly insisted on giving Eleanor and me his pair of orchestra seats while he joined Robin and Drew in the balcony. Eleanor sat enthralled through the triumphal march but fell asleep before Aïda was entombed, which was probably just as well since she has a horror of being trapped in dark places.

I am afraid Arthur was prevented from enjoying the opera by the presence of an active young boy at either elbow. I was unable to leave my seat at intermission as Eleanor had fallen asleep against my shoulder, so I did not see my three escorts again until the curtain came down for the final time. When I told Arthur good night, he said he had not fully realized until today how much he and his wife had missed by not having children—but he said it without any visible sign of regret. I know he thought the afternoon had been wasted on the children, but when I tucked Robin in bed tonight, he put his arms around me and said, "Good night, Celeste Mama." I was amazed and asked him how he knew what that word meant. He answered, "Mr. Fineman told me the man was singing about a beautiful woman like my mother." So I cannot agree that the afternoon was wasted—on any of us.

The Baltic cruise you and Dwight are planning for summer sounds delightful, but what will you do about the house in Vermont?

Tell Dwight that Arthur says there is a fortune to be made in South American silver mines for anyone willing to take a risk. Unfortunately I am not in that position—yet.

Je t'embrasse,

Bess

May 1, 1920
Dallas

Mr. Eben Stone
Tophill Farm
Devon Road
Woodstock, Vermont

Dear Mr. Stone,

My friends Mr. and Mrs. Dwight Davis have informed me that they will not be renewing their lease on the farm we occupied so happily last summer. In the hope that it is still available, I am enclosing a check for the first month's rent. I trust this will be a sufficient deposit to reserve the farm for my family's enjoyment for the months of June, July, and August.

Sincerely,

Bess Alcott Steed

June 1, 1920
Dallas

Dear Papa and Mavis,

We leave for Vermont at the end of the week and when we return to Dallas in September, a new home will be waiting for us. I am now the owner of a spacious, two-story brick house with attached garage. Since the fire I have never felt safe in a frame house, and though I know your house was considered a showplace in its day, I cannot help worrying about your safety.

I bought my house from an elderly couple looking for a place to retire. Dallas has become too large a city for their taste, so I suggested they think about East Texas and persuaded them to accept my title to Mama's cotton farm outside Winnsboro as a down payment on the house. Since I could never oversee this property personally,

I am happy to exchange it for an investment more suited to my immediate needs.

Farming is an occupation that will never hold much interest for me, since I am a city dweller at heart (though it took eighteen years of my life and marriage to an ambitious man to realize it). I cannot imagine Dallas ever becoming too large a city for my taste, so I have never looked upon the cotton farm as a possible setting for my old age. When I reap my final harvest, I hope to have a lot more than cotton to show for my effort in the fields of life.

Annie has decided to enter nursing school in the fall and I have agreed to supplement her savings so she can meet the cost of tuition. Her decision came as a blow to Hans who had hoped financial necessity would succeed where Christian charity had failed, forcing her to forgive him and welcome him back as head of the household. But Annie is determined to make her own way and I can only applaud her resolve. Frankly, now that Hans has agreed to pay a fixed amount of his income each month for child support and to commit a certain number of hours each week to their care, Annie feels better provided for than she did when they were living together as man and wife.

Manning and Lydia moved to Denton last month. They will begin academic life in the fall—he as a graduate student and college instructor, she as a high-school teacher—but I have persuaded them to spend at least part of the summer in Vermont with us. Mother Steed declined the invitation, preferring to stay home alone. I have missed them since they moved—and regret that we wasted so much of the time when we were all living in the same city. Life causes estrangement enough—why do we add to it out of misplaced pride? I am glad we will be sharing the summer.

Much love,

Bess


June 3, 1920
Dallas

Dear Cousin Josie,

Miss Saunders has been writing me at regular intervals to keep me informed of your condition, and I was delighted to learn from her last letter that you had regained consciousness long enough to inquire about me.

The children and I are well—and on our way to Vermont for the summer. I was disappointed we never got a chance to see you last summer and I would like to stop in Syracuse next week and pay you a brief visit. In the meantime, I trust your condition will continue to improve so that we can have a nice talk when I arrive.

Your devoted cousin,

Bess


June 15, 1920

Woodstock, Vermont

Dear Papa and Mavis,

Forgive me for not writing sooner but there has been so much to do since we arrived last week.

In New York City I parted ways with Manning and Lydia and the children. They took the first train for Vermont while I made a brief excursion to Syracuse for what I fear was a farewell visit with Cousin Josie.

When I learned that she had regained consciousness, I had hoped we might have a real visit, but what passes for consciousness in that place is a far cry from my definition. I did all the talking and Cousin Josie sat across from me dozing. I didn't think she had any idea who I was, but when I stood to leave, she suddenly opened the drawer of her bedside table and pulled out a handsome gold locket which she thrust into my hands.

I fumbled with the catch but finally succeeded in opening it—and found myself staring into my own face. Cousin Josie had taken an old photograph I had sent her years ago and fitted it into the locket. Upon examining the locket further, I discovered my picture had been placed over a picture of her dead parents. A sort of justice, I suppose. They took care of her at the beginning of her life and I took care of her at the end. But what did she do with all those years between? Was there ever another picture in the locket? A friend? A lover?

Cousin Josie made it clear I was to take the locket with me. It was the only thing left for me to inherit and would have been sent to me automatically at her death but I was touched to receive it directly from her. I kissed her good-bye and thought I saw a tear rolling down her cheek, but the nurse assured me it was a chronic allergy for which there seems to be no cure.

I had planned to stay the night in Syracuse, but once I left Cousin Josie I was determined to keep moving. I feared anyone who fell asleep there would awaken like Rip Van Winkle—twenty years older and nothing to show for it.

So I boarded an early evening train for Vermont. There were no Pullman accommodations, but it did not matter since I was in no mood to be alone. There were many stops, and I did not reach my destination much sooner than I would have if I had waited till morning for an express, but the motion of the train and the presence of the other passengers was very reassuring.

I so seldom travel alone I had forgotten how it feels to be surrounded by people and yet separate from them. I cannot imagine ever being lonely in such circumstances. There are so many possibilities for contact—knowing this and yet choosing to ignore all of them gives me a consoling sense of power. Alone on a train, I feel my life could go in any direction and at journey's end when I rejoin my family, I am filled with elation at the wisdom of my choice. Though they never know it, I have considered every possibility and once again chosen them. Of course I realize I am only playing a game; my choices were made long ago. I wonder how many other times when I truly thought the choice was mine I was playing the game without realizing it.

My excursion to Syracuse spared me the work of getting the farmhouse in order and by the time I arrived Manning and Lydia had everything well under control. All four children are bunking happily in the loft and the adults have the two downstairs bedrooms—a happy arrangement which affords me more privacy than I have known since we left St. Louis. How I look forward to moving into our spacious new home when we return to Dallas in the fall.

I hope your summer proves to be as pleasant as ours promises to be.

Much love,<br>Bess

June 25, 1920
Woodstock

Dear Arthur,

I accept with pleasure your invitation to join you in Boston for the July 4 weekend. It was kind of you to include the children but they cannot be coaxed into forsaking the country for even a day in the city. However, my sister-in-law and her husband are here with them so I am free to leave for a few days and I doubt that I will even be missed.

I am in ecstasy at the thought of all the theater and concerts awaiting us. I bought a Boston newspaper and have already written to make reservations. I know you must be occupied with all the business details of the trip, so I thought I would spare you the inconvenience of arranging our entertainment. Also please let me assume the responsibility of reserving our hotel accommodations, since I am so much closer to Boston.

I look forward to celebrating our country's independence in the city where it was conceived—and to enjoying a few days of freedom myself.

Fondly,

Bess


June 25, 1920
Woodstock

Dearest Totsie,

Welcome home!

I am anxious to hear all about your trip. Why don't you meet me in Boston for the July 4 weekend and we can catch up on each other's lives?

I know Dwight is so happy to be home again I would not presume to include him in the invitation, but I do hope you can get away for the weekend. On the chance that you can, I am reserving a room in your name at the Ritz.

If you cannot come, just send me a note at the hotel. Do not bother trying to reach me here. But please do not disappoint me. I long to see you.

Je t'embrasse,

Bess

June 25, 1920
Woodstock

Hotel Ritz
Boston, Massachusetts

Dear Sirs:

I would like to reserve three single rooms for the nights of July 3–5, two adjoining, and the third at a distance from the other two, possibly even on another floor.

The adjoining bedrooms are to be booked in the names of Mrs. Elizabeth Steed and Mrs. Dwight Davis and the third room is in the name of Mr. Arthur Fineman.

I'm enclosing a deposit to insure that the rooms will be held for our arrival.

Thank you in advance for your prompt attention to this request.

Sincerely,

Elizabeth Steed

July 4, 1920
Boston, Massachusetts

Dear Lydia,

I am so grateful to you for making it possible for me to get away for the weekend. My friend Totsie was already unpacking in her room, which adjoins mine, when I arrived.

We were having tea downstairs when I suddenly caught sight of my friend and financial advisor from Dallas, Arthur Fineman, who travels to Boston frequently on business. He was astonished to learn that all three of us were staying at the same hotel. However, he soon recovered his aplomb and invited us to join him for dinner and the theater.

We got along famously, disproving the old adage that "three's a crowd." And traveling in a trio had advantages for all of us: Totsie's presence spared Arthur and me any awkward moments at finding ourselves alone together in a strange city, and Arthur's presence enabled Totsie and me to travel freely about the city without fear for our physical safety.

We are all having such a good time we have decided to extend our trip by two days, so I will be returning on July 8 instead of July

6 as originally planned. I know Manning is anxious to get back to Texas but I trust he will not mind delaying his trip until my return. I am sure he would not like the thought of leaving you there alone with the children any more than I would.

Happy Independence Day!

Love,<br>Bess

July 6, 1920<br>Boston

Dearest Totsie,

You should just be getting home by now. I wish you could have stayed with us, but I can understand Dwight's desire to have you at his side. I will never stop missing Rob but now that I no longer have to answer to anyone for my actions, I do not think I would ever consider marriage again.

I finally confessed to Arthur that I had invited you for the weekend and you had accepted in complete innocence, knowing nothing of the circumstances. He said he had guessed it as soon as he saw us in adjoining rooms but decided to say nothing. I am continually amazed at his restraint and good manners; I just hope I can continue to count on them in your absence.

Give the baby a hug for me and thank Dwight for lending me your presence for three days.

Je t'embrasse,<br>Bess

July 8, 1920<br>en route from Boston to Woodstock

My dear Arthur,

All last night as I listened to you voice sentiments that went straight to my heart, I longed for pen and paper to give shape to the thoughts that were crowding my mind. I fervently hope nothing I write now will make you regret a single word you uttered.

I met my late husband when we were children. We reached adulthood together and continued to grow even after we were married. We were like two explorers taking turns in the lead as we made our way across uncharted country. But you and I have both made this trip before. We each think we know the way and would find it difficult to allow the other the lead.

I am just beginning to learn how to live alone as an adult. Can we not continue as we are? A man and a woman leading separate lives except for the moments they choose to share? There will always be times I would rather share with you than with anyone else in the world, dearest Arthur—please do not deprive me of the privilege of choosing to share them by demanding my constant presence as proof of my affection for you.

I will not breathe easily until I hear from you and you assure me that what we had has not been lost by what you hoped to gain.

Love always,<br>Bess

July 20, 1920<br>Woodstock

Dearest Totsie,

Your guess proved completely accurate. How strange that Arthur's intentions were so clear to you from the start. In no way did I anticipate a proposal of marriage. If so, I would have had time to ponder all my reasons for saying no. As it happened, I said it first, then spent the trip back to the farm trying to understand why.

I was terrified of losing Arthur as a friend when I refused him as a husband, but the letter I received from him today was so warm and understanding I think our relationship may even profit from the experience. I suppose whenever a single man and woman start spending time together, there comes a point at which marriage must be discussed. What I had not realized before were all the possibilities inherent in the relationship once the subject of marriage was closed. I am sure Arthur felt he owed me a proposal out of respect—but the tone of his letter indicates he was rather relieved when I refused.

How many unhappy marriages must result from that unholy sense of obligation that leads a man to propose and a woman to accept when both would be much happier continuing as they were. But fortunately society can impose its conventions only on the meek, and, like any bully, can be surprisingly docile when someone politely but firmly refuses to submit.

I hope Dwight did not feel you had in any way deceived him when he learned of Arthur's presence in Boston. It was terribly important to me that you be there and I could not run the risk of having you refuse by informing you of all the circumstances in advance. I pray I have not imposed on our friendship to the detriment of your marriage. How complicated life can become when loyalties intertwine. Sometimes I feel we are all marionettes and each string is controlled by a different master. I wonder if men feel as divided as women by conflicting obligations to husband, to parents, to children, to friends, and—the obligation too often sacrificed in the hope of effecting a momentary truce among the others—to one's self.

I cannot bear to end this letter because it means telling you goodbye for awhile. Is there any chance you could bring the baby here for a visit? My brother-in-law left today for Texas, so for the rest of the summer we will be a community of women and children. How I would love you to be part of it—for as long as you could stay.

Je t'embrasse,

Bess

July 25, 1920

Woodstock

Dear Annie,

I am shocked you have allowed Hans to move back in the house, though I frankly feared this would happen in my absence. I trust you have considered all the consequences of this decision and will regret none of them. If you had informed me of your intentions, I would have advised you to set down in writing certain conditions governing Hans' right to cohabit with you. It is still not too late to formulate some written agreement regarding your mutual rights and obligations. The longer these boundaries are left undefined, the greater the chance of future conflict between you.

I trust that your decision to enter nursing school in the fall has not been affected by the events of this summer. You cannot expect Hans to accord you any more respect than you accord yourself. If you do not keep your goals steadfastly in front of you, do not depend on anyone else to remind you of what they were. As long as you have ambitions of your own, your husband will never again be your judge, only your partner as you are his.

I hope I do not sound too harsh, but I have your happiness at heart. Remember, marriage is a privilege both husband and wife must earn—not a convenience to be enjoyed by one member at the expense of the other.

Give Hans my best wishes. If you are happy he is there, then so am I.

Affectionately,

Bess

August 15, 1920
Woodstock

Miss Abigail Saunders
Riverview Convalescent Home
Syracuse, New York

Dear Miss Saunders,

I was deeply saddened to learn of the death of my cousin, Josephine Farrow—and shocked to discover that she was only sixty-four. She seemed so much older. She slipped into senility with no visible show of resistance, as if grateful that life could no longer make demands upon her.

I have decided to relinquish my right to the four-poster bed in which she died. It represents the only physical claim she made on life, and I would like to leave it with you as a memorial to her. Would it be possible to affix to the headboard a small brass plaque engraved with her name?

I would be very happy to provide a few other pieces of furniture taken from her family home to create a "Josephine Farrow Memorial Room." This could establish a fortuitous precedent for your other residents, resulting ultimately in a welcome spirit of individuality, with each room reflecting the style and background of a former occupant.

I do not intend to criticize your methods, but I was struck by the unrelieved sameness of everything I encountered on my last visit: food, furnishings, and, sadly, even faces. Many of your residents might welcome the thought that their room would live after them and that their names at least would be remembered.

Since my cousin died on the tenth of the month, I would appreciate receiving from you the balance of the August payment, which I sent in advance, minus the cost, of course, of any funeral expenses not covered by my initial deposit for "death dues."

Sincerely,
Bess Alcott Steed

August 25, 1920
Woodstock

Dear Arthur,

I have not written sooner because I was not sure what tone my letter should take. I can no longer write as I did before, as a friend seeking advice and recounting anecdotes. Since Boston, an intimacy exists between us even in our silence—an intimacy I treasure and trust I have not betrayed by rejecting its marital translation. Please do not think it vain of me to want to continue just as I am now, like one of the maidens on the Greek urn so admired by Keats, suspended for eternity in the moment of pursuit.

My friend Totsie is here with me. The weekend we shared in Boston may prove to be a turning point in her life. After those few days of freedom with us, she found marriage an impossibly confining relationship. As far as her husband is concerned, all she is doing now is spending a few weeks in the country with her old school friend, but she is actually restructuring her life.

Her plan is to take an apartment in Boston when we leave here after Labor Day. She realizes now how much she has missed by living in the country for the past decade. Fortunately she has had her own income since college but her husband assumed the responsibility for investing it when they married. I have urged her to obtain from him all information relevant to her portfolio before informing him of her decision to establish a separate residence. Once she has the portfolio in hand, I think she would benefit greatly from your advice and support. I trust you will not object if I encourage her to write to you.

By the way, I see in the *Wall Street Journal* that a new company has been formed in Texas to explore the market for natural gas. I foresee an unlimited future for any product that is a source of energy. Can I afford to be part of this venture? Please give careful scrutiny to my portfolio in terms of growth potential. I own nothing I could not be persuaded to sell.

Love always,

Bess

September 1, 1920

Woodstock

Dear Annie,

Enclosed is a check covering tuition for the fall semester of nursing school. I hope it is not too late for your application to be processed.

I regret that you did not inform me sooner of your decision to lend your savings to Hans. I admire his ambition in wanting his own business, and you are right in remembering that I made a sizable loan to my husband to establish his position in the business community. However, I did not divert funds already earmarked for my own use.

An act as unselfish as yours carries within it the seeds of future unhappiness. To me the only viable transactions are ones in which both parties have something to gain. Even though you were ostensibly only delaying your entry into nursing school until Hans got started in business, there is no way of predicting what the future will hold for any of us. In almost every case, if I had delayed doing what I wanted to do, I would never have done it at all.

It is haying time in New England—hard work for the farmers but a holiday for the children. They have been spending their days at a nearby farm—riding the haywagon from the field into the barn, then jumping up and down on the hay after it is stored in the loft. This is an activity the farmers encourage. The more the hay is trampled, the more of it can be stored in the loft. It takes a huge supply to keep the cattle fed during the long New England winter.

We will be arriving home next week. Since your classes do not begin until next month, I would be grateful if you could devote this time to preparing our new home for our arrival. The keys can be obtained at the real estate office.

Perhaps you could begin this weekend while Hans is available to help with the heavy chores. I am having all the furniture we left stored in St. Louis shipped to our new address. I have asked the transport company to notify you of its arrival date. Enclosed (along with the check for your tuition) is a rough scheme I made to show where everything should go. Please direct the movers accordingly.

My sister-in-law and her daughter will be traveling with us and will probably spend the night in Dallas before going on to Denton. So please be sure the guest room is in order.

This is undoubtedly the last time I will ever call upon you for assistance of a domestic nature—though I may require your services as a nurse. For me Labor Day always marks the beginning of a new year and this year we both have cause for celebration: a new home for me, a new career for you.

Happy New Year, dearest Annie.

Love,

Bess

September 25, 1920

Dallas

Dearest Totsie,

We are now settled in our lovely new home and once again I cherish the illusion that I am the "master of my fate."

Your letter confirming my wisdom in urging you to move to Boston and establish a separate residence was indeed welcome. An outsider often finds it easier than the people involved to judge a situation objectively. The success of your marriage clearly depended on your ability to accommodate yourself to your husband's wishes without any thought for your own. I was hesitant to say anything because I thought you were happy, but when you confessed to me at the farm how estranged you and Dwight had become emotionally, then physical separation seemed to be the inevitable next step.

In the weeks to come Dwight will be forced to define the terms on which he wants the marriage to continue, and for the first time since he proposed (and I remember the spring that happened—none of us were in any mood for defining terms then), you will be in a position either to accept or reject them. So you must not feel that you have left your husband—at least not yet. So far all you have done is restore the possibility of choice between you.

The apartment sounds charming—and how wonderful to be

located within walking distance of so many places. It must have given you an enormous sense of freedom to leave your automobile behind with your home and husband.

Though I know you are happy devoting all your time to the baby, do not allow him to become your whole life. The potential for tyranny exists in the most angelic infant. They are quick to take advantage of any moment when you are not otherwise occupied and unless you firmly assert your right to time of your own, they can become your total occupation.

You would be well-advised to find some young girl willing to help with the baby in return for room and board. In a city like Boston, there are undoubtedly any number of young girls from large Catholic families whose experience in caring for younger brothers and sisters is equaled by a desire to move away from home and start a life of their own.

Our homecoming was quite gala. We did not expect anyone to meet our train, but to our surprise Manning was waiting at the station, and to our even greater surprise Arthur was standing beside him. The two men had never met and it was only when we began waving from the window of our compartment that they realized they were meeting the same party of travelers. Arthur seemed a little overwhelmed to encounter so much family at one time but he was gentle and gracious as always and Lydia was quite charmed by his gallantry.

We are now seeing each other regularly. I insist on occasionally assuming the responsibility for our entertainment, though with a man like Arthur this requires complicated advance planning. Last week I invited him to be my guest for dinner at the Dallas Country Club. He seemed very hesitant to accept, and I was afraid I had offended him by asking him to accompany me to a club where he would not be admitted on his own. I explained I only chose the country club because I knew he would never allow me to pay the bill in a public place but if it made him uncomfortable I would find other means of entertaining him. He said it was not the place that made him uncomfortable but the idea of my assuming the expense of the evening.

Once he offered that explanation, I promptly went ahead with the reservations, and we had a delightful dinner. I was somewhat apprehensive that country club cuisine might not measure up to his high standards, since most of the members are less concerned with what they eat than with who sees them eat it. However he pronounced the "sole bonne femme" superlative and I thoroughly enjoyed my porterhouse.

Arthur said he had not heard from you concerning your financial future so I urged him to take the initiative and suggest some income-producing investments to meet your immediate needs. His advice has made such a difference in my life, and I know he would be glad to do the same for you. And since his business requires him to make frequent trips to Boston, he could meet with you personally at your mutual convenience.

I hope all goes well with you and the baby. The next few months will be the most difficult to endure. Like me, you went directly from your parents to a husband, and it is only now, as an adult woman with a child, that you have had to make decisions entirely on your own. You may not believe me yet, but your own experience will soon confirm my assurance that you are as qualified to make decisions as those you have previously allowed to make them for you. Indeed I predict that you will soon enjoy the process as much as I do.

Je t'embrasse—et courage,

Bess

November 2, 1920

Dallas

Dearest Papa and Mavis,

I have been reading the newspapers with such interest all fall, preparing to cast my first vote for President of the United States. There is no question in my mind who is the better man—Governor Cox earned my vote with his stand on the League of Nations—but how many times in the past have we seen the better man go down to defeat? I hope that will not happen this year, now that women have finally been allowed a voice.

I have been fortunate to secure the services of an above-average colored woman to supervise the household. She is a good cook and with my encouragement has begun to show an interest in enlarging her culinary vocabulary. Last night she prepared very passable "suprême de volaille" (boned breast of chicken in cream sauce). I was more nervous than she about the undertaking, since I had invited my friend Arthur Fineman for dinner, but the evening was a triumph.

She is also an experienced seamstress and we spend many afternoons profitably employed in redoing my fall wardrobe. While we sew, I share with her my opinions on a wide variety of subjects. Recently we have been concentrating on topics of a political nature in order to prepare ourselves to exercise the long-withheld privilege of voting.

At first my housekeeper insisted she would not vote in this election, thinking it presumptuous to claim the privilege the same year I did. She reminded me of how many years her forebears stood by mutely and watched their white masters vote before finally earning the right to do likewise. She felt it would imply disrespect on her part not to allow me to set a precedent in this area. But I was quick to point out that at least in the matter of voting rights the color barrier had long since been broken, and the two of us are equals in the current battle against discrimination on the basis of sex.

I discuss the merits of both candidates as we hem my petticoats and we are adamant in our support of the Democratic ticket. Not only does Governor Cox appear to be a man of high ideals and firm convictions, we are equally impressed with his running mate, Franklin Roosevelt. I will be very proud to cast my first vote for their ticket and I trust the two of you will do the same.

Your loving daughter,

Bess

December 1, 1920
Dallas

Dearest Totsie,

I was fascinated by your first article. The society section of a newspaper is the perfect place for someone of your background to seek employment. In addition to income, your new position will provide a legitimate introduction to the social life of the city. And for me, it is most comforting to see that someone with no professional training or experience can find a satisfying means of making a living. I have always felt that a liberal arts education and the experience acquired through travel equal the value of any purely technical training.

I knew Arthur was planning a trip to Boston in November but I was surprised that you could persuade him to stay and spend Thanksgiving with you. I had decided against taking the children to Honey Grove for the holiday weekend, not wanting to leave Arthur alone, and had even made reservations for the lavish holiday buffet at the country club.

However, I am glad the two of you could spend the holiday together, and the children and I did not lack for company at the club. I was surprised to see so many people dining there on a day traditionally reserved for family but apparently I am not the only one who enjoys leavening the conversation of family with the company of friends. I am now convinced that the holidays are better enjoyed in the combined company of family and friends and to that end I am planning a large open house for Christmas Eve. It will be the first time I have entertained formally since we moved into our new home, so I am inviting not only those I owe but also quite a few whom I would like to have indebted to me.

I await Arthur's return to make a final decision on the menu since I consider his taste in this area infallible. I would ask you to give him this message but surely I will be seeing him before you read this letter.

Je t'embrasse,
Bess

December 15, 1920
Dallas

Dearest Papa and Mavis,

Once again I find myself dreading the approach of the holiday season. Scrooge is not the only one haunted by the ghost of Christmas past. On an ordinary day it is possible to be totally and mercifully absorbed by the present but at Christmas my mind is layered with memories. Perhaps that is why it is so difficult to be alone during the holidays. One's thoughts are peopled by all the family and friends who ever shared the occasion and solitude is unbearable.

I am so disappointed you cannot be with us this year. I hope it is not the Christmas Eve party I am planning that is keeping you away. I know in the past we always have had a quiet family Christmas but at this time of the year, when the past stalks the present, I cannot escape the fact that, without Rob, we are not a family. Pretending that we are is more painful than admitting that I am a woman living alone with her three children and seeking a less traditional way to celebrate. When Rob was seated at the head of the table carving our Christmas turkey, I could happily close our doors to the rest of the world. But since his death, no gathering of relatives, however devoted, can keep me from missing my friends. And does not an "open house" reflect the true spirit of Christmas, reminding us of the night when every door was closed except those of a stable?

The children will miss having you here for Christmas morning and so will Santa Claus. Like any entrepreneur, he thrives on an audience. Perhaps you will drive down later in the week when the holiday pace has slackened and our thoughts are turning toward a New Year hopefully unburdened by memories of the past.

All my love,

Bess

January 10, 1921

Dallas

Dearest Totsie,

Dwight gave you the best possible Christmas present by returning your stock portfolio and renouncing all interest in your investments, though I can guess the cost to his pride. I hope you see now how wrong it would have been for you to take the baby home for the holidays. Surely spending Christmas alone was a small price to pay for financial independence.

Our open house on Christmas Eve was a huge success, as you can see from the enclosed clipping. Unfortunately the reporter from *The Dallas News* does not have your eye for detail but at least the photograph will give you some idea of the house. It is not a very flattering picture of me but it does show my dress to advantage and I think Arthur looks very handsome.

Though his name was not on the invitation, Arthur graciously acted as host, which relieved me of a great deal of responsibility. He of course knew most of my friends in a business way, but now that we are seeing each other regularly, they have come to accept him socially as well and seem to enjoy his company as much as I do. And to my surprise, we are accepted as a couple here with no questions asked.

The party was much larger than I originally planned and I was afraid the children might get lost in the crowd but they were the center of attention. They spent all week deciding what to wear and the night of the party spent more time getting dressed than I did. When I was first planning the party, I thought of inviting a few children but all three were vehemently opposed to the idea. I have discovered that children settle for the company of other children only when there is no alternative. Given their choice, they much prefer the society of adults. On Christmas Eve they were the objects of enraptured attention and the three of them were still glowing from it the next morning when they came downstairs to see what Santa Claus had left.

The best present I received on Christmas Day was the unexpected arrival of my father and his wife from Honey Grove. They planned to spend only the afternoon with us but we prevailed upon them to stay the night. It is so rewarding when one is finally able to enjoy a friendship with one's family.

Now that you are in charge of your own finances, I can wish you nothing better than a happy and *prosperous* New Year!

Bonne Année,

Bess


April 10, 1921

Dallas

Mrs. Martin Banks
Program Chairman
Dallas Shakespeare Club
Dallas, Texas

Dear Exa,

I am putting this suggestion in written form so that you may submit it directly to the program committee—providing of course that it meets with your approval.

I have discovered to my surprise and delight that my colored housekeeper has an impressive acquaintance with and deep appreciation for the works of Shakespeare, and I would like to propose that we include interested members of our household staffs in some of our activities.

For example, on the days when the club invites a guest speaker, the servants could sit in the audience—in a special section reserved for them, of course, and suitably located toward the back so they could exit inconspicuously before the social hour began. In addition to their edification, such an arrangement would provide a built-in staff for the club, enabling us to serve more substantial refreshments than we are able to do at present. Indeed I have long felt it would be appropriate and quite pleasant to follow our meetings with a light repast. Food and fellowship would undoubtedly enhance our enjoyment of the scholarship that preceded it.

I hope you will give this proposal your full and immediate attention. I look forward to your response.

My best,

Bess

April 18, 1921
Dallas

Dearest Totsie,

How happy you must be—back in Boston as a free woman! Though I know this was a long and difficult winter for you, at least your enforced residence in Nevada allowed us to show you a little Texas hospitality en route.

I trust you are profiting from Arthur's presence in Boston this week. Once you start receiving the increased returns from your reinvested capital, you will again be able to live in the manner to which marriage accustomed you—and still enjoy all the advantages of living alone.

The baby sounds adorable. Two is an exciting, albeit exasperating age, as one enters the world of the spoken word. What a sense of power language instills in anyone not afraid to use it. No child is ever reluctant to employ any word with which he has even a passing acquaintance. It is only as adults that we shrink from employing the full power of our vocabulary.

Arthur must have been enchanted to hear the baby speak his name. He has always treated my children rather like foreigners, addressing them with the utmost courtesy but with no hope of achieving true communication. However, it is undoubtedly easier to make friends with an infant.

I will miss seeing you this summer, but my life has become so centered in Dallas that I have no wish to leave for even a week. I am learning to play tennis. It is a very demanding sport—both in terms of time and energy—but the sense of well-being that follows an afternoon on the courts is unlike anything I have ever experienced.

The man who is undertaking my instruction is an attractive engineer named Sam Garner who recently moved here from Philadelphia. We met at the home of mutual friends, Grace and Frank Townsend. He was married to a doctor who interned with Grace, but I gather he is in the process of getting a divorce. He is a kind and sincere man, despite rather strong views on the subject of professional women, and I see in him a zest for life that matches my own. He has made his own way in the world with great success—and I suspect before long he will make a substantial place for himself in this community.

Has spring arrived in Boston? It is everywhere I turn today. The azaleas have worked their annual alchemy upon the drab banks of Turtle Creek, their beauty doubled by their reflection in its green water. And flowering fruit trees are everywhere, their blossoms promising a harvest that never comes. (I have yet to pick an edible piece of fruit from any tree in any garden I have ever had.) But in this season a promise is cause enough for celebration.

My own garden is in full bloom. I planned it very carefully last fall, but the most spectacular colors this spring have come from the iris which emerged uninvited between my neat rows of tulips. I suppose they were set out according to a careful scheme by some former owner, but now, independent of my design, they appear of their own volition, in wild and glorious profusion. How arrogant we are to think the survival of any life that begins in our shadow depends upon our continuing physical presence. Indeed our shadow too often stands between the new life we create—in whatever form —and the sun's life-giving rays. Like the former owners of this house, would we not do better to go where our lives take us, with no thought to the seeds left planted in the soil we once owned? How can we not rejoice in the knowledge that strangers are now admiring beauty that began with us?

Next Saturday I am having a large afternoon garden party with a string quartet for dancing on the terrace. With the passage of that unfortunate prohibition legislation, invitations to afternoon tea have become increasingly popular here, though the gentlemen always accept in the hope that their hostess will provide an unadvertised beverage of a stronger nature. And any hostess who hopes to provide male dancing partners for her guests will, of course, oblige.

I do wish you could be here to take part in the festivities and then take note of them for the newspaper. I love reading your clippings and envy all the places your job has taken you. You are the only woman I know who can attend parties without having to reciprocate. A single man is always welcome—his mere presence considered payment enough for any invitation he receives. But a woman not only must repay an invitation, she also must attempt to outdo her previous efforts if she hopes to continue on the social circuit. It is indeed exhausting, even for someone who enjoys it as much as I do.

My best to Arthur. How much longer does he plan to be away?

Kiss the baby for me and teach him to say "Bess." It's surely easier than "Arthur."

Je t'embrasse,

Bess

May 5, 1921

Dallas

Dear Lydia,

Your letter caught me completely off-guard. I had no idea you and Manning had any interest in buying the farm in Vermont. Have you considered the difficulty in overseeing property located at such a distance from your place of residence? It is not that I have any proprietary interest in the farm. My life is here—at least for now. It just seems like such an impulsive move on your part. Except for the pleasure it will provide, I cannot see that the farm has much potential as an investment. Leasing it for the summer is one thing, but buying quite another.

When will you be leaving? Please keep me informed of your plans so that I may share at least vicariously in the pleasures of your pastoral summer.

Love to you all,

Bess

June 7, 1921
Dallas

Dear Dwight,

It was a surprise to hear from you but nothing compared to the shock of learning from Arthur and Totsie that they plan to be married at the end of the month. Their letter preceded yours by several days but I have yet to answer it, not knowing what to say. I believed with all my heart that Totsie was on her way to an independent life and it was to this end that I introduced her to Arthur. I never dreamed their friendship would even approach the area of marriage. Indeed when they met, I myself was enjoying a rather special relationship with Arthur, but obviously in recent months I have failed to convey to him just how much his friendship meant to me.

It feels strange to be confiding in someone who was the object of so many of the conversations Totsie and I shared last summer. However, I suppose intimacy between two people can be achieved in any number of ways, and events of the past year have brought you and me closer than we ever expected to be. We both have a stake in the decision just made by two people we loved and trusted (or at least *I* loved and trusted both of them), and we must now decide what course of action is still open to each of us.

I never thought you would lose Totsie when she decided to live alone. Indeed I was convinced that once you became accustomed to leading separate lives, your relationship would resume on a more equal footing. But I guess some people are just meant to be married and Totsie clearly falls into that category. If I had known it at the time, I would never have encouraged her to leave home and I certainly would never have introduced her to Arthur, since apparently he belongs in the same category.

I suppose we have no choice now but to broaden our thinking to embrace the two of them as a couple. I realize this will be easier for me than for you since each of them has already earned a place in my affections. Though Totsie will never be your wife again, surely you will choose to keep her as a friend. Please do not allow your pride to add to your loss.

Dear Dwight, try not to be unhappy. You have nothing to gain from despair. But thank you for writing me. Even though your letter began in anger, I felt it ended with the promise of affection, and I am a woman who holds a man to his promises.

In writing you, I have discovered what I want to say to Arthur and Totsie. Thank you for helping me find the words.

My love,

**Bess**

June 8, 1921

Dallas

Dearest Arthur and Totsie,

I still cannot quite believe that I am writing one letter to the two of you and that from now on, I will not be able to think of one without the other. I look forward to arriving at some new equation which will allow our friendship to flourish.

Does this mean you will be making your home in Dallas? I fervently hope so. Ever since college, I have prayed that one day Totsie and I would be able to share our lives as intimately as we did as schoolgirls. But I never imagined it would be Arthur who would provide us with this opportunity.

I understand your desire for a quiet wedding and I am very touched that you want me to be your witness. Of course I will be there. How could I miss such an occasion?

Manning and Lydia arrived in Vermont last week. They are leasing the farm this summer with an option to buy if the experience proves satisfactory. Your wedding will provide me and the children with just the excuse we needed for crossing the country also. I will leave them at the farm, of course, while I come to Boston for the wedding. Was it just a year ago that the three of us spent such a happy weekend together?

My best to you both,

et je *vous* embrasse,

**Bess**

June 8, 1921

Dallas

Dearest Manning and Lydia,

I find myself in the unusual position of accepting an invitation before it has been extended. However, propriety is shaped by circumstances and the children and I have just been provided with the occasion for a trip to New England, and an opportunity to visit you at the farm. The trip is prompted by the admittedly impulsive decision of my two dearest friends, Arthur Fineman and Totsie Davis, to join their lives in marriage. It was a little less than a year ago that I introduced them, and I frankly had no idea their friendship was heading toward such a conventional conclusion.

I never told you at the time, but it was not by accident that I met Arthur in Boston last year. He wrote and asked me to join him there for the purpose, I learned later, of proposing marriage. I did not think our relationship would prosper in an atmosphere of exclusive loyalty, and so I refused. We continued to see each other and I was convinced experience was confirming the wisdom of my decision. However, I had not counted on the attraction offered by another woman's need for his advice. I suppose there is not a man alive who can remain oblivious to the charms of a damsel in distress.

I do not mean to burden you with all the details of my involvement in this most unexpected event but I do want you to understand my reasons for making the trip. Arthur and Totsie are my closest friends and I love both of them. They have asked me to be a witness at their wedding and I cannot refuse, whatever the cost. If I am to find a form in which our friendship can not only continue but thrive, then it is imperative that I prove my good will by being present at their wedding.

Marian had such a good time visiting us alone last spring that my three are eager to have the same experience. Would it be possible for them to stay with you at the farm while I go to Boston for the wedding? Forgive me for acting on the assumption that we are welcome, but time is so short it would be impractical to assume otherwise.

I trust Manning will forgive us for this invasion, but I could not bear to journey to Boston alone when the children would rather be on the farm at this time of year than anywhere else in the world. How fortunate for all of us that you followed your impulses and leased it in spite of my reservations, which I only voiced out of concern for you. But I have often proceeded without regard for well-meant words of caution, and I am delighted you had the foresight to do likewise.

Much love—and à bientôt,

Bess

Dearest Papa and Mavis,

The children and I are packed and ready for an early-morning departure for New England.

Robin complained of aches and pains all day but begged me not to delay the trip on his account. The doctor said we could leave on schedule if he promised to rest on the train so that he will be completely well when we arrive. I expect it will be easier to keep him amused in a berth than it would be in a bed. Where else can you lie perfectly still and watch the world pass by your window?

Robin has already reached our destination in his mind. Today, lying in bed, he drew scene after scene of the farm, as if he were summoning it into existence by giving it form. He talks as he draws, even if no one is listening, describing every detail of our life there. Tonight he propped the picture he drew of Pinetree Lodge on the table beside his bed and pretended he was falling asleep there. Pinetree Lodge was the name the children gave to the shelter they discovered beneath the low branches of a huge pine tree. The ground was soft with pine needles and on warm nights they would spread blankets and stay till morning.

I have never known anything but happiness in Vermont, and I am looking forward to our arrival as eagerly as the children.

Good-bye for awhile,

Bess

June 24, 1921
New York City

Dear Arthur and Totsie,

I tried to reach you by phone but there was no answer, and it is just as well, for I do not think I could bear to hear the sound of your voices.

By the time we reached New York my precious Robin, who had left Dallas with an undiagnosed illness, was delirious with fever. Fortunately my brother-in-law had taken a train down from Vermont and was waiting for us at the station. We went straight to the hospital where I learned Robin was suffering from spinal meningitis.

At my insistence Manning has taken the other two children to the farm. There is nothing any of them can do here and my suffering is only augmented by seeing it reflected in their eyes.

Though I cannot witness your wedding in person, all my good wishes will attend you. I know you will find joy and solace in each other's presence even in moments of pain and sorrow. Until now I could not admit how much I envied you. Forgive me.

Bess

JUNE 25, 1921
NEW YORK CITY

MRS LEONARD MAXWELL
5620 WATERMAN AVENUE
ST LOUIS   MISSOURI
ROBIN DIED THIS MORNING   AM BRINGING BODY TO TEXAS FOR BURIAL   PLEASE ARRANGE TO HAVE ROBS COFFIN AT STATION TOMORROW READY FOR SHIPMENT   I CANNOT BEAR FOR ROBIN TO BE ALONE

BESS

June 27, 1921
Dallas

Dearest Lydia and Manning,

Two nights have come and gone but the nightmare does not end. The only way I have survived is by cultivating a sense of complete detachment. Mentally I assume a stance far away from the scene at hand and then watch the proceedings with the uncaring eye of an outsider.

It was kind of you to offer to make the trip to Texas with me but I am happier thinking of you in Vermont with the children. Nothing can be gained from getting close to death. Death is the enemy and every instinct urges us to keep our distance. I am so glad the children are there with you. It would take more courage than I possess now to find words of comfort for them, and even my silence reverberates with anger.

I am not sure I could have boarded the train without the unexpected assistance of Arthur and Totsie. They were married in Boston as planned and came into New York that afternoon. They were to sail for Bermuda the next day on their honeymoon. Instead they came straight to the hospital and spent their wedding night sitting with me. They were still there the next morning—the anniversary of my own marriage—when the nurse took me to Robin's bedside to tell him good-bye. I have never seen a fever create such a sweet dream. Robin thought he was lying in Pinetree Lodge and he made me promise he could sleep outside all summer under the stars. He said even if none of the other children wanted to stay there with him, he wouldn't be afraid to sleep alone.

Arthur and Totsie were with me all day after he died and never mentioned that their ship had sailed without them. Without even asking, they arranged to accompany me on the train back to Dallas and to spend their honeymoon looking for a place to live.

There was a large crowd waiting at the station in St. Louis when our train arrived. I had forgotten how many friends I made there. The conductor was kind enough to allow me to remain in my compartment during the long layover and my friends boarded in small groups to pay their respects.

There was a great deal of confusion about which baggage car was going on to Dallas and the conductor was calling, "All aboard," when I suddenly realized Rob's coffin was still on the platform waiting to be loaded. I gave a shriek, more of anger than of sorrow, as I realized nothing is accomplished in this life without constant supervision. I was not even to be allowed the luxury of total surrender to my grief.

Several well-meaning friends, thinking I was hysterical with emotion, tried to restrain me as I bolted down the aisle of the train. I broke free and leapt onto the platform, throwing my arms around the coffin. Finally the conductor understood and the large coffin was quickly loaded onto the baggage car to lie beside the smaller one.

I boarded the baggage car with it and refused to leave. I felt I belonged there with my husband and our son on the last trip the three of us would ever make together. I cannot explain the strange sense of calm that came over me as I sat in the darkness between those two coffins, wrapped in the blanket Arthur insisted on bringing me. At that moment I knew it was not possible to lose completely anything I had ever loved. I spent a sleepless but tranquil night and was not prepared the next morning when despair descended over me like a shroud, smothering in its dark folds all the hope I had felt the night before.

A very simple funeral service was held at the mortuary—just a few prayers and a hymn, all Robin would have understood since he had not been confirmed and thereby educated in the more elaborate rituals the Church has devised to disguise the brutal truth of our mortality.

The minister closed with the prayer Robin said every night: "Now I lay me down to sleep, I pray the Lord my soul to keep"; then continued with the words I never taught him: "If I should die before I wake, I pray the Lord my soul to take." By that omission I had hoped to spare him any thought that death could take him unaware. In that at least I was successful. For, more than the other two children, he accepted his father's death as part of life and never considered the possibility of his own. He was truly alive for every moment of his allotted decade. Even in his sleep his mind was always active, creating settings in which his restless spirit could roam, looking for adventure. I cannot believe even death will put an end to his happy dreams.

I find it difficult to bring this letter to a close. Somehow the effort of shaping my thoughts into sentences gives me the illusion I am in control of my feelings. But I know when I put down my pen all will be chaos again.

Kiss Drew and Eleanor for me and hold them close. Do they understand at all? But how unreasonable of me to expect that they would when nothing makes sense to me.

I must sleep now and hope the night will free me from the nightmare of this day.

Bess


June 30, 1921
Dallas

My precious lambs,

I have just finished reading your letters, and it is the first time since I left you that I have felt like smiling. It was so good of Aunt Lydia to ask you to write down everything you have been thinking and feeling. All we have is each other and we must share as much as we can.

Darling Drew, where did you ever learn a long word like "condo-lences"? It is such a sad-sounding word to me, much too long and sad for a little boy who was as happy as Robin. I am glad the two of you are there at the farm he loved so much. Marian loves having you there and Aunt Lydia hopes you will stay all summer.

I am very tired now so I have been staying in bed and trying to rest. Annie comes every day to take care of me. She tells me she is at the head of her class in nursing school and I can see why. She is so calm and efficient no patient would dare contradict her. I take all the medicine she gives me, even though I am not really sick, just very tired.

Grandpa and Mavis are here too. Sometimes after supper we talk Annie into joining us for a game of bridge but she is such a bad player we usually end by just talking. Grandpa has been telling me stories about his boyhood, most of which I had never heard before. I realize more and more that we have to work at making friends with members of our family the same way we do with strangers, by asking them questions and relishing their answers. I have asked Grandpa to remember all the stories he is telling me so he can repeat them to you when you get home.

Eleanor, I think your cat is about to become a mother, though I have no idea who the father is. However, she seems to have no further interest in him anyway and is quite content to sleep at the foot of my bed all day. I am very grateful to have her company, the sound of her purring helps me fall asleep. Which I am about to do right now.

Goodnight, my angels. I will come to you when I can.

Love and kisses,

Mummy

July 10, 1921

Dallas

Dear Lydia and Manning,

I am eternally in your debt for your care of the children this summer and anxious to join all of you there.

Today I left the house for the first time since attempting to turn it into my own tomb ten days ago. I have my friend Sam Garner to thank for leading me into the light again. He has been so kind and solicitous, stopping by the house every day on his way home from work. He never asks to see me, simply leaves a note accompanied by a basket of fresh fruits or vegetables from the farmers' market near his office.

I have not felt like facing anyone outside the family. I am not strong enough to put on a brave front, and no one can possibly share my sorrow. But yesterday I happened to be downstairs when Sam appeared with a bushel basket of tomatoes, so I felt I had to speak. He apologized for the size of the basket but said it was not possible to buy a smaller quantity. He stops at the market several times a week and usually makes his supper from the produce he brings home.

He seemed so lonely that I invited him to stay and share our fried-chicken supper. He insisted on slicing the tomatoes as his contribution to the meal. He is very awkward at expressing his feelings and seemed grateful when I directed the conversation toward impersonal topics.

Except for our friends, the Townsends, who introduced us, and his associates at work, Sam knows no one in Dallas. However, he seems more interested in places than people. I envy the firsthand knowledge of our area that he has already acquired. Compared to him, I feel like a foreigner. He is quite taken with this part of the country and the opportunities it has to offer. In his enthusiasm I see the spirit of the pioneers, and his unshakable optimism seems able to withstand even my despair.

This morning he arrived at my door with a picnic basket he had packed himself and informed me our destination was a new dam being constructed to the north of town. For the first time since I have known him he became almost eloquent as he described the far-reaching effects of the dam. To have refused to accompany him would have been an affront to his enthusiasm and so I went upstairs and got dressed for the first time since my precious Robin was laid to rest.

This afternoon when I returned home Arthur and Totsie were waiting. They have found a small house in Highland Park perfectly suited to their needs, and they are returning to Boston next week so that Totsie can close her apartment and reclaim her child. She had arranged for a nurse to care for him during the two weeks she and Arthur had planned to be on their honeymoon.

I was amazed to hear myself proposing that I travel to Boston with them and bring the baby to the farm with me. I feel I owe them a honeymoon, and I know it will be a great comfort to me to have the daily care of a young child. Drew and Eleanor adored having the baby visit us last summer and, as I remember, you and Marian were equally entranced with him. I hope I have not imposed on you unduly with my impulsive offer, but Arthur and Totsie accepted gratefully, and of course it will help fill for a short while the aching void in my heart. I will keep the baby in the guest bedroom with me.

My love to you all. See you next week.

Bess

July 25, 1921
Woodstock, Vermont

Dearest Papa and Mavis,

I was overcome with emotion at seeing my two precious children again, and I know now I should have rushed right to them instead of staying in Texas as long as I did. Somehow I thought it would be easier for all of us if we remained apart until I found the strength to go on living. But how foolish of me not to realize that they are the source of any strength I may still have. We flew into each other's arms and when they saw me cry, they gave way to the sobs they had been afraid to let anyone see.

Later that day they showed me the scrapbook they made with Lydia's help, describing their summers on the farm. Lydia has written a charming narration describing the adventures of my three children and their cousin, using illustrations supplied by the children, including the last sketch Robin made on the train. He is so alive and happy as a character in the story, and the children included him in all their pictures. I am so grateful to Lydia for finding a way of keeping him alive a little longer for all of us. Here on the farm it is hard to believe he is not out in the orchard playing hide and seek, just waiting for someone to call, "Home free," before bounding into sight.

Totsie was very happy to entrust her little boy to my care so that she and Arthur could spend a quiet week alone on Cape Cod before returning to Dallas to begin life as a family. He is a darling child and his eccentric two-year-old behavior makes us all laugh. I welcome the diversion he creates.

Lydia and Manning have decided against buying the farm, and after this summer I doubt that any of us will return here. The children have made a permanent claim on it with their memories and no matter who holds legal title, part of it will always belong to them.

I have decided to take the children back to Dallas on the train with Arthur and Totsie. Our help with the baby should compensate for the added responsibility of our company. I simply cannot face the thought of traveling alone with the children. Sometimes Arthur must feel he married two women. Since the wedding he has devoted as much time to me and my family as he has to Totsie. Fortunately they both knew me before they knew each other so neither resents my prior claim. Marriage does not begin to prepare us for the complicated relationships that can exist between men and women. Friendship, perhaps because it is less defined, can be a far more demanding responsibility.

My love,
Bess


July 26, 1921
Woodstock

My dear Dwight,

I was very touched by your letter of sympathy, and all it reflected of your feelings toward your own son. Be assured that Totsie has no wish to deprive you of his affection but he is so young he will forget you unless you make it a point to see him whenever you can. I realize this will become difficult once he is living in Texas but I am taking care of him this week while Totsie and Arthur are vacationing at the seashore and I hope you will take advantage of the opportunity to pay him a farewell visit. Having just lost a son, I beg you not to turn your back on the one you still have. Do not let your pride deprive you of more than even death could.

Little Dwight will be here all week. Please feel free to call on us at any time.

With deepest affection,
Bess

July 28, 1921
Woodstock

Dear Sam,

You were so kind to write and send separate letters to both children. Drew plans to hold you to your promise to take him fishing the first weekend we are home. Eleanor would not tell me what you promised her, but it was obviously a source of great satisfaction. After she read the letter, she locked it in her box of pine cones and other treasures.

I am delighted you have become a member of the country club. If I had known you were interested, I would have been happy to write a letter in support of your application. However, you seem to have managed sufficiently without my help. I must confess I had taken pity on you as a stranger in town but it is clear that you are not without influential friends. In our part of the country I can assure you that counts for more than wealth or family background.

New England now seems like a closed chapter of my life and I am anxious to bring the children home to Texas. It is nice to know you will be there waiting for us.

Affectionately,

Bess

July 29, 1921
Woodstock

Dearest Papa and Mavis,

Our pastoral existence was enlivened most pleasantly this week by a visit from my friend Dwight Davis. He drove up from his home in Connecticut, intending to spend only the afternoon at the farm with his son. But as afternoon lengthened into evening, it was clear he had no wish to leave. We invited him to stay for a supper of country ham, corn from the garden roasted in its own husks, and homemade bread and preserves from Mrs. Stone's larder. His two-year-old son took him by the hand and led him into the garden to help the children gather vegetables for the salad.

He admitted after supper that this was the first time he had ever been alone with his son for longer than a few minutes. Totsie was always standing by, ready to spring to attention at the first show of impatience on the part of either father or son. And, as almost any father will, he took advantage of her constant presence to evade those parental responsibilities that ultimately result in a precious intimacy which can be achieved no other way.

At my suggestion he booked a room in the village inn so that he could have another day at the farm. When he told us good-bye for the night, Little Dwight suddenly clung to him and begged to go with him. No one was more amazed than Dwight, but he quickly agreed. I packed the baby's nightclothes and favorite soft toy in a satchel and off they went. I fully expected to see them back here by breakfast the next morning. I suppose I am as guilty as the next woman of thinking father and child cannot stay friends for long.

However, it was late afternoon before they returned, bearing gifts for everyone. They had spent all morning shopping in the village and had then gone back to the inn for lunch. That act won Dwight to my heart completely. Any man brave enough to dine in public with a two-year-old has my total admiration.

I have always found Dwight a rather stiff and reserved person, but the children have taken a great liking to him (and the presents he brought from town did nothing to discourage their growing affection). We persuaded him to keep his room at the inn for the rest of the week—till Arthur and Totsie return from the Cape. It is ironic that he did not discover his son until he was on the verge of losing him but that may well prove soon enough.

I am reminded every day that there are greater tragedies than my own—the greatest being not knowing what you have until you lose it. How much of what passes for grief in the world is really nothing more than regret? Of course there are moments of unbearable sadness every day when I think of Robin and long for his loving presence, but some mornings I awaken astonished at the elation which fills my soul in gratitude for the years he gave us.

All my love,

Bess

August 5, 1921
St. Louis

Dear Lydia and Manning,

We are between trains here and the memory of my last stop at this station is so overwhelming I am taking refuge in a letter to you, hoping the lively events of the last few days will displace the dark thoughts that fill my mind.

Arthur and Totsie are still talking about the scene which greeted them on their return to the farm a day ahead of schedule. I am not sure who was the more shocked: Dwight to see Totsie with her new husband or Totsie to see Dwight so happy in the company of their son.

It was nice of Dwight to drive us to the train, though Totsie was quite undone at having to tell him good-bye face to face. And the baby cried loudly at having to leave behind someone he had just learned to love. When they married, Arthur told Totsie he would like to replace Dwight as the baby's adopted father and give him his name. Neither expected Dwight to offer any objection since he had been vehemently opposed to the idea of adoption in the first place and only consented to please Totsie. But when Arthur broached the subject to him on the day of our departure, Dwight was adamant in his refusal to discuss the matter. Totsie, however, has discussed little else this entire trip. She is distraught that the child will have one father in name and another in fact.

Arthur assures her that he is equally upset, but I have observed signs of barely concealed relief at the thought that another man is willing to share the responsibilities of fatherhood. Why do women make the mistake of exacting such total commitment from the men they marry? I have a feeling fatherhood is only one of many responsibilities most men would be glad to share. Marriage places such an unfair burden on the husband and I am only one of many young widows paying the price.

Thank you again for all you have done to make the pain of the last few weeks easier to bear. The children are still safe in the cocoon of fantasy you spun for them each night out of fables and fairy tales and I pray they will not break through the sheltering walls of their imaginary world until their wings are strong enough to hold them aloft. Would that we all could soar forever out of reach of the earth —beyond dangers waiting to destroy us the moment we alight.

Even though this trip revives unhappy memories, the train is a form of escape for me. I dread our arrival and the relentless ritual of daily life that awaits me.

Much love,

Bess

Dear Papa and Mavis,

I know you must be glad to be home again, cultivating your own garden, so to speak. It was generous of you to spend so much of the summer here, first with me and then again with the children when we returned from Vermont. Your cheerful presence sustained us in a way words cannot describe.

Ever since our return my friend Sam Garner has devoted himself to the children and their welfare. I chide him about spending so much time with us when I am in no position to make promises concerning my future, but he merely smiles and says he always does business by extending credit freely. The more I ponder this remark, the more unsettling it becomes.

However, Drew and Eleanor openly adore him. From the day we returned home he set about to win their friendship and within the week his efforts were completely successful. Children give their hearts so easily. Little more than a smile and they are yours forever —or at least until your attention lags. But as long as they have your total attention, you have their total devotion.

Sam has just bought a new rowboat and every Sunday we drive to a different lake, with the rowboat bouncing along behind us on a trailer. While Sam takes the children out on the lake, I read under a shady tree. I pay with endless teasing for my preference for shade and solitude, and I am beginning to feel more alone in their combined company than I do at home in my room. I know it is stupid of me but there are times when I feel the three of them are the family and I am the stranger in town.

Forgive me for letting my feelings show so shamelessly, but though I am seldom alone, there is no one in my life now with whom I can share my deepest thoughts. My friend Arthur Fineman and I used to prolong the dinners we shared for hours, discussing each new face and idea we had encountered since the last time we met. Now that he and Totsie are married, we still see each other frequently but the conversation seems to center on furnishing a house and hiring a staff, topics which none of us considered of even passing interest when we each had a separate and special friendship. And the intimacy which Totsie and I have shared since college suddenly seems nothing more than an ordinary friendship between two middle-class matrons now that we are neighbors.

I do not know what is causing this storm of unrest within my soul, but it is much worse than the sorrow that consumed me when Robin died. With death comes an awareness of life so intense that for a brief moment the world is radiant and beautiful to behold. But how quickly we slip back into our old ways and allow it to become drab and ordinary again. I grieve for my lost child now in a way that would have been abhorrent to me in the days immediately following his death when the world spoke to me in a thousand tongues and everywhere I turned I saw evidence that life had meaning. I grieve for Robin, but even more I grieve for the vision I could not keep.

I do not mean to hurt either of you by saying this, but how I wish my mother were alive.

Bess

November 1, 1921<br>Dallas

Dear Lydia and Manning,

It is All Soul's Day and I feel closer to the dead than I do to the living. I am amazed, though of course grateful, at the unquestioning way the children have accepted the death of their brother. The only time Eleanor has cried since she came home was the night before she was to go back to school. I took her in my arms to comfort her and she confessed, "Everybody's going to ask about Robin and I'm going to be so embarrassed."

They have survived the loss of their father and now their brother with an equanimity that finally challenges my own existence. Until now my purpose in life has been provided by the needs of other people but I am beginning to realize none of us is really necessary to anyone else. There is always someone to replace us. In a sense I rejoice at the new freedom afforded by this discovery. But I also grow more detached each day from everything and everyone around me.

However, the more alone and apart I feel, the more objectively

I witness the curious interdependence that seems to connect every-one else. For instance, my friend Sam Garner. It was his sympathy for my loss that involved him so deeply in my life this summer, but it is his own loneliness that keeps him there. He is as devoted to the children as if they were his own, and they have taken the place in his life of the children his own wife refused to give him, choosing instead the rewards of a career. The topic of professional women is one of the few that threatens his usually cheerful disposition, in spite of the fact that we were introduced by Grace Townsend, who is a respected orthopedic surgeon.

Sam stops by the house nearly every afternoon on his way home from work. The children are always delighted to see him and beg him to stay for dinner and when I add my insistence, he usually does. Last weekend, Drew was staying overnight with a friend and I had retired to my room with a headache when Sam arrived. Eleanor was about to sit down alone to a light supper of soup and sandwiches when to her delight he invited her to dine with him at a restaurant. She quickly put on her best dress and off the two of them went. She had cherries jubilee for the first time in her life and pronounced the whole experience unforgettable.

Sam is an expert photographer and the first person I know to buy a motion picture camera for home use. He follows the children around trying for candid footage, and now they begin clowning whenever they see him, while I sit watching their antics with an eye as cold as the camera.

Sam is going to Philadelphia for Christmas to sign the papers that will make his divorce final. I suspect he will ask me to marry him when he returns, and I am afraid the children will not allow me to refuse. When does a woman cease to be the hostage of her family?

Love,
Bess


December 17, 1921
Honey Grove, Texas

Dear Sam,

My father has been in ill health so we are spending Christmas here with him and his wife. We put a huge Christmas tree up in the hallway yesterday and your lovely packages were the first to go under it. It was kind of you to remember us. I thought you might forget your new friends in Texas once you rejoined your old ones in Pennsylvania. Returning home can make all the time spent in another place seem like a dream. I have been sleeping in the bedroom where I spent my childhood, and this morning I awoke thinking I still had my whole life ahead of me. What a shock to confront my two children at breakfast and realize how much of my future had already been committed.

I am glad you have no regrets about ending your marriage and hope you will enjoy all the freedom your new status affords. You are in a position now to restructure your whole life according to your own desires, with no obligation to accommodate your decisions to anyone else's needs. You must make the most of this opportunity and not assume any unnecessary burdens at this point in your life.

The events of last summer left me more emotionally exhausted than I realized, and I am finding the unhurried tempo of life in a small town very soothing. I play bridge once a week with girlhood friends grown old. It is ironic that the less they have experienced the older they look. And yet I am also amazed to realize that people who have never left Honey Grove can be more content with their lot than I am. My father and his wife belong to a bridge club, many of whose members graduated from high school with me, but they enjoy each other's company as if they were contemporaries. Perhaps that is why my father had no qualms about marrying a woman younger than his daughter. In a small town there are only children and adults. Once you finish school, you're as old as everyone else.

I try to spend several hours a day at my father's bedside. His failing health has made me realize how much of his life is still unknown territory to which he is the only guide. He loves answering my questions, and we sometimes talk for hours before my stepmother tiptoes in to suggest a nap. While he sleeps I rummage through bureau drawers filled with unidentified photographs, and when he wakes, I am armed with new questions.

The children are happier here than they have been anywhere except Vermont. My father rents the property adjoining his house to a farmer, and both the children and I marvel at the many uses to which so few acres can be put. He keeps cows and goats, and Drew and Eleanor provide an admiring audience every day for the afternoon milking. He has a cotton field and a fruit orchard, and has promised them a job as field hands this summer. Neither of them has ever accepted an offer more eagerly.

We envy you the snow in Philadelphia—we all would have enjoyed ice skating on the lake with you. The children were surprised to learn that in some parts of the country people do more than just sing about a "one-horse open sleigh."

I hope your holiday will be filled with all the peace and joy this season can provide. The children join me in sending you our best wishes.

Happy New Year,

Bess

December 19, 1921

Honey Grove

My dear Dwight,

Your letter was forwarded to me from Dallas. Unfortunately, I will be here for the holidays, so will miss seeing you during your brief stay.

I am delighted by your desire to spend Christmas with your son. And I can assure you of a warm reception from Arthur and Totsie, have no fear. Totsie has told me many times this fall how much it means to Little Dwight when a letter arrives from you. Did you know that ever since last summer he has insisted on being called Dwight? Anyone who forgets and refers to him as "Din-Din" risks the terrible wrath that only a three-year-old can unleash upon the world.

It occurs to me that in my absence you might enjoy the use of my house. I have a full-time housekeeper in residence, and she would be delighted to have you there. Little Dwight is a frequent visitor, always heading straight for the cookie jar, which has won him an enduring place in the heart of my housekeeper. I know he would enjoy being with you there, and a home is certainly preferable to a hotel room when it comes to celebrating Christmas. I will write my housekeeper tonight to get everything in readiness for you. Please do not disappoint us.

How marvelous that you are moving into Manhattan. If I were alone, I would not hesitate to find a small apartment in the heart of

the city and pursue every event of interest to me. I never open a
New York newspaper without seeing a hundred places I'd like to go.
How I envy your independence—physical, emotional, and financial.
I hope you are as happy as your situation allows you to be.

Affectionately,

Bess

December 19, 1921

Honey Grove

Dear Marthareen,

I hope you are enjoying a well-deserved rest in our absence. My
father's condition shows no sign of improving so I cannot make any
plans for returning home. However, my friend Dwight Davis, Mrs.
Fineman's former husband and the legal father of her adopted son,
is coming to Dallas for Christmas, and I have invited him to stay in
our house. He will be spending most of his visit in the company of
his son, so I hope you will do as much as possible on such short notice
to give the house a holiday appearance.

I am enclosing a check to cover the household expenses his arrival
will incur. Please spend part of it on a tree for the living room and
a wreath for the front door. In case you have forgotten, the Christmas decorations are stored in the small attic room just opposite the
stairs.

I am driving the children into East Texas this afternoon to gather
pine cones and cut branches to decorate the house here, and I will
send a box of greenery for you to arrange around the living room
as attractively as possible. Be sure to lay a fire and light it when Mr.
Davis arrives. Any free time you have should be devoted to making
Christmas confections. Men of all sizes love the taste of sweets.

In addition to the household check, I am enclosing a Christmas
bonus which I trust will compensate for the inconvenience of having
to delay your trip to Sulphur Springs to visit your sister. I am sure
she will be just as happy to see you after the holidays.

The children send you their love.

Merry Christmas,

Bess Steed

December 21, 1921
Honey Grove

Dear Lydia and Manning,

I very much appreciate your invitation to Christmas dinner, but Papa is confined to his bed and I do not want to leave him. I am filled with the fear that this is his last Christmas, and I feel I owe him my total attention.

The last time he was seriously ill, I was living in St. Louis and could not abandon my husband and children to come to Honey Grove. But now life has stripped me of conflicting responsibilities and left me free to play the role of dutiful daughter. And in a way I am grateful for the obligation. It gives me an excuse for avoiding any decisions about what I should be doing with my life. The children are very happy here, and I see no reason for returning to Dallas after the holidays. They can go to school here, and I can give Papa the time and attention I have too often denied him in the past.

I trust my friend Sam Garner will profit from my absence as much as Papa will from my presence. Now that he is legally free to form other relationships, I hope he will explore all the opportunities for friendship open to any man or woman of independent spirit and not merely seek a conventional commitment.

I have become interested in completing my unfinished college education and wonder if Manning would be kind enough to furnish me a catalogue of the courses open for enrollment next semester. I could easily drive over once or twice a week for classes. Even a limited academic career would be a welcome diversion from the restricted life I lead here, yet would not interfere with my familial obligations.

We mailed our presents for your family last week. I hope they arrive in time for Christmas. The children are so enraptured with the puppet theater they made for Marian they will be happy to come share it with her any time.

Christmas cheer to all of you,
Bess

January 3, 1922
Honey Grove

Dear Dwight,

Christmas came late for me this year. In fact it arrived only yesterday when I opened the stack of exquisitely wrapped packages from Bonwit Teller's. I felt like Cinderella, exclaiming in wonder at the silk scarf, the kid gloves, and finally the magnificent fox fur muff. I only wish you could have witnessed my delight. No fairy godmother could have done more to make me feel like a princess. I have always felt there was an art to giving, and you have clearly mastered it.

I am so delighted my home could be the setting for your first Christmas alone with your son. What better present could you have received than the discovery that he is already an interesting person at the age of three. The happiness of your reunion does a great deal to ease the pain of my own loss.

Happy New Year,

Bess


FEBRUARY 1 1922
HONEY GROVE

MR AND MRS MANNING SHEPHERD
1263 UNIVERSITY AVENUE
DENTON TEXAS
PAPA DIED PEACEFULLY IN HIS SLEEP LAST NIGHT    MUST RE-
GRETFULLY WITHDRAW FROM COLLEGE ENROLLMENT AT THIS
TIME    PLEASE REQUEST REGISTRAR TO RETURN DEPOSIT AT EAR-
LIEST CONVENIENCE

BESS


February 10, 1922
Honey Grove

Dear Lydia and Manning,

I cannot tell you what your presence meant to me all week. And I will miss you more than you imagine. To lose my husband, my son, and now my father in the space of three years is more than a woman should be asked to bear. I feel so completely alone. I think of the woman I was just a week ago, filled with confidence about the future, and she seems like a stranger to me.

Our parents—and the older generation they represent—provide a barrier against death, and when both of them are gone, as both of mine are now, there is nothing between us and our own mortality. Now it is my turn to stand as a shield between my children and the enemy. The cannons of death echo in my ears and I wonder how long I can stand firm without someone at my side to catch me if I stumble and start to fall.

However, for the moment I refuse to think about the future. We are welcome here, and indeed my presence is required for the legal untangling of my father's estate. Mavis has had no experience in the business world and relies heavily on my advice, which of course I am happy to give.

I deeply regret having to withdraw from your course on the Transcendentalists, Manning, but recent events have confined my attention to more mundane topics. I have decided to sell my house in Dallas and continue living here with Mavis at least until the children finish school in June. After that we will have to find a home of our own, but I do not know yet where it will be—or with whom.

My love,

Bess


February 15, 1922
Honey Grove

Dear Sam,

The children were delighted by your unexpected visit last weekend. I am sorry I was unable to share more fully in all the activities you planned, but lately I just seem to go through the motions of living.

Even the children find it difficult to claim my attention any more, but fortunately they are thriving on the undivided devotion of my father's widow. Having no children of her own, she finds their constant clamor a welcome diversion in a house otherwise silent with loss. She is so happy with them and they with her, I have neither the heart—nor the motive—to add to her bereavement by returning to Dallas.

So I have decided to sell my house there and put my furniture in storage. Forgive me for not apprising you of this decision last week-end when we were face to face, but I was afraid such an announcement might lead you into a commitment you would later regret. I am very grateful for the kindness you have shown to me and my children, but please do not feel it should have permanent consequences.

I am sure by now you have made many new friends, and I have no doubt you will be in great demand as an escort. I can certainly vouch for your many excellent qualities in that capacity.

Affectionately—as always,

Bess


March 1, 1922
Honey Grove

Mrs. Martin Banks
Treasurer
Dallas Shakespeare Club
Dallas, Texas

Dear Exa,

I have decided to sell the house I bought last year in Dallas and stay in Honey Grove—at least for now. Since my father's death last month, I have been in a state of indecision concerning my future. All I know is I do not want to go back anywhere I have been before.

In the meantime I am concerned about the immediate future of my devoted housekeeper, Marthareen Jenkins. She is, of course, fully occupied at the moment packing our things for storage and getting the house ready for its new owner. But her work for me will be finished by the end of the month, and then she will have to seek other employment. Of course she will have no trouble finding another position. Indeed, several of my closest friends have approached her in my absence about the possibility of coming to work for them. However, if I should move back to Dallas at some future time, I would like to think she would be available to return to my employ, and in the meantime she must have some sort of temporary position.

It occurred to me that the Shakespeare Club might profit from my predicament. The luncheons following the lectures were so successful last fall, I wondered if you have given any thought to expanding the social activities of the club. Marthareen is an efficient executive as well as an excellent cook, and the entire membership would benefit from her full-time presence on the staff.

In her free time I think she could be persuaded to conduct a class for the other members of our unpaid catering staff. She has complained to me in the past of their lack of attention at lectures, and indeed I am aware that the presence of domestic servants at meetings has provoked some unfavorable comment from the membership at large. Perhaps this unfortunate situation could be remedied—and not at the expense of the accompanying social activity which we all enjoy—by providing some basic instruction for our servants in the appreciation of Shakespeare. I cannot imagine anyone better equipped to perform this service than my capable housekeeper.

No one who has had a conversation of any length with her can doubt her fine intelligence and keen grasp of language. She was raised on Shakespeare, and I must candidly say she is more comfortable with his idiom than many of us. But she also has a great sense of responsibility toward her "brethren," as she calls them, and has often questioned whether she is meeting her obligations to her fellow man by continuing in domestic service. I know she would be thrilled at the opportunity to make the glories of Shakespeare accessible to friends whose upbringing did not afford them the literary advantages she had, and I would be very grateful to feel I still had an option on her future services. I look forward to hearing from you.

My best,

Bess

March 5, 1922
Honey Grove

Dear Dwight,

I have received more letters of sympathy in the last three years than anyone my age has a right to expect, and they are all beginning to sound alike. Very few people are capable of supplying real comfort in times of loss, but your letter succeeded in lifting my spirits to heights I have not approached since my husband died.

The thought of a trip to New York fills me with delight. My

world, which has shrunk to the size of a front lawn since Christmas, has suddenly become globular again.

I am accepting your invitation with great anticipation—but on the strict condition that I will be responsible for my entertainment once I get there. Of course I would love to explore the city with you whenever you are free, but I am not afraid of being alone. Indeed the experience of solitude is one I would cherish.

I will be arriving next Monday—and staying as long as my circumstances will allow. And it goes without saying I will arrange my own accommodations. It is kind of you to offer to meet my train. In case you fail to recognize me, just look for the lady with the fox fur muff.

A bientôt,

Bess

March 5, 1922
Honey Grove

Dear Sam,

I was delighted to find a letter from you in the morning mail but puzzled to see only a single sentence inviting me to dinner on Saturday.

I am sorry I cannot accept but I will be on my way to New York that night. An old friend impulsively invited me for a visit and just as impulsively I accepted.

I know you cannot understand my abrupt departure from your life, but it would not be fair to you to continue our relationship. I have reached the point where my life has so little value for me, I cannot believe it has meaning for anyone else. Please do not allow this confession to negate in any way my gratitude for your continuing solicitude, but I cannot look to you to restore my eroding sense of identity. Self-esteem comes from within, not from without. I must have some time away from the routine of family life to see if I am still a person I would care to know.

The French say "au revoir" to someone they hope to see again. Only "adieu" means good-bye forever. Their language can express so much more than ours in the same amount of space. So instead of good-bye, let me just say, "Au revoir, Sam."

With enduring affection,

Bess

March 10, 1922
Honey Grove

Dear Lydia,

It was kind of you to invite the children for a visit this weekend, thinking I would be in New York. I hope it will not inconvenience you if I come with them—and bring my reason for staying in Texas.

As I am sure you have guessed, the reason is Sam Garner. He appeared without warning last night while I was upstairs packing for my trip. He asked the children if they wanted him to marry me, and it was settled before I even knew he was here. The happiness shining from all three faces when they finally confronted me melted the cold stone I have carried for a heart these long months and I heard myself agreeing to all the plans they had made without me.

At my suggestion we are waiting to set a date for the wedding until we have found a house suitable for starting our life as a family. I hope that a few weeks of house-hunting will convince my husband-to-be that we will never find the house we want unless we build it ourselves. Since he is an engineer by profession, the prospect of incorporating his own ideas into his home should appeal to him as much as the delay it would involve in our wedding plans appeals to me.

Why am I so reluctant to abandon my single state when there is a kind and devoted man not only willing but actually anxious to share the obligations of parenthood? Perhaps it is because I suspect no one will ever love me as much as Rob did, and I would rather live alone than with anything less. And yet I hope you will forgive me for adding this final truth. I also suspect Sam loves the children more than Rob ever could—or at least he makes them a larger part of his life. The more I look around me, the more I am convinced that husband and father are often unrelated roles, and a man can be splendid in one capacity while barely adequate in the other. Of course the same observation can be made of women. Why does society insist we share every experience in life with the same person? We are all so much more complicated than we allow ourselves to appear.

I look forward to seeing you this weekend. Now that you know he can never take your brother's place in my life, I hope nothing will keep you from according a warm welcome to the man I am going to marry.

Fondly,

Bess

May 1, 1922

Honey Grove

Dear Totsie,

Sam and I abandoned our search for a suitable house last month and since then we have been looking at lots on which to build a house of our own design.

Yesterday we saw the acreage of our dreams—a secluded spot of land bounded by a wooded park with a stream running through it. The lot next to us is owned by Harold D. Perkins, an editor at *The Dallas Morning News*. I could not have chosen more prominent neighbors if I had been given my pick of the entire city. However, he apparently bought his land as an investment, so we will be the first to build.

Sam was so enchanted with the property he made the down payment out of his own savings account and insists on assuming full responsibility for the balance. Owning land clearly has special meaning for a man raised in impoverished circumstances. However, I feel a home should be the joint responsibility of the man and woman who share it, and so Sam has agreed to let me finance the construction of the house that will stand on his property.

As a precaution, I have decided Sam and I should come to some agreement in writing concerning the terms of the partnership we are about to undertake. He was offended when I suggested the idea, as if it implied that his intentions toward me were less than honorable.

However, I quickly pointed out that in business a legal contract implies no lack of trust. The only difference as I see it is that a business contract is a short-term agreement covering a limited area of mutual interest whereas marriage is a lifetime covenant. It is my opinion that every couple contemplating marriage should be required to sign a contract before being issued a license. Then divorce would be simply a breach of contract without the bitterness that too often attends the dissolution of marriage.

Enclosed is a rough draft of the contract I have drawn up to cover all the contingencies of married life as I see them from this vantage point. Would you mind reading it and, on the basis of your experience, suggesting any revisions or additions that occur to you before I show it to Sam and ask him to sign it?

Now that we know where we will be living, Sam thinks there is nothing to stop us from being married immediately. I do not know how much longer I can deny him access to my nights as well as my days. Frankly, I am almost as eager as he is to resume married life.

Je t'embrasse,

Bess

Enc.

PROPOSED MARRIAGE CONTRACT
between
Elizabeth Alcott Steed
and
Samson Arlington Garner

I. Place of residence: a home to be constructed at the expense of Elizabeth Alcott Steed on property owned by Samson Arlington Garner.

II. Income: husband and wife will continue to maintain separate bank accounts.

A. Elizabeth Steed will retain sole responsibility for managing the estate inherited from her parents and her first husband.

B. Samson Garner will retain sole possession of all income received for his services to Daltex Steel Company and from investments current and future.

III. Household expenses:

A. Elizabeth Steed will assume responsibility for all expenses of running a home, including utilities, insurance, food, and household staff.

B. Samson Garner will pay Elizabeth Steed a monthly sum roughly equivalent to one-fourth of the above costs.

IV. Furnishings:

A. House will be furnished from family possessions now owned by both parties. Any additional furniture deemed necessary will be selected and paid for by Elizabeth Steed—and remain her permanent property.

B. Any furniture specifically requested by Samson Garner will be acquired at his own expense and considered his property.

V. Automobiles: each party shall retain title to and assume financial responsibility for his/her own automobile—including costs of insurance, maintenance, and fuel—and shall replace it at his/her own discretion.

VI. Life insurance: both parties will carry a life insurance policy of equal value, naming the other as beneficiary; however the value of any additional policies naming other beneficiaries (i.e., the children of Elizabeth Steed) will be left to the discretion of the policyholder.

VII. Dependents: Elizabeth Steed will assume full financial responsibility for the needs of her two children, including clothing, medical costs, education, and social obligations. In the event of her death, these needs will become the responsibility of Samson Garner.

> June 10, 1922
> Honey Grove

Dear Totsie,

The architect has submitted his final set of plans and we have approved them, with perhaps more enthusiasm from me than from Sam. At least on the surface we are in agreement, however, and work is scheduled to begin immediately.

With the plans approved, I capitulated completely to Sam's insistence that we set a date for the wedding. He suggested tomorrow but I persuaded him to wait till July 4th, which will give us the long holiday weekend for a honeymoon. Besides, the idea of getting married on Independence Day appeals to my sense of irony. I am not sure where we will live until the house is ready, but I rather like having a few unanswered questions in my future.

I am glad you approve of the marriage contract. I showed it to Sam today on our way downtown to apply for our license. He read it without a word, signed it, then handed it back to me and said in a voice so devoid of emotion it sounded as if it had been recorded on another planet, "I never want to see that damn thing again as long as I live."

I must admit I was caught off-guard by the one question you raised. I did not realize how completely the contract ignored the possibility of offspring resulting from this union—perhaps because it is a possibility I have never contemplated and Sam has never mentioned. My reproductive processes have been in such a state of rebellion since Robin's death I doubt if I could conceive now even if I had the desire—which I do not.

I love my children at the age they are now, and I have neither the energy nor the patience to shepherd a new one to this level of perception and response. And neither does Sam, though he may not realize it. Nor, frankly, would I risk his affection for my children by presenting him with one of his own. This is not a matter we have discussed, and I trust Sam will never put me in the position of opposing him outright. However, no matter how equally a man contributes to a child's conception, it is the woman who is left to bear and often to raise it alone. So the decision must finally belong to her.

Darling Totsie, how happy I am you will be standing at my side to give me courage as I commit the rest of my life to yet another man.

Je t'embrasse,

Bess


June 28, 1922
Honey Grove

Dear Lydia and Manning,

Sam and I are to be married next Friday evening in Dallas, and we hope the two of you can be there—and of course Mother Steed and Marian if they care to come.

Grace and Frank Townsend—the friends who introduced us— have graciously offered to have the wedding in their home, followed by a champagne supper. It will be a very intimate affair. So 'ar I have only invited you, Mavis, Exa and Martin Banks, Totsie and Arthur Fineman, and Sam has asked a few associates from the office.

Of course I will not be mailing engraved wedding invitations, but I am sending announcements to all our friends. None of the usual wording seems quite appropriate since my parents are dead and this is a second marriage for each of us. So I have decided to compose my own announcement. A draft is enclosed. Please give me your candid appraisal—from the point of view of social acceptance as well as literary style. I will not place my order with the printer until I have your approval, so do let me hear from you right away.

My love,

Bess

Enc.

---

*Elizabeth Alcott Steed*
*daughter of*
*Andrew and Abigail Alcott*
*of Honey Grove*
*widow of*
*Robert Randolph Steed*
*of Dallas and St. Louis*
*mother of*
*Eleanor Elizabeth and Andrew Alcott Steed*
*is pleased to announce*
*that she has joined her life in marriage*
*to Samson Arlington Garner*
*of Philadelphia and Dallas*

*on the Fourth of July*
*nineteen hundred and twenty-two*
*in Dallas, Texas*

July 3, 1922
Dallas, Texas

Dear Mother Steed,

Lydia and Manning arrived this afternoon with Marian. We are all staying at the home of my friends Totsie and Arthur Fineman, and it is quite a gala house party. Totsie graciously offered to keep the children this weekend while Sam and I are away on our honeymoon, and I do not know who accepted her offer more eagerly—Sam and I or Drew and Eleanor.

She and Arthur have been so kind and generous to us from the day we announced our engagement. They are hosting the rehearsal dinner tonight, taking care of the children after the wedding, and then—most thoughtful of all—giving us their house for a month while they vacation in Colorado. I think they more than any of our other friends understand the mixed feelings that accompany a second marriage, and they are doing everything they can to make it easier for both of us.

I was very sad when Manning and Lydia arrived today without you, and I trust that even though we will not have your presence at our wedding tomorrow we will have your blessing. No one loved Rob as I did or mourned his passing more—not even you—so no one has the right to judge me for committing what is left of my life to another man. No one would rejoice more than Rob to see how happy his children are in the presence of the man who is about to become my husband, and if you love your grandchildren as much as you say you do, then you will rejoice with us tomorrow—even though you have chosen to do it alone.

Affectionately, as always,

Bess

July 8, 1922
Dallas

Dear Mavis,

I was so glad you could come for the wedding. Somehow, looking at you, I could almost see Papa standing beside you giving me his blessing. The reverses of fate are difficult to accept and I still find it unbelievable that I am with a husband when you are without one.

Sam and I had a lovely weekend in Galveston. He had never been there before and I had only seen the city in transit so it was an adventure for us both. Galveston shares with all seaports an air of mystery and excitement and even though it is located in Texas, it seems closer in spirit to Naples than to Dallas. I could never look at the Gulf of Mexico without imagining that Jean Laffite and his pirates were anchored out there somewhere.

We played tennis every morning before breakfast. Sam is determined to improve my backhand, though I am not sure it can be done. In return for my sincere effort to master a sport for which I clearly have no aptitude, he has agreed to submit to my tutelage in the fine arts. At this point the only place our interests meet is at the movies. Sam has always been interested in photography and he is fascinated by motion pictures from a purely technical point of view. As for me, I become so absorbed watching John Barrymore as "Beau Brummel" and Rudolph Valentino as "Monsieur Beaucaire," I completely forget a camera is involved.

We were away only three days, but they were spent in such leisure the trip seemed much longer. Time has a different meaning in an unfamiliar setting. Each new experience seems to stretch an hour to several times its normal capacity. If I were told I had only a short time to live, I would spend the weeks left to me traveling, making each hour hold as many new sights and sounds as possible. And how much easier to leave loved ones behind when adventure is ahead. I would like to believe that the soul sets out on a journey of its own long before the body ceases to breathe so that by the time those left behind begin to mourn, our traveler has already embarked in another country.

How strangely the mind works! I started this letter by describing my honeymoon and I end it by discussing death.

Much love,<br>Bess

July 22, 1922<br>Dallas

Dear Dwight,

What an extraordinary wedding present!

When I opened the box and saw the beautiful leather-bound book, I assumed it was some rare edition and wondered why there was no title imprinted on the binding. Then I opened it and saw the exquisite vellum pages—all blank except for your inscription. Who else but you would know the excitement I would feel on being presented with a book of blank pages? Our thoughts are among the few things we can leave behind us in permanent form and I am anxious to begin writing—though somewhat awed at the thought of opening that handsome volume and seeing my own efforts enshrined.

Why is it never enough for me just to live my life? From the time I was a child and started my first scrapbook, I have always looked upon my own experience with the eye of an artist trying to shape it into something more interesting than it was. My scrapbooks are filled with newspaper clippings about other people, some of whom I barely knew, as if their activities could somehow extend the boundaries of my own experience or perhaps, less than satisfied with my own achievements, I hoped to share vicariously in theirs.

Sometimes I think it is that same frustration with life as it is lived day by day that compels me to write such long letters to people who seldom reply in kind, if indeed they reply at all. Somehow by compressing and editing the events of my life, I infuse them with a dramatic intensity totally lacking at the time, but oddly enough I find that years later what I remember is not the event as I lived it but as I described it in a letter. I find the very act of writing turns fact into fiction and for that I thank God with all of my heart. And I thank you for the book that will preserve my life in the form I impose upon it. It occurs to me we are all capable of adding another dimension to our daily lives if we would but look upon the people around us as characters in a drama devised for our amusement. There is no life too dull to be transformed into art by a lively imagination. Even Rumpelstiltskin began with straw.

I am anxious for you to meet my new husband, but who knows when we will travel east again. He is appalled that I have crossed the Alps but never seen the Rockies, and is planning road trips across the western United States that should keep us busy for several summers. In the meantime I am subscribing to *The New York Times* so at least I can be with you in spirit.

With abiding affection,

Bess

September 5, 1925
Dallas

Dear Lydia,

Promise you will destroy this letter after you read it.

This morning I looked in the mirror and saw a woman Rob would not recognize. The slender, high-spirited girl he married is as dead as her handsome and adoring first husband.

In the three years since I married Sam, I have gained thirty pounds. Dear Sam . . . I must not blame him—at least not entirely—for what I have become. He is still the same man—weight included—that he was on our wedding day. In fact, he seems to thrive on the domestic routine that marriage enforces on unsuspecting individuals.

My first marriage survived many storms—from within and without—but no turbulence can compare to the agony of being becalmed, with no wind in sight. Like the Ancient Mariner, I inhabit "a painted ship upon a painted sea."

Marriage to your brother did nothing to prepare me for life with Sam. Rob and I had our battles in the beginning, but I was more in love with him when he died than on our wedding day. Poor Sam! How can he compete with a memory that is not only perfect in itself but allows me to exist in perfect freedom?

The camping trips Sam plans each summer are my only escape from a daily existence that grows more oppressive each year. We returned from New Mexico yesterday and have no plans to leave home again until next summer, when Sam hopes to explore Utah. After shepherding the children and me west for three years, he is finally beginning to feel we qualify for American citizenship.

Last year I added a screened-in sleeping porch to the house—at my own expense—so that Sam could recapture the sensation of camping outdoors and I could remain in the bedroom, reading as late as I liked. Sam loves the breeze but expects me to fall asleep at his side. And not at the hour of my choosing but when he is ready to retire—on the dot of ten every night of his life. If I ask to leave on my light and read, he does not forbid it but laments that he cannot fall asleep for the sound of the moths flailing their wings against the screen in a futile effort to reach the light.

Last night I lay beside him staring into the dark till he fell asleep, then crept stealthily back into the bedroom and read till dawn.

Unfortunately I succumbed to sleep with the book still in my lap so my absence from his bed did not go unnoticed. Though he did not dare confront me directly, he took particular pleasure in summoning me to a breakfast I was in no mood to enjoy after only two hours of sleep.

The children start school next week, but I am not sure they are being properly challenged here and am considering sending Andrew East next year. His manners would profit as much as his mind. Naturally he is adamantly opposed to the idea, even though I have had a place reserved for him at Choate since he was a child. Like most of our friends, he believes the best of everything can be found right here at home. The more he argues, the more he convinces me I am right in wanting to broaden his outlook.

Though Sam objects in principle to a prep-school education, I do not think he would mind having the other male voice at the dinner table silenced and moved a polite distance away. Friction between father and son is to be expected, I suppose, but the tensions are exacerbated when the father is as new to his role as Sam. There are nights, after an especially vocal dinner, when I wonder whatever made me think it was best for the children if I married again. Or—dare I say it?—for me.

Now destroy this letter, dearest Lydia, and dismiss its contents from your mind, as I must do if I am to continue living within the bonds of holy wedlock.

I love you as Rob's sister—and mine,

Bess

April 5, 1926<br/>Dallas

Dear Dwight,

Andrew was notified by letter today that he has been accepted at Choate for the fall semester. I have never seen him so excited. Thank you for all your efforts in his behalf.

He is quite conscious of the fact that he is about to embark on a journey that no one in his family—or indeed no one he knows here—has ever made before him, and the thought fills him with pride, along with barely concealed apprehension. It is just as much of an accomplishment for a young man from this part of the country to travel eastward, back to the tradition-bound institutions of his ancestors, as it was for the pioneers to travel westward into uncharted territory. To be sure he will not face physical obstacles, but the intellectual challenges ahead of him are equally formidable.

As much as I would like to accompany him when he boards the train in September, I know I must stay behind. However, I am already looking forward to visiting him later in the year and then spending some time in New York. A dispassionate observer might even question my motives for sending my child away to school, seeing what an unassailable excuse it provides for frequent trips to my favorite city.

I have a feeling it is going to be a glorious fall. I can hardly wait.

A bientôt,

Bess

June 28, 1926

Dallas

Dear Lydia and Manning,

We are celebrating several separate occasions Saturday with a family picnic for all our friends, and I hope you can join us. Come for the weekend if you can and of course bring Marian and Mother Steed with you.

Sam and I will be observing our fourth wedding anniversary and concurrently, as usual, our country's independence. We will also be celebrating an eminent arrival and a departure. Our first neighbors, the newspaper editor, Harold D. Perkins, and his wife, will begin building a house on their lot next fall, at the same time Andrew will be leaving for Choate.

I am sure you will find it to your advantage to get to know a man of such widespread influence as our new neighbor. I have been looking forward to his prospective proximity from the day we bought our lot and have been disappointed by his continued delay in starting construction. I had the impression when we began building that he and his wife would soon be following our example, but the more I saw of them, the less definite their plans seemed to become.

When I called to invite him to the party, he first declined, saying he had houseguests. Then I explained the party was partly in his honor, to welcome him to the neighborhood, and the invitation of course included his guests. He hesitantly agreed to make a brief appearance at the party, reluctant, I am sure, to impose unduly on my hospitality. He confessed that he had never been inside the homes of any of his present neighbors and had come to depend on the privacy this lack of intimacy afforded. I assured him I agreed completely in principle, the only exception being a case where individuals share enough common interests to be friends at any distance. I also made the point that there was no reason why our friendship could not profit from our proximity—as long as it was not based on it.

We look forward to seeing all of you next weekend—fried chicken, fireworks, and new friends await you.

Love,

Bess

September 10, 1926

Dallas

My darling Drew,

Forgive me for reverting to a name you put aside long ago, with your teddy bears and toy soldiers, but it is hard for me to face the fact that I have lost my little boy forever. A young man with the same sweet smile is still sleeping in his bedroom but tomorrow even he will be gone.

I am driving this letter downtown to the main post office tonight so it will travel east on the same train with you. It is a comforting illusion to believe that part of me is making the trip with you, even if it is just a piece of paper. But a piece of paper can be a powerful presence. I have always had enormous respect for the written word and invariably find a letter more revealing than a face-to-face conversation. In a strange way I suspect I will get to know you better at a distance than I would if you had stayed home.

I will of course send you your allowance once a month but I expect you to earn it, just as you have to earn it at home, not by raking leaves or washing the car as you do here, but by writing to me. A letter a week—that is my price—and I can assure you your check will depend on it.

You will not read this letter until you have arrived on campus, seen your room, met your roommate, and learned the combination to your postal box. I wanted you to have a letter waiting on arrival so you would not for a minute feel abandoned by the outside world. I remember vividly when I went away to college, standing in the college post office watching the clerk sort the morning mail, my heart literally leaping with joy every time a letter hit the glass window of my box. I suppose the high regard in which I hold written communication dates from that time. In those months away at school the post office did more than the dining room to sustain life for me.

It is not uncommon for a person, years after graduation, to dream he is taking an exam for which he is unprepared. But I have never had that nightmare. My recurring dream is that I am back in school many years later, all the students and teachers I knew are gone, and no one can tell me the combination to my postal box. For some reason I know clearly which box is mine and I can see the letters stacked up inside but I can never get to them. I wake up with a sense of isolation more intense than I have ever known.

My life has not been without tragedy and at times my waking horror has stalked my sleep, allowing me no escape from the pain I was experiencing by day. But my only recurring nightmare is the one I have just described. It seems strange that I have never told you about it before, but I've never told anyone.

You see what I mean about writing letters. There is something about the process of writing—perhaps because it usually takes place in the privacy of one's room—that allows and indeed encourages the expression of thoughts one would never say aloud. So although in spite of my best efforts, I know I will cry tomorrow at the train station when I kiss you good-bye, by the time you read this, I will be in my room, happily writing you another letter and looking forward to our getting to know each other as we never could while living under the same roof.

All my love,
Mummy


November 19, 1926
Dallas

Dearest Dwight,

I cannot thank you enough for inviting Andrew to share your apartment during the Thanksgiving holidays. How I wish I could be part of the fun. I know many of his friends will be spending the weekend in the city, but I am very grateful he will not be staying in a hotel crowded with his contemporaries. I trust my son, but I do not trust crowds of any age—especially in a city the size of New York.

Andrew seems to be very happy at school, though his letters are so terse you would think he was sending telegrams and paying by the word. At my request he has sent me reading lists for all his courses, and I am currently renewing my acquaintance with Chaucer. I do not want him to consider me an illiterate stranger when we meet again at Christmas.

While you are entertaining my son, I will be spending Thanksgiving with yours. Arthur and Totsie have invited Sam and Eleanor and me to join them for the weekend at their cottage on a nearby lake. Sam is delighted by any invitation that includes a body of water, and I am pleased at the prospect of spending more than just a few hours in the company of my two closest friends. No matter how often we see each other for dinner or lunch, the knowledge that we will soon be going home to our separate residences prevents the kind of closeness that Totsie and I shared when we were roommates at school.

During our school years we share so much of our lives with our friends, perhaps because so many of the same experiences await us each day. Then we encounter the divisive responsibilities of adulthood and find ourselves alone in our separate lives. I fell in love with my first husband in the fourth grade, and though our intimacy found increasingly physical means of expression we were never more one person or so clearly led one life as we did at the age of nine when we met every morning outside the schoolhouse and did not leave each other's sight until sundown.

I suppose it is the thought of this weekend that has sent my mind wandering among the honeyed groves of my childhood. I would like to think it possible for two couples to share a friendship as close as that of two individuals, but I have yet to experience it. Why is it a woman who prizes her independence as much as I do is at the same time consumed by the longing to be part of some larger pattern?

Please take Andrew to the theater at least once during the holidays —even if he protests. I want this to be my treat, so I am enclosing a check to cover the cost of four tickets, in case either of you wants to bring a friend.

My love,

Bess

April 18, 1927

Boston

Dearest Lydia and Manning,

It is a lovely spring afternoon—the kind more appreciated in New England than in Texas by contrast to the severe winter that preceded it. I am glad now that Andrew refused to come home for spring vacation, though at the time I was hurt by what appeared to be an outright rejection. But now that I am here with him, I am grateful he has learned to feel at home in this part of the country.

He was stunned to see the whole family arrive by car at his dormitory on the afternoon school was dismissed, since he had made plans to stay with his roommate Roger Wainwright at his home in Boston. However, I assured him we had no intention of interfering with his plans, we would simply be staying in Boston at the same time. I invited the two boys to travel with us, since we shared the same destination, and they accepted with a surprising show of gratitude.

I trust my son's growing affinity for all things eastern will include the good manners displayed by his friend. Young Master Wainwright had obviously imagined his roommate's family to be part of some primitive culture totally unknown to him—an impression Andrew apparently had made no effort to correct—and his surprise at encountering three civilized human beings was clearly evident. He must have conveyed his feelings to his family, for soon after we checked into our hotel, his mother called to invite us to dinner.

The family lives in an unpretentious but elegantly appointed house on Beacon Hill. The husband is a regular contributor to the *Atlantic Monthly* so the conversation took a literary turn early in the evening and, delightfully, stayed there. Sam and the children were soon bored and disappeared after dinner into an adjoining billiard room. Once I had established my credentials as a descendant of Louisa May Alcott, my opinions were received without a trace of condescension, and we discovered a shared enthusiasm for Scott

Fitzgerald. They were less familiar with my favorite contemporary author, Willa Cather, having only read her Pulitzer Prize winner, *One of Ours,* but I urged them to base their critical appraisal on her earlier novels, *My Antonia, O Pioneers,* and *The Song of the Lark,* which to my mind stand unsurpassed in modern fiction.

This afternoon Sam has taken the children boating on the Charles River and I am meeting Mrs. Wainwright at the Fogg Museum. Both her father and her husband attended Harvard, so her son is assured a place there. I have not made up my mind where Andrew will go and so far he has not expressed a preference, but I fully intend to come to a decision before he does.

Love to all of you,

Bess

June 19, 1927
Dallas, Texas

Mr. and Mrs. Adam Wainwright
211 Chestnut Street
Boston, Massachusetts

Dear Adam and Priscilla,

Andrew has written Roger extending an invitation for the summer, but I would like to add my insistence. My husband is determined to balance Andrew's experience in the East with further exploration of the Far West. We are planning a motor trip to the Grand Canyon and Yosemite National Park in August, and we would love to include Roger. My conversation with him in the spring led me to believe his firsthand knowledge of this country is still somewhat limited, and I am sure he would derive much profit as well as pleasure from extending his horizons further west. From a purely selfish point of view, let me say how welcome his presence would be to all of us on the trip. Indeed I fear my son would be a most unwilling passenger without him.

I still look back with delight on our visit to Boston. I have visited the city before, but never in the company of people who were so clearly part of it. Though I have been favorably impressed with the curriculum at Choate, Andrew's friendship with your son has been a source of greater pride to me than any of his academic achievements. The ability to choose friends wisely was his father's greatest asset in business and of all his admirable traits, that is the one I am most happy to see his son inherit. When I sent him away to school last fall, I was still not sure in my heart that he was ready to leave home. But in this year he has proved to me he can make a home anywhere. Your son had a far shorter distance to travel—Choate is located within the boundaries of the world he knew as a child. We look forward to having him visit us this summer so that he too can experience the satisfaction of making an alien land his own.

Affectionately,

Bess

March 5, 1928

Dallas

Dearest Mavis,

It has been far too long since we have had a glimpse of you. My life seems strangely divided ever since Andrew went away to school. My thoughts are with him even when I am not.

I am planning to take the children to Europe this summer. Sam, of course, is welcome to join us but I doubt that he will. For some reason he feels his parental responsibility ended at the Rocky Mountains, while I, on the other hand, do not feel their education is complete until they have crossed the Alps.

Several of Andrew's friends, including his roommate, will be seeing Europe for the first time this summer under the chaperonage of their history professor at Choate and his wife. Andrew wanted to join the tour, but I felt he should share the summer with his family. And after all, unlike most of his friends, Andrew has been abroad before. Of course, since he was not yet two at the time, he has no memory of our first trip, but memories have to be cultivated like anything else. As we travel, I will remind him of the places we have been before and describe the things he said and did, so that by the time we return home he will truly feel that he has been to Europe twice.

Sam and I hope to see you some day soon. We usually go for a drive on the weekend. Sam brings home a bushel basket of farm produce, and I return with the title to a new piece of property. All the young people growing up on the farms and in the little towns around Dallas are eager to sell the land they have inherited and move to the city. Why can't they see that the city is moving to meet them and the way to make their fortune is to stay where they are? Fortunately I can.

We look forward to paying you a visit soon.

Love,

Bess

June 23, 1928

aboard the Aquitania

Dearest Sam,

The steward says this has been the worst June crossing in his memory, so I cannot in all honesty say I wish you were here.

Eleanor and I have not left our stateroom since we sailed and have subsisted on chicken sandwiches and hothouse grapes brought to us in bed by our delightful steward. He is our only link with the outside world and with our trays brings us rollicking stories about other crossings. I wish he could accompany us on the rest of our travels.

We have not seen much of Andrew since he joined forces with his Choate friends. I deliberately booked passage on the same ship with his school tour but I did not expect to lose his company completely. Fortunately the stormy crossing does not seem to have affected his stomach at all, and he has not missed a meal. He described the first night's dinner to us in graphic detail—beginning with shark fin's soup, which I suspect he ordered for the name rather than the taste—but Eleanor and I proved so unresponsive to his rapturous account that we have not heard a word from him since.

Our leavetaking was very gala. I wish you could have come as far as New York with us but I am holding you to your tentative promise of a Paris rendezvous. You must get over the idea that you will be helpless in a country whose language you cannot speak. We are always at the mercy of strangers when we travel—even in our own country. In Europe we are just a little more so.

My friend Dwight Davis drove us (with our ten pieces of luggage following in a taxi) to the Cunard Pier at the foot of 14th Street where the *Aquitania* was waiting in all her majestic splendor, so there was at least one friendly face in the crowd that waved us good-bye. Your sweet telegram was waiting in the stateroom. You are indeed a man of few words, my dearest, but the words you choose I cherish. I have your orchid pinned to my bed pillow. I trust it—and I—will look well enough to attend the dance the captain is giving tomorrow night.

All my love,

Bess

June 25, 1928

aboard the *Aquitania*

Dear Lydia,

Thank you again for the lovely guidebooks you gave us as a going-away present. I had an opportunity to enjoy them sooner than I expected, since a stormy crossing has sharply curtailed all physical activity. I spent the first two days in my stateroom getting my sea legs (and losing my stomach).

Yesterday I was determined to get dressed. The sun appeared for the first time and so did I. It was very pleasant on deck, and I claimed a deck chair next to a most attractive man from Atlanta, Georgia, who is traveling with his son. His name is Richard Prince and he recently retired as president of a large manufacturing company. He lives on a 500-acre estate outside the city and, in addition to a Rolls Royce, owns a private yacht. The more we talked, the more we discovered how much we had in common, including marriage partners who dislike traveling abroad.

He invited me to join him at the captain's table for dinner. I wore my new silver lamé evening dress with my orchid from Sam pinned to my shoulder. Judging from the response I received when I sat down to dinner, I would say the effect was quite stunning. Throwing discretion to the winds, I indulged freely in the lavish lobster dinner that was set before us.

Then the dance began and in two hours I made up for the two days I had spent in seclusion in my stateroom. There are a great many charming men aboard and I danced with all of them last night. It was not until midnight that I had cause to regret the lobster. I said a precipitant good-night to my partner and left the dance floor as the waltz ended. Fortunately I reached the deck in time to return my lobster to its natural habitat before retiring to my stateroom for the evening.

I felt fine again this morning and persuaded Eleanor to leave the safety of her bed and venture outside with me. She made it as far as a deck chair before her legs gave way, but felt better after a little bouillon. Richard Prince brought his son over to be introduced. He is a splendid-looking young man, over six feet tall already and only sixteen years old. He invited Eleanor to play a game of deck tennis but unfortunately she was not feeling well enough to accept. She said the sea air was making her sleepy so we left her alone to nap. Richard and I strolled the deck and when we finally returned to our deck chairs he showed me by the pedometer strapped to his leg that we had walked over a mile. I am not used to that much exercise, which is probably the reason I have felt so breathless all afternoon.

Must stop now and get ready for dinner. My orchid has faded but I have just begun to bloom.

Much love,<br>Bess

July 10, 1928<br>London

Dear Lydia,

After two weeks of motoring through the English countryside, we were as excited as provincials at our first sight of the capital.

We were greeted at our hotel by very welcome letters from you and Sam and messages from shipboard friends who arrived ahead of us—including one from Richard Prince inviting me to dine with him at the Savoy Grill. He is a delightful dinner partner who spends several weeks a year in London and knows everything that is happening here. But since I became a regular subscriber to *The London Times* several years ago, so do I. I was fascinated by his appraisal of the current political situation and he was visibly astonished at my knowledge of the events that had precipitated it.

After dinner we walked along the lighted banks of the Thames watching the boats (in England even the barges move with a kind of majesty). We soon discovered we shared another passion: the theater. He plotted my theater schedule for the rest of the week and even arranged to book all my tickets.

The next night the two of us attended an intriguing mystery play called *Alibi,* and I was introduced to the remarkable acting of

Charles Laughton. Only an Englishman could give such a delightfully wicked portrayal of a French detective. After the theater we had a late supper at a charming restaurant on the edge of Covent Garden and made our way home through crates of cabbages. It was a cheery scene with fires burning in metal cans to ward off the night cold and a chorus of cockney voices calling good-night as we climbed into a taxi.

I invited Richard and his son to be our guests for dinner the next night at Ye Olde Cheshire Cheese where Dickens used to dine, but unfortunately they had a prior commitment. However, Andrew's history master and his wife accepted the invitation readily, obviously grateful for an evening in the company of anyone over sixteen.

Sunday Andrew accompanied Eleanor and me to services at Westminster Abbey on the condition he would never have to enter another cathedral on the entire trip. Sometimes I think back wistfully to our first trip to Europe when he never objected to anything I wanted to do. Whatever happened to that cheerful, agreeable little boy? I have lost him to life as surely as I lost my beloved Robin to death.

Tomorrow we take the Golden Arrow express train to Paris. It has been fifteen years since my first visit. I never dreamed I would have to wait so long to see it again. I keep hoping Sam will be there to meet us. If I were traveling alone, I do not think I would miss him so much but I feel our marriage has made him responsible for the children—or is it that the children were responsible for our marriage? In any case he should be with them. The three of them are invariably interested—and bored—by the same things.

However, my heart sings at the thought of seeing Paris again—with or without Sam.

> Much love,
> Bess

> July 16, 1928
> Chez Madame Sèze
> 44 Avenue Wagram
> Paris

Dearest Sam,

Your telegram was waiting for us on arrival. We were happy to hear from you but it would have made us happier to see you. The children say they are no longer interested in seeing the Italian lakes without you to take them rowing.

Our accommodations here are very pleasant and quite a bargain. Madame Sèze has placed her entire apartment at our disposal (even the drawing room where she sleeps on a daybed during our occupancy) for the sum of 125 francs per day (francs are four cents now). I hope you are impressed with our economy. A shipboard companion of mine from Atlanta, Georgia, is paying thirty-five dollars a day for a suite in a fashionable hotel.

We had made reservations and paid in advance for a tour of Versailles the day after we arrived, realizing too late that it was Bastille Day. The travel agency was closed, naturally, and it was too late to get our money back, so there was no choice but to join the mob that stormed the palace.

Paris, along with the rest of the continent, is suffering from a record heat wave, and Louis XIV would have been shocked to see the deplorable condition of his gardens. The grass is brown everywhere and the streams almost empty. Only the Grotto of Apollo looked cool and inviting, but the descendants of Robespierre soon spoiled even its quiet seclusion, filling the air with raucous laughter and the stench of garlic. I have never been more in sympathy with poor, bewildered Marie Antoinette, and I am thankful for the few happy moments she enjoyed playing shepherdess in her adorable hamlet. (I hope you are reading *The Letters of Madame de Sévigné* which I left on the bookshelf by your bed so that you may at least share our adventure in spirit.)

We made an early return to the city and watched the dancing in the streets below from the comfortable perspective of our balcony. The Eiffel Tower was illuminated in the distance and I went to sleep feeling I had arrived at the center of the universe.

All my love,

Bess


July 21, 1928
Tours, France

Dearest Dwight,

It was so kind of you to escort us to the ship, and I cannot thank you enough for the foreign currency computer you tucked into my pocket as you kissed me good-bye. I do not mind traveling in a country where I cannot speak the language as long as I can understand the money.

We have just concluded a strenuous three-day tour of the Loire Valley. To my delight Andrew and Eleanor have become fascinated by all the court intrigue contained within the walls of each chateau, and they have followed the checkered history of Catherine de Medici from one royal residence to another with as much interest as my laundress reads newspaper serials. They were thrilled to see the secret cabinet where she kept her poisons in a paneled room at the Château of Blois and applauded her audacity in banishing her husband's mistress, Diane de Poitiers, from the "dream palace" of Chenonceaux after his death and claiming it for her own. Though I cannot admire her I do envy her way of life. A woman of wit and intellect was much more appreciated in a royal court in Renaissance France than she is today in a living room in Texas.

Tonight we are staying at a country inn that is very much to your taste. I wish you were waiting below to join us for dinner.

My love,
Bess

August 5, 1928
Amsterdam

Dearest Sam,

We allowed a week on our itinerary for Amsterdam, so we would have time to enjoy the Olympic Games, but we all wish we were staying longer.

It is thrilling to see our flag raised when our athletes win. Unfortunately we will be leaving before the swimming finals but we were impressed by Crabbe's perfect form in the semifinals. I hope his Australian competition will not get the better of him in the finals.

We shared a sightseeing excursion with a group of Irish Olympic players, and one of them, a student of medicine at Trinity College, Dublin, was quite attentive to Eleanor. I invited him to join us for dinner and he came gladly. Unfortunately his team was defeated the next day—due largely to poor decisions by the referee, we felt.

Andrew has missed his weekly tennis game with you, but he found plenty of partners here—unfortunately all better than he is.

We miss you.

Love,

Bess

August 25, 1928
Villa d'Este
Cernobbio, Italy

Dearest Lydia,

From the day I discovered Byron, I have dreamed of the Italian Lakes, but my first glimpse of Lake Como convinced me that there are times when even the most unrestrained imagination fails to match the artistry of nature.

The enchantment of the setting was further enhanced by the unexpected appearance at our hotel here of my shipboard companion Richard Prince. He travels without an itinerary so is free to go wherever his mood takes him. I had furnished him with a copy of my itinerary when we parted in Paris, however, so I suspect he was not as surprised to see me as I was to see him.

By happy coincidence we have adjacent rooms with balconies overlooking the lake. Last night we shared the spectacle of a sunset whose splendor was doubled by its reflection in the lake. How wise we would be to multiply all our pleasure in life through the simple act of reflection, allowing memory to serve as the mirror in which the original moment can be recreated at will. I feel with Wordsworth that an event "recollected in tranquillity" has an intensity it often lacks in the present. My stay in Europe is at an end but I expect to make the trip many times in memory, unencumbered by children and baggage.

Richard and I spent this morning rowing on the lake. Fortunately our children are happy in each other's company and old enough to plan picnics without us. It is a delight—and a new experience for me —to spend time in the company of a man who is better educated than I am. Most of the American men I know have been too busy earning a living to pursue any aesthetic goals, and my friend freely admits he devoted his early years to acquiring a fortune. But he is just as rigorously devoting the rest of his life to enjoying it.

His interests are unbounded and he approaches each new country as if it were a company he had decided to acquire. He studies its historical contribution and if he feels it merits his attention, he commits himself to learning the language. He is renting a villa in Fiesole this fall in order to attend the language institute in Florence. I have resolved to study Italian on my own when I return home, and we have sworn that the next time we meet we will converse only in the language of the country we are visiting.

I have missed Sam on the trip but if he had been with me, I would never have gotten to know Richard Prince. It seems unreasonable to expect—or indeed even to want—to share every experience in life with the same person. We are more complicated than that and capable of pledging lifelong devotion to any number of different people of different sex and age. Why does society restrict a man and a woman to only one such pledge per lifetime? I hope I will never break any promise once made, but if I were free and clear at this moment, I would never again promise my exclusive devotion to anyone.

I trust you are not shocked by the feelings I am expressing. I can assure you they were foreign to me when I was married to your brother, though perhaps the passing years would have tested even that seemingly perfect relationship. I am now married to a man I love and respect but that does not mean I would not enjoy a similar relationship with other men.

Sometimes I think the world would be a much more interesting place if on coming of age, everyone moved into a house of his own and shared his life with a variety of other people at mutually arranged times and places. Of course there are the children to consider, but I sometimes suspect monogamy is an invention of the male, designed to protect his exclusive claim to the children he fathers. Nature assigns no role to the father once conception takes place. It is a refinement of civilization to make the father an equal partner in the child-rearing process, and I wonder if this division of responsibility is in fact an improvement on the natural order of things. Any society depends on an acceptance of a twofold responsibility: to one's self and to others. Perhaps it is to enforce the second that nature denies the male any physical ties to his children. Could it be that the male is not given a demonstrable claim on his own children in the hope that he will assume a spiritual responsibility for all children?

Forgive me for this intellectual excursion into territory I have never dared explore in the past. But now that this physical journey is almost over, the only voyages ahead of me in the immediate future are in the mind, and in that area I am an intrepid traveler. But I trust that, like any traveler, I will enjoy my homecoming all the more because of the distance I have traveled in order to reach my point of departure.

> A bientôt,
> Bess

September 20, 1928
Dallas

Dear Lydia,

A state of armed truce has existed in our household since my return. Sam greeted me with the announcement that he had had me followed by a private detective from the time I left Paris. I was careful to avoid any mention of my friend Richard Prince in my letters to him, but it never occurred to me to censor the children's letters home and apparently they described our friendship in sufficient detail to arouse Sam's already suspicious nature.

We had no sooner stepped off the train than Sam triumphantly presented me with evidence of adjacent rooms at the Villa d'Este. I was so enraged by his lack of trust I went to my room without a word in my own defense and stayed there for five days, admitting only the children and having my meals brought to me on a tray. On the sixth day a letter arrived for me from Richard Prince in Fiesole.

Sam brought it to the door of my room and threatened to open it and read it aloud if I did not emerge at once. With all the dignity I could muster, I opened the door and demanded the letter. Sam finally agreed to relinquish it on the condition that any further correspondence between us would be subject to his scrutiny. I met his condition with one of my own: I would not reply to the letter if he would refrain from further accusations. He agreed, appearing grateful to have the matter closed, and that night, for the first time since our return, the dinner table was graced with my presence, if not my appetite.

The children are back in school and I have begun my independent study of Italian. I should soon know enough to conduct a private correspondence with someone who will understand what my wayward heart is saying despite my woeful grammar.

Ciao,
Bess

October 14, 1930
Dallas

Dearest Andrew,

I am glad you are so happy at Yale. Your letters home do more than your diploma to convince me Choate did a good job of preparing you for college. I was especially touched by your note of gratitude to me for everything I have done to make you feel the equal of anyone in your class, no matter how impressive his family background. From now on, you will be measured on the basis of your own achievements and that is the only standard you must employ to judge others.

I have some very sad news to report. Arthur Fineman died yesterday of a heart attack. He was only forty-five. Though he has been in poor health for the past year, his death came as a complete shock to all of us—but can be counted a casualty of the stock market crash as surely as any suicide. The sense of responsibility he felt toward his family, which would never have allowed him to take his own life, killed him in the end. He not only watched his past savings disappear, he foresaw little hope for future income from his chosen profession.

I stopped trying to make sense out of the stock market some years ago and began to buy land, but Arthur continued to chide me and insist there was logic to the buying and selling that was his livelihood. When the crash came, he felt he had not only been lying to himself but also deceiving people who trusted him.

You were too young to realize how much I profited from Arthur's advice after your father died. He took the place of a husband at a time when I was very much alone in the world and even after each of us married someone else, his wise and cultivated presence continued to be an important part of my life. Life in Dallas will be desolate without him.

I am buying a seat in his name in the new civic auditorium so that in spirit at least he will continue to be part of the performances that meant so much to him. My contribution carries with it the stipulation that the seat be reserved for me during the opera season. I cannot bear to think of attending alone, but neither can I imagine anyone else sitting beside me and visibly trembling at a piece of music the way he did. If there is indeed a choir of angels in heaven, I am sure Arthur is applauding even now.

I think it would be very nice if you wrote to Totsie, not a letter of condolence—what a mournful phrase that is—just some acknowledgment that Arthur touched your life in a way no one else did. Try to describe some incident that will make him live for her again, if only for a moment. Life is our only defense against death. I know.

All my love,
Mummy

April 16, 1931
Dallas

Dear Lydia,

It was a joy to spend Easter with you in Denton. With Andrew at Yale and Eleanor getting ready to go to Vassar, I feel our life as a family is coming to an end—or at least changing form. How fortunate you and Manning are to be teaching where Marian is learning —to be joined in a continual process of give and take and spared the estrangement that so often occurs when a child starts college.

I am giving an afternoon tea at the country club on May 10 in honor of Eleanor's graduation from Hockaday. I hope you and Marian will be able to attend. I expect the occasion to receive full coverage in *The Dallas News* now that Totsie Fineman has become a society reporter. When she was first widowed, she refused to consider going back to work, feeling it would reflect unfavorably on Arthur's provisions for her in his will. But I insisted she join us one night when our neighbors the Perkinses were here for dinner and she had a job before we had finished our lemon soufflé.

I look forward to seeing you at the tea.

Love,
Bess

September 10, 1931
Dallas

Mr. Richard Prince
Greenhill Estate
Atlanta, Georgia

My dear Richard,

I know you will be surprised to hear from me after a silence of three years. The letter you wrote me from Fiesole the week after we parted enabled me to relive more than once all the sunsets we shared. Forgive me for waiting so long to reply, but I was not in a position to provide you with the answer you wanted and anything less would have seemed a reproach to the tender expression of affection offered freely on your part and embraced wordlessly by me.

I think of you often and of your handsome son. When we met, he was planning to attend Princeton after two more years of prep school. My daughter, Eleanor, leaves next week for Vassar. I am sure she would enjoy seeing your son again, and I hope he will be pleasantly surprised to learn of her proximity.

It would give me great pleasure to think our relationship could continue through our children. But whatever the future holds, the past survives, and souvenirs of my last trip furnish my memory more richly than my home.

With abiding affection,

Bess

NOVEMBER 8 1931
DALLAS

ELEANOR STEED
VASSAR COLLEGE
POUGHKEEPSIE   NEW YORK
SHALL I SHIP YOUR BLUE CHIFFON FOR PRINCETON COTILLION
PLEASE ADVISE IMMEDIATELY

LOVE

MOTHER

ELEANOR STEED

VASSAR COLLEGE

POUGHKEEPSIE   NEW YORK

BLACK VELVET HIGHLY INAPPROPRIATE EVEN FOR PRINCETON

BLUE CHIFFON ON ITS WAY

LOVE

MOTHER

June 10, 1932
Dallas

Miss Eleanor Steed
S.S. *Statendam*
Pier 24
New York City, New York

My darling,

How strange it feels to be saying "bon voyage" from Texas. In fact, how strange it feels to be saying "bon voyage" at all. I am used to being on the receiving end of such sentiments, bravely waving good-bye and writing warm letters of reassurance to my loved ones left at home. Now that I know what a bereft feeling it is to be left behind, I marvel that either of my husbands allowed me to travel to Europe without them.

However, I know you will enjoy touring the continent in the comfort of a private automobile, and I am sure "Europe on Wheels" will enrich your education as much as any course you could take in college.

I trust the past weekend in New York with Henry Prince was everything you hoped it would be. I know how disappointed you are that his mother's illness will prevent him from joining you in Paris as planned. But there will be many young people traveling abroad this summer, and you will be pleasantly surprised to learn how fast any English-speaking stranger can become a friend in a foreign country.

I miss being there to share a final glass of champagne on deck before hugging you good-bye, but I hope the roses I ordered for your stateroom will be a constant reminder of my love and pride in your continuing growth. You are somebody I would look forward to knowing if we were just meeting for the first time. What greater compliment can a parent pay a child?

I have bought a scrapbook which I hope to fill with your letters and photographs, so please write often. Your letters will sustain me now—and you in years to come.

Bon voyage, ma petite. Amuse-toi bien.

Au revoir,
Mummy

July 6, 1932
Dallas

Miss Eleanor Steed
c/o "Europe on Wheels"
München, Deutschland

My darling,

Just received your first epistle from abroad and went straight to my desk to pen a reply before the post office closes.

I am happy to hear you did not lack for male companionship on the crossing, and I can tell your young sculptor friend laid siege to your imagination as well as your heart. Little wonder your college escorts seemed dull by comparison. But do not be disappointed if you do not hear from him again. For an art student newly arrived in Paris, the present is everything. Faces from the past, even a face as pretty and trusting as yours, soon fade from memory. Though Paris lovers are legendary, an artist at work there quickly becomes the prey of the intellectual passion that pervades the city and finds little time for personal sentiment. In France it is ideas that set men on fire. So beware of losing your heart there—it may not be returned to you intact.

I was enthralled by your description of the lovers bicycling side by side along the canals in Amsterdam, the man touching the woman's handlebar. That is an image to remember as you choose the man to accompany you on your journey through life—two figures advancing through their own efforts, neither propelling nor impeding the other, simply reaching across the space that separates them for reassuring proof of the other's presence.

I imagine you now traveling through Germany, seeing through suddenly adult eyes the sights we shared four years ago. I hope there are other shared excursions ahead of us but for now I delight in every description you provide.

All my love,

Mummy

July 20, 1932

Dallas

Miss Eleanor Steed
c/o "Europe on Wheels"
Villa d'Este
Cernobbio, Italia

My darling,

I had to write a letter to this address, which holds so many happy memories for me.

I trust your green Franklin phaeton made a successful passage through the Dolomites. Crossing those mountains by car must be an undertaking filled with suspense.

I am glad you are getting along so well with your traveling companions. I am now firmly convinced that a long trip abroad should precede an engagement. Travel is certainly the test of any relationship. If the honeymoon came before the wedding, I suspect there would be a considerable reduction in the divorce rate.

As soon as I read your last letter, I went to the music store in search of a recording of Albert Schweitzer playing the organ. I am listening to it now and the whole room resounds with the music of Bach. Schweitzer plays as if God were listening to every chord. What joy a man must take in a talent so immense. I am so happy you were able to hear him play in person.

How I envy the afternoon you spent exploring the Deutsche Museum in Munich. It must have been like taking a trip into the future —seeing machines most of us have never even imagined in operation. I wonder how long I will have to wait to see television.

I have been reading newspaper accounts of Nazi activities and I am glad I did not know at the time you were attending a rally. I can understand your curiosity about Hitler but I for one would not pay one pfennig to hear him speak. I find him such a ridiculous figure it is hard to believe anyone takes him seriously and I would be troubled to hear a crowd cheer him.

It gives me such pleasure to think of you in Italy. Enjoy every moment. Each new experience will be enriched by time. The best dowry a woman can bring to a marriage is a set of memories she acquired alone.

All my love,<br>Mummy

August 10, 1932<br>Dallas

Miss Eleanor Steed
Cas' Alta
Firenze, Italia

Darling,

Your last letter assaulted our placid horizon as unexpectedly as a bolt of lightning and I am braced for the thunder to follow.

I can understand the emotions Italy has awakened in you but your impulsive decision to remain in Florence for the winter has taken all of us by surprise. Your chaperone wrote me that you had stayed behind in Florence to recover from a sore throat but she fully expected you to rejoin the tour in Rome for a final week of sightseeing (paid in advance, I might add) before returning home.

It was very responsible of you to write Vassar that you would not be returning in the fall, though I regret that you did not consult me before arriving at this decision. I agree that the purpose of college is to teach an individual to think for himself but you seem to have acquired that ability sooner than I expected.

Any argument I could offer in opposition would be contradicted by the choice I made twenty-three years ago to leave college and marry your father. I must admit in all honesty I never regretted my decision. I can only hope you will not regret yours. Too many college graduates regard their diploma as proof that their education is complete. I will never cease to be haunted by all the things I have yet to learn.

I am impressed with the arrangements you have made for living and studying in Florence this winter, but I trust you will confirm them with your art professor while she is still on the continent. Even though she will not have the pleasure of your company for the rest of the tour, I am sure she will be happy to give you the benefit of her advice and experience.

I have always had the utmost respect for your ability as an artist and I cannot help being thrilled by your response to the great works of art you have seen this summer. Though I have no talent in that sphere, I must admit that the sculptures of Michelangelo have made even me want to seize a chisel and attack the nearest block of marble. And your decision to leave school, as ill-considered as it first appeared to me, can clearly be traced to the afternoon you spent staring at Michelangelo's unfinished sculptures for the Medici tombs. Who could fail to identify with those figures struggling to free themselves from the stone which gives them substance and at the same time denies them form? All of life for me is contained in those emerging figures—for what is life but a brief assertion of a unique identity between womb and tomb?

Forgive me, my darling, for being so angry when I began this letter. Sometimes being a good mother gets in the way of being a good person. I will close now and start packing a trunk with your winter clothes. I have never been in Italy in the winter but I understand it gets very cold. Please do not go out alone at night—but do go out.

All my love,<br>Mummy

October 12, 1932<br>Dallas

Mr. Richard Prince
Greenhill Estate
Atlanta, Georgia

Dear Richard,

I have just learned of the death of your wife last summer, and I did not want you to think I would let such a loss go unacknowledged. Though your separate interests often kept you apart, I am sure the pride you shared in your son was a bond to the end, and it is sad your wife will not be at your side for all the happy occasions your son is sure to provide in the future.

I suppose Henry told you that Eleanor has forsaken a college education in favor of independent study in Florence. Though she is living with a family who have been highly recommended, I cannot help worrying about her. I know you have many close friends in Florence and I would be very grateful if you would ask one of them to call on her and make sure she is all right. Is there any chance you will be traveling to Europe this year?

It was a pity Henry had to cancel his trip abroad last summer, but I am sure his presence at home was a great comfort to his mother. He has many fine qualities but the one I find most impressive is his devotion to his family, and I hope Eleanor has profited from his example. It gave me great joy to see the close friendship he and Eleanor formed last year and I trust her decision to study abroad will not cause any unnecessary estrangement. She does not discuss her correspondence with me, but I know she would enjoy hearing from Henry, if he has not written already. I am enclosing her address along with a snapshot taken this summer at the Villa d'Este. As you can see, she has changed quite a bit since the summer we met. I flatter myself that I have not, however—and that at the age of forty-one, I look at least as young as I did when we met four years ago.

Again, please accept my sympathy for your loss—and my abiding affection.

Bess


March 1, 1933
Dallas

Miss Eleanor Steed
Cas' Alta
Firenze, Italia

Darling,

Just received your letter announcing plans to spend spring vacation in Sicily with Count d'Annunzio Fabrini and his family. I am sure he is as anxious to meet your family as you are to meet his so I am joining you in Rome for Easter and we will travel to Sicily together.

Exa Banks is accompanying me abroad with her new green Lincoln and her chauffeur, so we will be traveling in a manner befitting friends of Italian nobility. Since her husband's death she has little interest in staying home and who can blame her?

I have made reservations at the Hassler, so we will meet you on Easter Sunday at the top of the Spanish Steps. How glorious it will be to put my arms around you again. This year I will have my own reasons for singing Hallelujah!

All my love,

Mummy

APRIL 1 1933

DALLAS    TEXAS

MISS ELEANOR STEED

CAS ALTA

FIRENZE   ITALIA

IMPOSSIBLE TO DELAY TRIP TILL SUMMER   ARRIVING AS SCHEDULED ON EASTER SUNDAY   DO NOT LEAVE FOR SICILY WITHOUT ME

MOTHER

April 18, 1933

Hotel Hassler

Rome, Italy

Dearest Sam,

I doubt if my lifetime will offer a more historic opportunity for visiting Rome than this nineteen-hundredth anniversary of the crucifixion of Christ. I would swear all of Italy was standing in St. Peter's Square on Easter Sunday, waiting for the Pope to appear on his balcony and give his blessing. We were fortunate to have rooms waiting for us since we hear tourists are quartered in bathrooms and closets all over the city.

The drive down from Genoa took longer than we expected. From the moment it was unloaded on the dock our green Lincoln attracted admiring hordes, and we caused a traffic jam in every small town en route to Rome. We arrived here exhausted from our ordeal, but our spirits revived at once at the sight of my beloved daughter. She brought a bouquet of flowers to our hotel room, but the blossom I cherished was her own smiling face. She seems so much older and self-assured than the young girl we kissed good-bye last summer— and yet much more open in her affections. No wonder she has captured the heart of an Italian count—I have fallen madly in love with her myself.

Count Fabrini is a charming young man and fortunately not nearly as forbidding as his title. I do not know how we would have made our way around the city this week without his able assistance.

On Easter Sunday he managed somehow to steer us through the mob that packed St. Peter's and to procure a place for us across from Michelangelo's *Pietà,* where we waited almost two hours for the Pope to arrive to celebrate Mass. Though the Catholic ritual is as foreign to me as the tongue in which it is conducted, I could not help being moved by the devotion of the crowd and the reverence in which they hold "Il Papa." I envy the faith that allows them to submit so completely to the authority of a man who is only human in spite of his high position. There is something so touchingly child-like about the Catholic faith. We all long for an infallible father figure but finally come to realize our parents are no more perfect than we are.

Still, despite my doubts, I shared with the adoring masses an overwhelming sense of awe and mystery as the Pope was carried down the center aisle of the cathedral on his white-and-gold cano-pied throne. Whether it was the sight of his noble features or the sculptured devotion of Michelangelo's Madonna across from me I do not know, but I was filled with the love of parent for child which is as close as we come on this earth to experiencing the love of God for man. I felt blessed to have my child beside me, and for the first time since she sailed last summer I dared admit to myself how much I have missed her.

Thank you for your Easter cablegram. It was very thoughtful of Mrs. Perkins to invite you to share their Easter dinner. She has been rather distant with me ever since my last trip abroad. I am sure she thinks I have abandoned you once again. I trust you do not agree.

Exa has not been abroad since her honeymoon and although she is a more timorous traveler than I am, her curiosity about life on the continent grows hourly. At the end of the week we are driving down to Sicily with Eleanor and her Italian count. From there we will make our way back across the continent, ending in England in time for the Ascot Races. It is my fervent hope that Eleanor will come with us, but I have not dared broach the idea. I am so happy to have found her again, I cannot risk losing her. So for now we maintain the illusion that we will be parting again after our trip to Sicily. But in my heart I have made a secret vow not to return home without her.

My love,

Bess

April 24, 1933
Sorrento, Italy

Dear Lydia and Manning,

To see the Blue Grotto is never to be satisfied with a picture postcard again. The one I am enclosing does not begin to do it justice (but save it for me anyway—at least it will prove I was there).

Exa and I are traveling in great comfort in her green Lincoln, but Eleanor prefers to travel at faster speeds with her friend Count Fabrini in his open sports car. We say good-bye at breakfast and meet again each night for dinner at a new destination. I miss her company during the day but at least I have the comfort of knowing where she is at night.

Count Fabrini took charge of our sightseeing during our stay in Rome and insisted we balance each ancient ruin with a modern accomplishment. He is convinced Italy will soon surpass its ancient glory under the stewardship of Mussolini.

This country seems to require figures of absolute authority at the head of both church and state. Between "Il Papa" and "Il Duce," an Italian has very little opportunity to think for himself. However, there is no doubt Mussolini has made enormous improvements in the economic life of the country, and apparently he has just begun.

Count Fabrini assured us a trip to Sicily like the one we were planning would have been much more dangerous before Mussolini. Under his regime all three thousand members of the notorious Black Hand gang have been captured and successfully convicted, and they are now doing hard labor in prison. Apparently they had been captured before but no judge would convict them. This time Mussolini added his weight to the scales of justice by threatening any judge who did not convict with the loss of his job.

But despite Count Fabrini's enthusiasm for Mussolini's many accomplishments, I find Rome's past more interesting than her future. I could happily spend the rest of my life here, descending layer by layer into history, imagining the architecture that once encompassed every arch and the chronicles witnessed by every column.

A gala ball was held in our hotel one night to raise money for Russian refugees. After a strenuous day of sightseeing, Exa rebelled at the thought of dancing a step. However, Eleanor and I were fascinated at the sight of so much royalty assembled under one roof, and we bought tickets for twenty lire apiece (the dollar is now worth seventeen and dropping hourly). The Cossack choir sang and Rachmaninoff played the piano for the glittering crowd which included the king of Greece and an Indian rajah and his entourage.

When the dancing began, our hotel manager graciously introduced Eleanor and me to a series of handsome partners. I was particularly charmed by an Italian history professor. He spoke more gracefully than he danced, however, and we soon left the dance floor for a quiet stroll outside. Before we said good-night, I had signed up for his lecture series, "Walking and Talking in Ancient Rome."

He proved a delightful guide, making every scheduled site come to life with his vivid commentary. In addition to the lecture tours for which I suscribed, he took me on a private tour of the gardens at Tivoli. I have never responded to a place with such a keen sense of physical pleasure. I was actually trembling in the midst of that myriad of fountains. I finally had to rest on a marble bench secluded in a grove of cypress trees in order to recover my equilibrium. Professor Panetti was most kind and solicitous, saying that to someone of a Latin temperament the feelings I was experiencing for the first time were a common occurrence. Finally my knees stopped shaking enough for me to stand and we continued our tour.

On our way back into the city Professor Panetti pointed out to me the Villa Sciarra, formerly owned by an American woman. She gave it to Mussolini, who in turn gave it to the people of Rome, but the peacocks she bought still stroll in the garden. Italy clearly had the same effect on her that it is having on me. I came to Italy to rescue my daughter but instead I seem to have succumbed to its spell just as she has.

Love to all of you,

Bess

Andrew Steed
Calhoun College
Yale University
New Haven, Connecticut

Dearest Andrew,

This is the first time I have been to Europe without you and your ever-present sketchbook. I miss your wicked habit of sketching the tourists looking at the sights as a way of avoiding the sights yourself. I still treasure your sketch of the fat German tourists staring with such visible lack of appreciation at the *Mona Lisa*. One wonders why those people bother to travel at all.

We are on our way back to Florence after a weekend in Sicily with Count Fabrini and his family. Our visit did more to illustrate to Eleanor what marriage to an Italian is like than anything I could have told her. They were charming and gracious to us, of course, but no American woman could help but be offended by the authoritarian manner in which an Italian man rules his family. I cannot imagine any woman who is used to having her opinions received with respect submitting by choice to such arbitrary authority. Fortunately neither can Eleanor and, to my great joy and delight, she said good-bye to Count Fabrini and left him in Sicily with his family—forever, I trust. She is traveling back to Florence with us. At the moment that is as far as she plans to go but once there, I hope I can persuade her to pack her things and return home.

Your spring vacation visit with the Wainwrights sounds most pleasant. They must be proud of Roger. I am very impressed to be personally acquainted with the new editor of the Harvard *Crimson*. I had always hoped you would try for a position on the Yale paper but verbal expression appears to hold little attraction for either of my children. Have you considered submitting any of your drawings to the paper? Political cartoonists are also held in high regard.

Sam will be disappointed you have decided against taking the job he offered you at the plant this summer. Having attended a trade school himself, he considers hard physical labor a necessary corollary of a college education and feels everything you learn in books should be balanced by direct application of your knowledge in some salaried position.

However, I can sympathize with your desire to enjoy to the fullest your last summer of leisure, and you have my permission to join the Wainwrights on the Cape. On one condition: I will expect you to meet our ship when it docks in New York on June 29. In fact, why don't you invite Roger to be your guest for a weekend in Manhattan, beginning the day we arrive? It would be a gracious way to repay him and at the same time provide an attractive escort for Eleanor in the happy event she agrees to come home with me.

See if you can arrange theater tickets for *Design for Living*. I hear it is marvelous and I am always fascinated by unconventional living arrangements.

I look forward to our homecoming. One of the nicest things about traveling to Europe from Texas is coming back by way of New York.

Love,<br>Mummy

May 6, 1933<br>Cas' Alta<br>Firenze, Italia

Dear Sam,

The more I see of Italian family life, the happier I am to have a husband like you waiting for me at home, one who treats his wife as an equal, not merely an accessory. How I look forward to sitting across from you at supper again, listening to you describe your new profit-sharing plan.

I have been very encouraged about the state of our economy by Walter Lippmann's articles in *The New York Herald Tribune,* which I read every day. Even you will finally have to admit Roosevelt made a wise decision in taking the United States off the gold standard. However, I think you would be wise to put the wage increases you are proposing on a "contingency basis" until you are completely convinced that they can be justified by increased production.

The drive here through the green valleys of winter grass was beautiful. Mussolini is determined to end the importation of wheat and make Italy self-supporting, and judging from the amount of land under cultivation, I predict he will be successful. I worry about what will happen to the countries with wheat to sell when they lose Italy as a customer but that does not seem to concern anyone here.

I am living like a lady of leisure in Florence. The strenuous sightseeing of the previous weeks has left me exhausted and unable to ignore any longer the recurring back pains that are the inevitable toll of cobblestone streets.

I have been greatly impressed with Eleanor's Italian "mother" of the past year, Signora Manolo, and the manner in which she runs her household. No wonder Eleanor has been so happy here. There is only one servant, but she is a marvel, getting up before dawn to clean the house and do the marketing, preparing three-course luncheons and four-course dinners, with a change of plates for each course.

I just wish I could bring an Italian domestic home with me. I asked Signora Manolo about wages and was amazed to learn she pays her servant only two hundred lire a month. At the old exchange rate of twenty lire to the dollar, which Eleanor was getting when she arrived, this is only ten dollars a month, but even at the current rate of fifteen lire to the dollar, that is still quite a bargain compared to the cost of household help in our country.

However, I could not be persuaded to make my home in this country at any price. Even in a private residence like Signora Manolo's, guests are required to show their passports to the police. Apparently there have been numerous attempts on Mussolini's life (none of them reported in the Italian press, which is only interested in love triangles), and the police are constantly on the lookout for political dissidents. Private citizens are subjected to strict laws governing all aspects of their behavior. For example, it is against the law for an unmarried woman of any station to receive a gentleman caller in her bedroom. Police have the right to enter any home whenever they have the least suspicion any of these laws are being broken.

Eleanor has finally agreed with me that it is dangerous to continue living in a country where the government has the right to intrude so freely on the private life of its citizens, so we will be sailing home at the end of June. It is thrilling to see how much she has grown in the five years since our last trip together, both as a person and in her appreciation of all that Europe has to offer. I was overwhelmed with pride as we stood in the dimly lit Church of St. Carmine and she pointed out to me the first stomach muscles in Renaissance art (on Masaccio's Adam).

She is very serious about continuing the study of art she began here and would like to take an apartment in New York in the fall. I cannot bear to think about losing her again so soon but at least we will have her in Dallas for the summer. It will be nice to be a family again—albeit briefly and without Andrew.

All my love,

Bess

June 15, 1934

New Haven

Dear Lydia and Manning,

Sam and I watched with great pride while Andrew received his diploma today. I just wish his father could have been here. When I think of the mark he made in the business world with only a Texas diploma, I rejoice at how many doors a Yale degree will open to his son. Andrew is still undecided about a career. All he knows for certain is that he will never set foot in another classroom, so graduate school of any kind is out of the question.

Eleanor met our train in New York and we spent several happy days there with her. Her apartment is tiny but she has made the most of the available space. She would rather be alone in a crowded apartment than share a spacious one and I heartily concur. Dwight Davis, who is now a successful decorator and much happier than he was as a stockbroker, generously provided advice and professional discounts, so the apartment is exquisitely furnished.

Eleanor insisted on cooking dinner for us one night. Her culinary skill is limited to one menu—steak and artichokes—but that is one more than I ever mastered, so I was quite impressed. After dinner she showed us a portfolio of her costume sketches—the result of her study this year at the Design Institute. I think she has real talent in this field and could compete on a professional level; however, she appears to have no interest in a career.

She accompanied us to Yale for Andrew's graduation, then traveled alone to Princeton for the commencement activities of her friend Henry Prince. I would love to have gone with her—I have seen neither Henry nor his father since we said good-bye in Italy almost six years ago—but Sam felt we belonged here with Andrew.

Eleanor has spent a great deal of time with the Prince boy since moving to New York last fall but insists they are simply good friends and says I must not expect anything further to develop from their relationship. I know she is only trying to prevent my future disappointment, but nothing will keep me from being heartbroken if they cannot find permanent joy in each other's company.

The two of them are making plans to travel through Germany this summer—on foot where possible and by train everywhere else, no itinerary, only impulse to guide them. Under any other circumstances, I simply could not permit Eleanor to make a trip of this kind, but I have the highest regard for Henry Prince and I can only hope this will be the first of many adventures the two of them will share. Henry and his father are the kind of men who are at home anywhere in the world, and I could ask nothing better for my daughter.

Congratulations to Marian on all her academic honors. You must be very proud of her.

> Love to all of you,
>
> Bess


SEPTEMBER 9 1934
DALLAS TEXAS

MISS ELEANOR STEED
ROTHENBURG-OB-DER-TAUBER
DEUTSCHLAND
IN ANSWER TO YOUR CABLE YOU WERE BORN AT 4 35 P M AUGUST 25 1913  ARE YOU BEING INTERROGATED  AM FRANTIC WITH WORRY  IF YOU ARE IN TROUBLE GO TO AMERICAN EMBASSY AT ONCE  PLEASE ADVISE OF YOUR SITUATION IMMEDIATELY

> LOVE
>
> MOTHER

Miss Eleanor Steed
Rothenburg-ob-der-Tauber
Deutschland

Darling,

I was so relieved to get your letter and to learn you needed the hour of your birth for astrological purposes only. However, I was stunned that, according to the stars, you have yet to meet the man you are going to marry. I thought you and Henry were having a wonderful summer. What has gone wrong?

I can understand his ambition to be a poet and it is a profession he can certainly afford. The examples of his work that you sent me are indeed impressive and I imagine he will find in England just the intellectual climate his work requires in order to grow and flourish. But why is he going to England alone? And what is keeping you in Germany?

I had hoped you would be coming home in time for the fall social season. The president of the Idlewild Club has called me several times to see if you are interested in making your debut. I have taken the liberty of assuring him that you are—anything less would seem insulting—though I did warn him it might not be this year.

You have acquired a rather glamorous reputation in absentia but it is time to reinforce it with your presence. People are admittedly intrigued at first by someone who stays away, but finally distance becomes an affront. However, someone who chooses to come home when there are clearly so many other choices available, is accorded a welcome unknown to those who never left.

It has been a joy to have Andrew living at home again. He has not had any luck finding a position equal to his education, but times are difficult and he was grateful to get a job with the gas company last week. Unfortunately the hours are not very compatible with his heavy social schedule, but any job that would allow him to sleep until noon would also require his presence after dark and of course that is out of the question—at least until after the holidays.

Please let me know your plans in detail. I am delighted you are acquiring such fluency in German. In spite of Annie's patient efforts with all of us, it is a tongue I could never master. I am dazzled to think you will soon have four languages at your command. That is a greater fortune than anything you will inherit from me. However, what finally matters is *what* you are saying and not in which language you are saying it. At this moment I must confess I do not understand you in any language. But I love you in all of them.

Mother

November 23, 1934<br>Dallas

Mr. Richard Prince
Greenhill Estate
Atlanta, Georgia

Dearest Richard,

Today is my birthday and I feel my life is over at forty-four. The end came this morning with a birthday greeting from my daughter, now studying sculpture in Munich. She told me she and Henry made a vow in September when they parted—to renounce the limited pleasures of earthly love and consecrate their lives to art. In the same letter she told me you had remarried. My past and my future have been taken from me with one blow and without them my present has no meaning.

I long ago abandoned the hope that you and I could have a relationship within the boundaries of this country and the responsibilities to which our previous lives had already committed us but, until I was deprived of it this morning, I did not realize how much I cherished the illusion that our children would continue what we began. Without it, I am lonelier than I have ever been.

I know that you and your new wife are now on an extended Mediterranean cruise but since your Georgia address is the only one I have, I am sending my letter there in the hope that it will be forwarded to you abroad. I do not know your itinerary but I am sure you will be seeing your son in England. Please remind him that the greatest poets have been inspired to new heights of achievement by the love of a woman. Where would Dante have been without Beatrice?

Though it would have thrilled me to announce the marriage of my daughter to your son, I would be quite content at this point with a less permanent arrangement. I can understand how a poet might resist any relationship that threatened to disintegrate into domestic routine, but Henry and Eleanor share so many of the same elusive goals, it seems a pity they cannot pursue them in tandem if not united in marriage. Besides, as you and I both know, a union of souls is often more easily accomplished outside of marriage.

However, I trust this is not the case with you at present. Please accept my congratulations. I will try to take comfort in the knowledge that someone who traveled alone for so much of his life has at last found a partner to share his excursions. I suppose it is because I have been deprived of this experience that I seek it so desperately for my daughter.

Why do I suddenly seem so old at forty-four—and wise only by default? I know I will feel better in the morning, but how will I get through the night? (That is merely a rhetorical question. Unfortunately my nights are not your affair.)

Adieu,

Bess

April 18, 1935
aboard the *North Star* at Helsinki

Andrew darling,

Eleanor was thrilled to learn of your engagement and will be coming home with me for the wedding.

This trip has made both of us realize how little we really know of the world. Eleanor met my ship at Southampton and we spent a week in London before embarking on the North Cape cruise. She was anxious to see Henry Prince again. They had corresponded faithfully all year, each encouraging the other's single-minded pursuit of his chosen art form, but it came as quite a shock to Eleanor, who has studied sculpture with the solitary devotion of a nun, to find that Henry composes his poetry in the company of a young man who shares his flat.

Eleanor felt so betrayed as both an artist and a woman that when she returned to our hotel, she threatened to destroy the terra-cotta madonna she had made for my birthday. Fortunately I got to it in time and it is now packed safely away, out of reach of her anger. I treasure it all the more knowing she will never again work at her art with so pure a motive.

We left London in just the mood to appreciate the stark beauty of the Scandinavian countries and as we approach our final destination —Leningrad—I am intrigued at the thought of penetrating a culture so different from our own. Though I had a hard time convincing Eleanor to come with me on this cruise, she is now very glad that she did. It seems the best way of getting her home to Texas is by way of a place she has never been.

As soon as we return I would like to give a party at the country club in honor of your engagement and Eleanor's homecoming. You choose the date and book the orchestra but do not extend any invitations until I have approved the guest list.

Love,

Mother

JUNE 5 1935

ABOARD QUEEN MARY

MR ALBERT HENDERSON
PRESIDENT
IDLEWILD CLUB
ADOLPHUS HOTEL
DALLAS   TEXAS
ELEANOR JUST GAVE VERBAL CONSENT FOR FALL DEBUT   HOPE
YOU ARE STILL FREE TO ESCORT HER

BESS STEED GARNER

October 5, 1935

Dallas

Dearest Lydia and Manning,

After so many quiet years when the children were away at school, our house has come alive again. Sam complains constantly of the noise but I cherish every sound—even the victrola music coming from the third floor at three o'clock in the morning.

From the beginning that floor has belonged to the children. Now all the furniture has been cleared from the large center area that was once a playroom to make room for dancing. Eleanor has claimed the two rooms to the left for her bedroom and studio and Andrew calls the two adjoining rooms on the other side his suite.

Last Saturday night they brought several members of the band home with them from a party and danced till dawn. When Sam and I awoke Sunday morning, we had twenty unexpected guests for breakfast. Fortunately my housekeeper is as happy as I am to have the children home so she was undaunted by the size of the crowd. She didn't even mind missing church. She said she could praise God just as well making pancakes as she could standing in a pew.

Eleanor has been feted like a returning prodigal ever since we got back from our North Cape cruise. A few weeks ago some of her friends got together and served her with a mock subpoena, charging her with monopolizing the attention of all the eligible young men in town. Her "trial" was held at the Manhole, a house shared by a half dozen promising young lawyers, one of whom undertook her defense. His name is Walter Burton and I gather he comes from a rural family of unknown origin somewhere in Maryland. However, in the year since he arrived here, he has earned the respect of some of the city's most prominent lawyers, and Eleanor was thoroughly delighted with his eloquent defense. After she was "acquitted," everyone at the trial was served dinner. All the men sharing the house contribute to the salary of a cook, and, according to Eleanor, an invitation to dine at the Manhole is one of the most sought-after in town.

I hope the two of you will be able to attend the dance I am giving in Eleanor's honor a month after the Idlewild Ball. Traditionally, her escort for the ball, in this case the president of the club, would escort her on this occasion, but she insists on according the honor to her defender, Walter Burton. This is a complete breach of etiquette and I am unequivocally opposed to it, though I like the young man in question very much. However, she says she would rather cancel the party than spend it in the company of someone who bored her so I suppose I have no choice but to give my consent. I have persuaded her, however, to keep her decision private until after Idlewild. I do not want anything to jeopardize her formal introduction to Dallas society on the arm of the club president.

I am anxious for you to meet Nell Cunningham, the young woman Andrew is going to marry. She is a direct descendant of one of the first families of Virginia, and I cannot help being flattered that she has agreed to marry my son. I just hope he properly appreciates his good fortune.

They have set the date of their wedding for February 21. February is usually a slow month on the social calendar and Andrew felt a big wedding would be a welcome diversion for all his friends. Nell and her family would prefer a small wedding. They have only recently moved here from Virginia and do not know many people. Also, although their background is impeccable, I suspect that like many aristocrats their resources may be somewhat limited. So I have suggested the wedding reception be held at the country club at my expense. After all, the wedding of my only son represents a certain social obligation for a woman in my position, and I feel it is only fair for me to assume the financial responsibility for an event that will be enjoyed primarily by my friends and family.

Nell and her mother and father are the only members of her family living here. Her brother Craig is a costume designer in Hollywood. He is designing his sister's wedding dress, and giving it to her as a wedding present. She showed me the sketch he sent from Hollywood and the dress is simply stunning.

You have not told me very much about Marian's young man beyond the fact that all of you are very fond of him. I hope Marian will bring him to Eleanor's dance and introduce him to us—and to Dallas.

Love,

Bess

November 10, 1935
Dallas

Dear Mr. Cunningham,

Though we have not been formally introduced, I have heard your sister speak of you so often I feel as if you are already part of the family. And your sketch of the wedding dress was all the introduction I could ask to your work.

Actually, it is your work that prompts this letter. My daughter, Eleanor, who is an artist in her own right (having studied painting in Italy, sculpture in Germany, and costume design in New York), is making her debut next week. At the end of the month I will be giving a dinner dance in her honor, and I would be very proud if she wore a Craig Cunningham original on this occasion. It is traditional for a debutante to wear her Idlewild gown again at her own party but my daughter is already flaunting tradition with her choice of escort so she might as well defy it in her dress.

Though I know you make a handsome living designing for films, I should think it would be to your advantage to develop a private trade as well. Surely it is unwise to depend solely on a profession as fickle as filmmaking for one's livelihood. The women who will be attending my daughter's dance are accustomed to paying a great deal of money for their clothes and I would be very happy to see someone so soon to be a member of my family profit from their extravagance.

I have on occasion purchased designer dresses in New York and I assume your prices are in the same range. However, I can afford to pay as much as any movie star, so do your best for my daughter.

Let me know at once if this proposition interests you and I will send measurements.

Sincerely,

Bess Steed Garner

February 2, 1936
Dallas

Mr. Harold D. Perkins
Editor
*The Dallas Morning News*
Dallas, Texas

Dear Hal,

I am distressed that you and your wife will be unable to attend my son's wedding next week, but of course I understand that the newspaper conference comes first.

However, the wedding is the subject of this letter. I do not know how carefully you read *The New York Times* but surely you have noticed that the society section, in cases where both families are equally prominent, often uses a picture of bride and groom leaving the church in place of the usual bridal portrait. Your society editor and my close friend Totsie Fineman informs me this is not the policy of *The Dallas Morning News,* but I am enclosing pictures of my son and his prospective bride on the steps of St. Matthew's Cathedral in the happy event that you decide to revise this policy before departing for the conference.

You might also suggest to your wife that those huge lilac bushes she planted as a border guard between our two houses would benefit from some judicious pruning. I would mention it to her myself but I never seem to see her.

Affectionately—as always,

Bess

July 18, 1936

Dallas

Mr. Walter Burton
The Manhole
4123 Amherst
Dallas, Texas

Dear Walter,

This letter is a formal apology for confronting you with an artichoke at dinner last night. No one should have to encounter his first artichoke in public and I am truly sorry for any embarrassment the experience may have caused you. However, I admired you for admitting so openly that you did not know what to do with it. To me education is a continuing admission of how much we do not know, and the more I see of the world, the more I realize how much I still have to learn.

I am very grateful for the happiness you have given my daughter in the past year, and I hope it will continue. She tells me the two of you have discussed marriage but you do not feel your financial position can support a proposal at this time. Caution is an admirable quality for a man in your position but, based on what I have seen of your character and ability in the past year, I would say your future in this community is assured. I would be very pleased to have you in the family, and my use alone of your legal services will assure you a substantial income. I have never had a lawyer I could consult freely, and I look forward to a professional relationship as well as a personal one.

I hope you and Eleanor will make an official announcement of your engagement soon and set a date for the wedding. Frankly, only a definite date in the immediate future can keep Eleanor at home. She has already written an art school in Vienna to inquire about their fall schedule. I have hidden her passport but she is threatening to apply for a replacement. Though I have twice brought her home from Europe, I might not be so successful the third time.

I would like to give you a corner lot I own on Mockingbird Lane as an engagement present and my wedding present will be the house we decide to build on it.

Devotedly,

Bess

June 20, 1937

Dallas

Mrs. Walter Burton
6824 Mockingbird Lane
Dallas, Texas

My darling,

Welcome home. I wanted a letter from me to be the first one you found in your mailbox when you returned from your honeymoon.

I spent the day after the wedding getting your house in order, putting away all your presents, making up your bed with your new monogrammed sheets, planting flowers around your front door to greet you on your return. I inspected every inch of the house and am well satisfied with it. The architect you chose made imaginative use of a limited space. You were right to insist on him, even though his fee seemed excessive to me at the time. It was wise of Walter to persuade you to delay the wedding until the house was completed. You would never have found an apartment with a double bathroom, and sharing a basin can create more friction in a marriage than sharing a bed.

I am glad now that you refused to go through with the big wedding I had planned and insisted on the small one at home. I will never again walk through my living room without seeing you in the exquisite dress you designed standing in front of the fireplace, with the sculpted angels you gave me for Christmas kneeling on the mantel, holding lilies in their clasped hands. In my mind they are praying for your happiness and each night now before I go upstairs I kneel there and add my prayer to theirs.

As we stood in the station waving until your train disappeared in the direction of New Orleans, Sam suddenly took me in his arms and announced we were leaving on a honeymoon of our own at the end of the week. In our marriage the usual order of things was reversed and Sam was a father first and then a husband. Now, with both my children married, we are husband and wife at last and already seeing each other through different eyes.

Sam has planned a wonderful trip by train through the Pacific Northwest and continuing by boat into Alaska, and to my delight and surprise, he insists on paying all our expenses. On all our previous trips we have shared costs, and of course I have paid for all the trips I have taken alone. I have no idea how much money he has. He always makes me sign our joint income tax return before any of the figures are filled in. However, I have a feeling he is on his way to becoming wealthy, and I look forward to sharing old age with him.

We will be gone all summer, so you and Walter will be able to begin married life without interference from in-laws. I could almost accuse Sam of planning this trip with that in mind, but whatever his motive, I'm glad we are going, and as soon as I seal this letter I will start packing my suitcase. So hello and good-bye.

All my love,

Mother

SEPTEMBER 3 1938
CIUDAD MONTE   MEXICO

MRS WALTER BURTON
FLORENCE NIGHTINGALE HOSPITAL
DALLAS   TEXAS
IF I HAD WINGS I WOULD BE THERE    BUT MY HEART TOOK FLIGHT ON HEARING OF SAFE ARRIVAL OF MY FIRST GRANDCHILD   WE ARE SAFE BUT STRANDED BY FLOODS   I ACHE TO SEE BABY

LOVE

MOTHER

SEPTEMBER 3 1938
CIUDAD MONTE   MEXICO

MR WALTER BURTON
SANDERS AND HARRIS LAW FIRM
210 MAIN STREET
DALLAS   TEXAS
BAD CONNECTION MADE PHONE CONVERSATION IMPOSSIBLE
STILL DO NOT KNOW IF GRANDCHILD IS GIRL OR BOY   WHAT-
EVER IT IS PLEASE AMEND MY WILL SO IT WILL INHERIT EQUALLY
WITH MY CHILDREN   I MAY NOT GET OUT OF MEXICO ALIVE

LOVE

BESS


SEPTEMBER 3 1938
CIUDAD MONTE   MEXICO

BURTON BABY
FLORENCE NIGHTINGALE HOSPITAL
DALLAS   TEXAS
MY DARLING GRANDCHILD
AM DESOLATE THAT I WAS NOT IN DALLAS TO WITNESS YOUR
ARRIVAL BUT TAKE IT AS SIGN OF INDEPENDENT SPIRIT THAT
YOU DO NOT WAIT FOR ANYONE   SAME CAN BE SAID OF ME
WE ARE GOING TO BE GREAT FRIENDS   I LOVE YOU ALREADY

GRANDMOTHER


September 7, 1938
Dallas, Texas

Dear Lydia and Manning,

I have just seen my first grandchild for the first time. At one week she already seems to know everything. She actually glared at me as if demanding to know why it took me so long to get here. I admitted she had the right to ask.

We were on the Pan American Highway headed for home on Monday, August 29, two weeks before the baby was due. Carefree, with no hint of what awaited us, we decided to stop for the night at Ciudad Monte. We drove to the best hotel only to find it surrounded by automobiles and restless, milling crowds. We discovered to our horror that heavy rainfall had flooded the rivers to the north of us. All bridges were down and there was no way to get through to Monterrey.

All the hotels in town were overflowing and we were sent to the dormitory of one of the biggest sugar mills in Mexico, where we were hospitably received by the owners, who happened to be Americans. We felt fortunate to have beds as the tourists who arrived after us had to sleep in their cars. The bridges could not be repaired until the waters receded, so we had no choice but to wait until the rivers that separated us from Monterrey were shallow enough to be forded.

We were stranded without any means of communication for several days. When telephone service was finally restored on Saturday, I learned that I had been a grandmother for three days. I could hear Walter telling me that Eleanor and the baby were both fine, but apparently he could not understand a word I was saying. I have never had a more frustrating conversation.

I was beside myself with anxiety when the governor of the state of Tampico came to my rescue. He appeared unheralded at our hotel, riding, not a white charger, but a huge road-digging machine which he said would get a limited number of us across the first river. I was the first to volunteer. Sam stayed behind with the car, waving dubiously as I climbed onto one of the lateral beams and crouched there. There were twenty of us seated in every conceivable spot on the machine when we left.

We forded the first river, then proceeded on foot over huge stones to the main channel where the current was very strong. There we got into hastily constructed flatboats and crossed to waiting cars in which we forded two more rivers before finally arriving in Victoria for the night. From Victoria we took a bus to the next river, then had to walk a plank, crawl over stones, and finally climb up a ladder to the one section of bridge still standing. We were then crowded into a much smaller bus and after fording another river, reached Monterrey.

In my haste to start for home, I had left my pocketbook containing my tourist card and most of my money in the car with Sam. I was carrying a small change purse in my pocket, which contained just enough for a second-class train ticket to Dallas with nothing left over for food or drink. During the past week while we were stranded in the sugar mill we had subsisted entirely on the crackers and canned goods we had been wise enough to store in the trunk of our car as emergency provisions. I thought I would never be able to look at another can of beans, but by the time I reached Monterrey I was so hungry I would have happily eaten the can itself.

The train was very crowded but I finally found a seat next to a Mexican woman with two crying babies. In halting Spanish I explained that I was on my way to Texas to see my first grandchild and I offered to hold one of her babies. She accepted gratefully and the baby was soon sleeping peacefully on my shoulder. As a means of thanking me, the woman offered me a banana from a large bunch she was carrying. I ate it so hungrily she quickly offered me another. Four bananas later, we were fast friends. I don't believe she had ever seen a starving American tourist before. She talked to me the whole trip, unaware that I could understand only a fraction of what she was saying. My hunger had made me seem like a sister no matter what language I spoke.

When we got to the border and I had no tourist card to show the official, I broke into tears trying to explain what had happened. The official was trying to make me leave the train when my new friend began an eloquent defense. Something about a baby was all I could understand, but it seemed to satisfy him. He gave me a paternal smile, patted the baby asleep in my arms, and let me continue on my way.

When I reached Dallas, Eleanor and the baby were just leaving the hospital. I drove home with them and for the second time in a week held a sleeping baby in my arms but this time it was my own granddaughter.

I am as exhausted as if I had given birth myself—and just as proud.

Love,

Bess

August 1, 1939
Dallas

Dear Mother Steed,

It seems very sad that we have had so little to say to each other in the last two decades. I know you have taken great pride in Lydia's family and we were all thrilled when Marian gave birth to your first great-grandchild two years ago. But let me remind you that you have another great-granddaughter here in Dallas whom you have seen only once since she was born almost a year ago.

She is staying here with us for two weeks while her parents vacation in New Mexico. We would love to have you come for a visit and share in the fun of having her to ourselves without parental interference. She is just on the verge of learning to walk. In fact, she could do it today if she had any confidence in her own ability, but her parents have done nothing to encourage her, insisting that she will take her first step as soon as she is ready and not before. However, today I purchased an ingenious little harness with a long belt attached to the back. I stand behind her holding the belt and, secure in the knowledge that I am providing total support, she literally runs down the front walk into the waiting arms of her grandfather.

Forgive me for conferring the title of grandfather on a man who earned it only through marriage, but, never having had a child to call him father, Sam is doubly grateful for the role of grandfather. And just as my first marriage was cemented by the arrival of children, my second marriage has been surprisingly strengthened by the presence of a grandchild.

When Eleanor got married, Sam and I were left alone as husband and wife for the first time since our own wedding fifteen years ago. Too often in the past I have taken for granted everything that lay within easy reach and sought adventure abroad. But in the last two years, exploring the mysteries contained within the familiar boundaries of our own continent, I have seen evidence of a glacial era in Canada, an ancient civilization in Mexico, and hitherto undetected ardor in the eyes of my husband.

Our newly discovered joy in each other's company has been sealed by the presence of a grandchild in our lives. I see now what a child of his own would have meant to Sam. He has been unstinting in his affection and concern for my two children, always treating them as his own, but this is the first time he has shared in the miracle of a baby.

He took such pride in her progress today. Tomorrow when I put on the harness I will only hold the belt for the first few steps then I will let go, and I am convinced she will walk alone. When she finally discovers that I am far behind, she will be too elated by her own ability to care. By the time her parents return, I am determined to have her walking everywhere. If I have my way, they will never see her crawl again.

The presence of a grandchild has mercifully diverted my attention from the absence of my only son. I know now how you must have felt when your only son married me and moved away. When Andrew told me he was moving to Kansas City to open an advertising agency, I was overcome by a feeling of loss unlike anything I have ever experienced. He is so far from where I want him to be.

The west bedroom is ready and waiting for you. It is still furnished with the organdy and chintz Eleanor chose when she was sixteen. After she left for college, she never occupied the room again, preferring the privacy of the third floor. For a while after her wedding, the house seemed much too big for us and I considered selling it, but now I look forward to filling it with grandchildren—and a visiting great-grandmother. It must be so thrilling to see your life descend into another generation. I am determined to have that experience before I die.

Hope to see you soon.

Much love—as always,<br>Bess

November 9, 1942<br>Dallas

Mrs. Hans Hoffmeyer
240 N. Cheyenne St.
Tulsa, Oklahoma

My dearest Annie,

How deeply I am grieving for you today. Last night I was reading the paper, feeling the war coming ever closer, when the name of Franz Hoffmeyer seized my attention. Above the name was the photograph of a captain in the United States Army, whose smiling countenance gave the lie to the accompanying news item "killed in action."

It does not seem so long ago that I was writing to another grieving mother whose son Franz had been killed in the war. But that was the First World War and your brother was fighting on the other side.

At that time you and Hans were understandably torn between your loyalty to the country that contained your past and your commitment to the country that promised you a future. But this time there can be no doubt about your citizenship; I only hope its privileges can compensate for the heavy price you have just paid.

Until I read your address in the newspaper I did not know you and Hans had moved to Tulsa. I hope that his automotive supply business is prospering and that you are continuing to pursue your chosen profession. I can vouch for your skill as a healer of wounded hearts as well as bodies. Had it not been for your devoted care after Robin died, I am not sure I would have found the courage to continue. I know too well the despair engulfing you at this moment. And the anger at a life denied. Franz was just twenty-five—with marriage and children still ahead of him. But at least he was allowed to reach the threshhold of life—to exult in all the choices that seem open to a person on reaching his majority. After that so much is compromise, with each choice narrowing the range of succeeding choices.

I do not mean to insult the sorrow you are enduring in the death of your son by comparing it to the disappointment I am sensing in my own life, but the subject of loss summons many variations to mind. And perhaps because I was forced to experience the death of a husband and a child so early in life, I am able to see more clearly the death that exists in life and, conversely, the life that survives death. The love I felt for my first husband continues unchanged by the fact that he is no longer at my side—and I must admit that there are moments I still prefer to share with him than with the man who greets me every morning at breakfast.

The power of memory is that it preserves every image intact, safe from the tarnishing effects of time. For me Robin remains forever a happy little boy of eleven even at those moments when I wonder what kind of man he would have become. At his death I still cherished the illusion that a mother could shape the destinies of her children, could will them into attaining their full growth as individuals. But with each passing year you expect less from them until one day you find you are asking for nothing more than their physical appearance at regularly appointed times and places so that you can pretend you are still as close in mind and spirit as you are in the flesh.

Nature as a process provides for no growth past physical maturity. Only the individual, through an effort of will and imagination, can add, enhance, enrich. Life unresisted merely subtracts. I no longer believe an individual can change the fate of other people, no matter how much she loves them, but I will not relinquish the responsibility for my own life until the day I die.

Dearest Annie, circumstances have conspired to keep us at a distance since I moved from the house and the life we shared into one of my own, but I think of you often and my heart aches for you and Hans in this time of loss. Please know a devoted friend shares your pain—and that as long as I am alive, you are not alone.

Bess

July 8, 1943<br>Dallas

Dearest Eleanor,

This is the most difficult letter I have ever attempted to write for it has to span the greatest distance—that ever-widening gulf that separates a mother from her married daughter. When you decided to make your home in the same city with me, I never dreamed I would one day feel further from you than I did when you were living abroad with only an ocean between us. But here we are almost within shouting distance and I am not even sure I can reach you by letter.

I had a lovely time at your luncheon today—despite having to ask to be included on the guest list. Until you are my age I fear you will not be able to understand what it means to be treated like a contemporary by members of the next generation. I have such fun with your friends I forget I am not as young as they are—until I am once again alone with you. Why do you insist on relegating me to the company of people my own age? I shared my friends with you when you were a child and delighted in seeing them treat you as an equal. Why are you so disinclined to return the favor now?

In the world of the arts people of all ages attend the same parties. Old playwrights advise young actors, promising artists question acknowledged geniuses, would-be poets fawn over literary lions. The only criterion for admission is talent.

How dare polite society segregate people on the basis of age? This injustice makes me angrier than discrimination on the basis of race or sex. The company of the young (or the younger) is our only defense against that cruel oppressor—age. How painful to see my own daughter aiding and abetting the enemy by denying me access to the next generation.

Has the fact that we are mother and daughter kept us from also being friends? Just because my company was imposed on you by birth should not prevent you from enjoying it as though you had chosen it deliberately. I must confess that I feel like a lively, witty conversationalist around everyone but you. However, in your presence I feel I am continually auditioning for the pleasure of your company, and I find myself apologizing for boring you with answers to questions you never asked.

I know children are supposed to be beyond the reach of their parents' rod once they are grown, but I cannot stand by silently while a child of mine deliberately inflicts hurt on someone who did nothing to deserve it—even when that someone happens to be me. When I am with you, I am too afraid of losing the small part of you I still possess to express to your face the disappointment I feel on being excluded so callously from so much of your life. Even this tirade began as a thank-you note for reluctantly permitting me to intrude into your life one more time. But my pen will not continue the charade we act out in person, and I realize now I have risked your contempt by accepting so gratefully the few half-hearted invitations I have forced you to extend. It is an illusion to pretend I am part of your life just because we occasionally occupy the same room. You have my word I have indulged in it for the last time. Be assured that I will not inflict my unwanted presence on you again.

I wish I had the courage to say all this aloud, but only in a letter do I dare express my feelings openly. At least when I am writing, I can pretend you are listening. When I am with you, I know better.

I love you desperately,

Mother

Totsie Fineman
10011 N. Torrey Pines Road
La Jolla, California

Dearest Totsie,

How dare you move to California when I need to talk to you so desperately tonight! Yesterday I wrote a letter to my daughter that may have lost me her love forever, and I have forsworn the written word—as soon as I post this mea culpa to you.

Until now the act of letter-writing has kept me sane and calm, allowing civilized expression of all the emotions that trouble my sleep. However, today, for the first time in my life, the written word has betrayed me.

I have never before lost my temper on paper and said things I would give my life to take back. I even went to the post office this morning and pleaded with them to return the letter before it was delivered, but neither rain nor sleet nor a mother's tears can stop the U.S. mail from reaching its appointed destination.

My only hope was to station myself on the receiving end and intercept the letter as it was delivered. But I was too late. Eleanor was holding the open envelope when I arrived. She stared at me without a word, then abruptly left the room. I followed her up the stairs, begging her to surrender the letter. But she informed me coldly that under law a letter once mailed becomes the property of the recipient, and she entered her bedroom with the incriminating evidence, closing the door behind her.

I know you moved to California to be near your son, but please do not make the mistake I did of expecting physical proximity to result in intimacy of mind and spirit. I have yet to experience from my family the welcome you receive each time you arrive for a visit. How I wish that once in my life my children would greet me as eagerly as if I had traveled a great distance to be with them. I must face the fact that I have stayed too close to them for too long, but where am I to go? If only this wretched war would end and allow me to escape outside my own life! When my son was drafted and taken from me, I turned all my devotion on the only child who remained within my reach, and I fear that when peace is declared for my son, I will still be at war with my daughter.

How can I make her forget—or at least forgive—all the harsh words I wrote in anger? Accusations hurled aloud are blurred by time and memory, but angry words on paper never lose their power to hurt. After tonight I will never dare put pen to paper again. A blank page to me is like a drink to an alcoholic. I do not know when to stop, and the next day I am overwhelmed with regret at all the things I said.

How I long to see you! Though we were born of different parents, we are connected at the heart like Siamese twins. My daughter may have turned her back on me, but you are the mainstay of my larger family. I will love you all my life.

Good night, sweet sister.

Bess


September 1, 1945
Dallas

Lt. Andrew Steed
Barracks C
Fort Sill
Lawton, Oklahoma

Dearest Andrew,

We are waiting anxiously to welcome you home. But once you have been properly welcomed, I plan to start traveling. In your absence I have faced the fact that my children no longer need or want my constant presence on the perimeter of their daily lives. So I plan to see as much of the world as I can in the years left to me. I am counting on at least another twenty on my feet and hopefully another decade after that in a reclining position to look back on my life and try to make some sense out of it.

How thankful I am that you will stay safely in Oklahoma until you are allowed to come home to Texas. I know you are frustrated not to have seen action on other fronts, but there are enough battles to be faced on the home front when you return.

I do not know whether her letters have prepared you or not, but the wife who awaits your homecoming is not the shy, submissive mate you left behind. I have had ample occasion to observe her during the course of our volunteer duty with the Red Cross, and I have been surprised and delighted with her growing independence.

She volunteered immediately for driving duty and has learned to handle huge trucks and buses with surprising ease for someone who appears so fragile. I would advise you to rethink the restrictions you applied so arbitrarily to her use of the car during the first years of your marriage—as well as any other nonreciprocal rules, spoken or unspoken, by which you attempted to govern her conduct—if you have any hope of celebrating a silver wedding anniversary.

I am very happy that you decided to move back to Dallas before entering the service. Though the reasons for your return were financially regrettable, I can assure you that you will profit from our proximity in the future.

I have just been by to see Eleanor and the new baby. They are doing fine and Walter does not seem the least bit disappointed to have a third daughter. I trust their family is complete now. Three children are enough for any couple, especially now with domestic help so difficult to arrange. I do not see how Eleanor survives with only a single servant, but she turns down all my offers of assistance, so I assume she has learned how to manage. In my day one would not dare ask the housekeeper to help with the children, but modern women, whether wives or servants, have to be prepared to do everything. I am not sure that can be called progress.

I am sorry Mother Steed did not live to see her fourth great-grandchild, but at least she derived much pleasure from the first three. Babies brought us together in the last years of her life just as they did in the early years of my marriage. We shared many happy visits at my house until a few months ago when she became too ill to travel.

I know you have been disappointed by the failure of your marriage to produce children, but there is nothing to keep you from adopting a child. Over the past few years I have made substantial contributions to a shelter for homeless children in Fort Worth, which would insure that your application received immediate attention should you decide to adopt. I trust you will give careful consideration to this alternative and not subject your marriage to the severe strains so often caused by the prolonged absence of children.

All my love,

Mother

July 21, 1947
Galveston, Texas

Dear Mavis,

Is there anything more exasperating than a rainy day at the seashore, especially when one has traveled a great distance to get there?

I finally persuaded my children that it was time for their children to see an ocean, and so a week ago Nell with her little boy and Eleanor with her three girls accompanied me on the overnight train to Galveston. None of the children had ever traveled by train or seen a Pullman compartment, and they were thrilled with the magic of a disappearing bed and washbasin. I wish our husbands could have made the train trip with us, but they are driving down later.

The weather was beautiful the day we arrived and we spent all afternoon on the beach. The children were fascinated by the never-ending movement of the ocean and crushed yesterday when we were confined to our rooms by heavy rain.

I volunteered to keep all four children while their mothers took refuge in a movie and decided to employ the time in an educational manner. I endeavored to explain the movement of the planets to them and climbed up on a chair so I could circle the ceiling lamp with an orange to illustrate the path of the earth around the sun. I became so enraptured with my own explanation, I forgot I was standing on a chair and suddenly stepped into space and fell to the floor.

I am afraid I did further injury to vertebrae already damaged by my leap to safety when our house caught fire so long ago. I have stayed in bed today while the rain continued and confined my instruction to French vocabulary, paying each child a penny for every word committed to memory.

Our husbands arrive tomorrow and sunshine is predicted. To celebrate their arrival, I have made dinner reservations for all of us, including children, at the Balinese Room on the pier. Eleanor and Nell were in favor of hiring babysitters and leaving the children behind but I find children behave as they are treated. If they are accorded the same respect as adults, they can be counted on to display comparable manners. Besides, none of them has ever seen food served on flaming swords, and it is time they got a glimpse of some of the wonders the world contains. Why is it I feel so much closer to my grandchildren than to my children? Perhaps because they are still young enough to consider me a peer—something their parents ceased doing years ago.

The children speak often of the week we spent with you in Honey Grove. They prefer traveling without their parents because I allow them to stay up as late as they like. Remember the night you and I talked until dawn with Betsy trying her eight-year-old best to stay awake with us? The others had long since fallen asleep when she suddenly saw the sun rising and burst into tears, terrified to realize morning would come whether she had slept that night or not. But better for her to learn early that nature does not ask our consent to continue its inexorable circuit.

Love,<br>Bess

June 10, 1948<br>Quebec, Canada

Dear Eleanor and Walter,

It is a joy to hear French spoken without having to cross the Atlantic. I wonder how many other cities as fascinating as Quebec await my discovery—and how many more I will never see. You must not spend too many more summers at home. Even though you are saving money, you are spending time, and what a waste to let a summer go by without a new experience to show for it.

I hope you are making use of my television set in my absence, even though you were opposed to its purchase. I cannot argue with your reasoning that television equipment is still in an early stage of development, but at my age I cannot afford to wait for technical refinements. You are undoubtedly right in your belief that the price of a set will be reduced considerably as production increases, but I will not deny my grandchildren the miracle of visual transmission for the sake of economy. Besides, I consider the privilege of owning one of the first sets in the city to have a value commensurate with the price I paid. The television set is only one of many occasions in my life when I have paid more than other people thought I should for something I wanted, but it is my considered opinion that I have never been cheated.

When you bring the children over in the afternoon to watch television, do not hesitate to use the window air conditioner I had installed this spring. I know you consider this another of my extravagances, but once you have enjoyed the oasis of a cool room on a hot Texas afternoon, I am sure you will deem the money well spent. And if you insist on staying in Texas all summer, the least you can do is take occasional refuge in a cool room that offers a window on the world.

From here we travel to Tanglewood and then on to Chautauqua.

Love,

Bess


August 29, 1949
La Jolla, California

Dear Eleanor and Walter,

California is indeed the Promised Land. In climate and scenery it surpasses anywhere I have ever been. If it were not for my grandchildren in Texas, I would be tempted to spend the rest of my life here.

We felt like pioneers, driving across the desert from Texas, traveling by night to escape the sun, sleeping fitfully by day. An automobile is a decided improvement over a covered wagon but the trip was not without hardship all the same. However, Grace and Frank Townsend proved to be gallant traveling companions and their good cheer got us through one long night when our engine locked and we were stranded for several hours with only coyotes and cactus for company.

Totsie Fineman has a charming house here and she is happier than I have seen her since Arthur died. Her son and his wife and two children moved to Los Angeles last year. They drive down several times a year to see her, but she is surprisingly content living alone.

Dwight opened a branch of his interior decorating business in San Francisco some years ago and it is so successful he now spends half his time there. Totsie met him quite by accident when she was in San Francisco last winter. It was the first time she had seen him since their son's wedding eight years ago, and what happened between them apparently took them both by surprise. Totsie said it was like meeting a stranger and suddenly discovering how much you have in common.

Their son has no idea they are seeing each other and they have decided not to tell him—at least for now. They seem to enjoy the clandestine aspect of their relationship and prefer to visit their son and his family separately rather than appear together in the conventional role of grandparents.

We are driving to Los Angeles tomorrow. Craig has graciously invited all of us to lunch at the studio and promised to introduce us to at least one movie star before we leave. I am sorry we will not be in Dallas to celebrate Betsy's birthday but we will drink a toast to her that night at the Cocoanut Grove.

I wish you were here with us. Next year we must all travel together. It is time for the children to realize Texas is not the only state in the union.

Love,<br>Bess

July 10, 1950<br>Ocean City, New Jersey

Dear Lydia and Manning,

The whole family has gathered here for two weeks at my expense and I am relishing the role of matriarch. All three families traveled by different routes from Texas, reliving moments from the past and finally arriving at a place new to all of us.

Eleanor and Walter drove by way of Maryland where his sister and her husband were waiting to meet the wife and children they had never seen. Andrew and Nell flew with their two children to Virginia and visited relatives still living in the county named after her maternal ancestors. They saw the college so dear to Nell in the Blue Ridge Mountains, then flew to Boston to visit Andrew's prep school roommate. Sam and I stopped first in Philadelphia where we were shocked to learn that Sam's first wife had died of a heart attack five years ago. It is so strange to have a large part of one's past obliterated without a trace.

I planned this summer in the hope that my grandchildren would begin to see how deeply their lives are rooted in people and places unknown to them until now. I am convinced that the more they know of the past, the more they will derive from the present.

Eleanor and Andrew were at first opposed to this trip on the grounds that it would be too expensive but I would rather have my grandchildren remember me for the experiences we shared than for the money I leave them to spend alone. I hope they will one day look back on this summer with the happiness I feel at this moment.

Children squander the present because they think it will never end. It is up to the adults who love them to impose the form and meaning that will make each day worth reliving in memory. But parents are faced with so many daily responsibilities for the care of their children, they have little time to consider their future and even less time to remind them of their past. It falls to us grandparents to enrich their present experience with stories from the past and dreams for the future.

The children are calling me to come play in the ocean. Their parents have gone back to their rooms and Sam is taking a nap, but I promised to stay out with them until the sun sets.

Love,

Bess

July 9, 1952

aboard the S. S. Caronia

at the Arctic Circle

Dear Totsie,

I do not know exactly when I began to plan this trip. I think it was soon after my sixtieth birthday that I was seized with a longing to see the land of the midnight sun.

It is now 11:55 P.M. and the sun is still several feet above the horizon. This is the lowest point it will reach in the sky and soon it will start its upward climb toward noon. Everyone around me is taking pictures by the light of the midnight sun but there is no way for a camera to capture the sensation of a day that never ends. The memory will illuminate all the nights left to me.

It is just as well Sam did not come with me. He would go mad to see the universe mock the pattern of day and night by which he has ordered his life.

I suppose I should go below now and try to sleep, but I have never been one to close my eyes while the sun is shining.

Give my love to Dwight the next time you see him.

Je t'embrasse,

Bess

March 24, 1953
aboard the S.S. *Lurline*
en route to Hawaii

Dear Mavis,

I felt like Magellan when we left Los Angeles harbor, sailing west to a whole new world. My only regret is that our final destination is Hawaii and not the Orient, but Sam would simply not hear of extending our itinerary beyond the authority of the United States.

The night before we left Dallas, Eleanor and Walter gave a gala bon voyage party for us, complete with leis and ukelele music. Then after all the guests had gone, my daughter surprised me with the announcement that I was going to have another grandchild. I am still in a state of shock.

Eleanor will be forty years old when the baby is born. How can she take such a risk—not to mention what she is doing to me? I have not had her complete attention since 1936, and I feel I am entitled to it in my old age. Of course her answer is that my old age is nowhere in sight, and I do have to agree. But another baby in the family may well bring it on at any moment.

I thought Walter was content with three daughters, but there must be some primitive part of his psyche that still yearns for a child formed in his own image. That is the only explanation I can find for an act so rash and irresponsible. No matter how civilized their fa-çade, men are savages at heart. Looking back, I marvel that I escaped the manacles of motherhood when I remarried. I sometimes forget how good Sam has been to me.

We are enjoying each other's company on this cruise, and yet not limited to it as we would be on a conventional trip. Among the many advantages a cruise offers to long-married couples is the constant presence of other people. You would be quite at home here with us. In many ways a ship is a little town that floats. There is only one movie but many card games. The only real difference between the

lives you and I are leading at this moment is that I have a destination
and it is different from anywhere I have ever been.

Much love,

Bess

June 10, 1954
aboard Pan Am Flight 81
New York to Lisbon

Mr. and Mrs. Dwight Davis
Monte Verde at 6th
Carmel-by-the-Sea
California

Dearest Dwight and Totsie,

Welcome home from the Orient. How wonderful it feels to be
writing one letter to the two of you. Just addressing the envelope,
I relive your wedding last fall. I was very proud to be witness at a
ceremony reconfirming a union as inevitable as it is unique.

Sam and I spent a week in New York before leaving for Europe.
We thought of you and your adventures in the Orient as we watched
*Teahouse of the August Moon.* I long to hear more about your nine-
month honeymoon. I am wild with envy to think of all the places you
have been that I will never see: Hong Kong, Singapore, Bangkok,
Tokyo, Pago Pago. Three score and ten years is barely time to scan
the table of contents of this world. I have not even begun to read
the book.

Our departure from Dallas was saddened by the sudden death of
Lydia's husband, Manning, the week before. She is being very brave
and insists on remaining alone in Denton in the house they shared
for so long.

It is thrilling to travel to Europe by air after so many trips by sea.
I trust the increased ease of travel will encourage people to move
about more freely. Sometimes I think the primary division in the
world is not between male and female but between people who
travel and people who stay home.

It is my great regret that I have shared so little of what I have seen
with either of my husbands. Sam and I have been married almost
thirty-two years and this is the first time he has consented to accom-

pany me abroad. And only on the condition that we confine our travels to Switzerland—the only country in the world outside our own that seems safe to him.

He has given his reluctant consent to spend a few days in Lisbon since we have to land there, but then we fly directly to Geneva. I tried to interest him in a quick tour of North Africa, but he would not hear of it so I fear that for me it will forever remain the dark continent.

However, I am content just to be in motion again, traversing the night with morning waiting to meet us and below us an ocean whose size seems suddenly comprehensible now that it can be crossed in a day. I must climb into my berth now so I will be rested for my first look at Lisbon.

Je vous embrasse,<br>Bess

August 5, 1954<br>Montreux Pálace Hotel<br>Montreux, Switzerland

Dear Grace and Frank,

Sam and I speak often of the pleasant trip we shared to California and wish each night we would find you waiting in the dining room here to join us for dinner.

I am seated on the balcony outside our hotel room, looking down at the lake and at the geranium-framed tennis courts where Sam is already engaged in a game. We have both gotten in the habit of sleeping late, then having our "petit déjeuner" brought to us on the balcony. I cannot tell you how much better a croissant tastes in Switzerland, served with fresh butter and jams made from mountain-grown berries.

I usually remain in my robe all morning, reading and writing letters on the balcony and watching Sam defeat a series of younger opponents at tennis. No one would believe he celebrated his seventieth birthday this summer. He is the picture of robust health and quite the most handsome tourist staying at this hotel. His only complaint is his eyesight. Occasional attacks of double vision cause him to lose a game to an unworthy opponent and when that happens he is not fit company for the rest of the day. His mind is as unaccepting of old age as his body and sometimes I am frightened of the years ahead.

I admire the two of you so much for voluntarily retiring from the active pursuit of your chosen professions and devoting yourself to interests too-long neglected and to each other. Old age should be regarded as a reward for a lifetime of hard work, but it can only be a punishment if one insists on doing the same things one has always done, measuring present achievements by past ones and inevitably falling short. If only Sam would retire now and devote himself to the music that has always been a Sunday pastime. He could play the flute with his eyes closed and never think about growing old.

I see that he has just defeated the young Englishman who has been his nemesis on the courts ever since we arrived, so we shall have a pleasant afternoon. When he is in a good mood, I suggest a picnic. The hotel provides us with an ample basket and we set out on our rented bicycles around the lake and into the woods.

After lunch I read aloud from a book of poems. (I prefer Byron but always bring along Walt Whitman for Sam.) The poetry usually puts us both to sleep and after a pleasant nap "al fresco" we awaken greatly refreshed and bicycle back to the hotel, where we bathe and dress for dinner downstairs. Coffee and liqueurs are served after dinner in the lounge to the accompaniment of chamber music. This is the most restful trip I have ever taken and sometimes I forget I am in Europe. Where I think I am I do not know, but at least I am not in Dallas.

Sam just came in from the courts and asks to be remembered.

Love from us both,

Bess

August 31, 1954
Villa d'Este
Cernobbio, Italy

Dear Eleanor and Walter,

After three weeks of tennis and chamber music at the Montreux Palace, I thought I would lose my mind if I had to remain there one more day. I finally convinced Sam to hire a chauffeur and car for our last week in Europe and see at least a little of the surrounding countryside.

Though he was extremely dubious about crossing the border into Italy, I could not leave Europe without one last look at the place which holds more happy memories for me than any other in the world. I have a strong premonition that this is my last trip abroad and it seemed appropriate to spend the last night of it here.

It was naive of me to expect nothing to have changed in the quarter century since my last visit and yet I could not help hoping I would find some physical connection with the past. The concierge was too young to have been more than a child on my last visit, but his face looked decidedly familiar. We began to talk and I learned that he inherited the position from his father.

I inquired if Signor Prince still stayed here regularly and the concierge said sadly he had not been back since the tragic occasion ten years ago when he came from America to claim his son's body. I know you will be as shocked as I was to learn that Henry Prince drowned in Lake Como. Suicide was suspected but nothing ever proved. The concierge says that as far as he knows, Richard Prince has not left Georgia since.

I miss all of my family very much. Sam and I have bought excellent watches for everyone, even the baby. Time has become very important to me and I cannot bear to lose track of a single second. We will be arriving at Love Field at five in the afternoon on Sunday, September 2. I will expect all of you there to meet us and then to be my guests for dinner at the airport restaurant. The food is always excellent and I have so much to tell you. I cannot bear to be met and then abandoned. After dinner we will reassemble at my house for the distribution of souvenirs, so please make no plans for Sunday evening.

Tell Betsy we will be drinking a toast to her tonight on her sixteenth birthday. The present would be unendurable if I did not have a family to keep my vision firmly fixed on the future. I cannot wait to hug each of you.

All my love,<br>Bess

Dear Sam,

Your letter was waiting on arrival here last week, but this is the first chance I have had to answer it.

I was shocked to learn of Hal Perkins's death. I suppose the word "shocked" seems strange to describe the death of a man eighty years old, but he seemed so vigorous the last time I saw him.

It was one morning this past March—very early, before even you were awake. I had had a restless night, and, too proud and stubborn to court sleep when it clearly had no intention of coming near me, I got dressed and went down to weed the rose garden. To my surprise our neighbor, fully dressed, was returning home from his morning constitutional. To my even greater surprise he stopped and talked to me, displaying a demeanor more open and expansive than I had ever encountered from him at a later hour.

His manner toward me was always completely correct, of course, yet extremely reserved, as if he wanted to make clear that the proximity of our two houses in no way implied a desire for intimacy between our two persons. I always had the utmost respect for him in his professional role of newspaper editor, underscored by a feeling of regret for the personal relationship that continued to elude me.

But on this particular morning he questioned me extensively about the Caribbean cruise from which I had just returned. I was quite flattered by his interest and we talked at great length about that troubled part of the world. He confided to me his regret that he had done so little traveling in his life. He did not blame his wife but did admit she was never comfortable away from home. I was always aware of her disapproval when I took a trip without you, and I am sure she would have been astonished to hear her husband say he wished she could share some of my enthusiasm for other ways of life. Perhaps he was already worried about what her life would be like without him. What a burden for a man to fear that his death will deprive his wife of her life as well.

We are back in Lima after a thrilling but very taxing excursion by air to Cuzco, the ancient capital of the Incas. Our DC-4 was not pressurized, so we had to suck oxygen from a tube during the two-hour flight over the Andes and sit quietly to avoid "seroche" (mountain sickness). In spite of these precautions, several of the younger members of our group became very ill during the flight and had to spend the rest of the trip in their hotel rooms.

The next morning we survivors, undaunted by the altitude (Cuzco is 11, 440 feet above sea level), boarded a funny little train which took us through a jungle where orchids grew wild on the trees to a station where Indians in native dress had gathered to stare. Guides were waiting to lead us on foot high into the mountains to the "lost city of the Incas," discovered in 1911 by a Yale professor (see *National Geographic* I left open on your bedside table).

I planned to stay behind at this point and watch the tour from a distance, not daring to subject my already aching vertebrae to the rigors of a mountain climb, but when the guide began to talk, I could not bear to let the tour leave without me. The excursion began with a steep ascent up the sides of a 200-foot canyon and the guides virtually had to lift me from ledge to ledge. They could not believe it when they realized my torso was encased in a steel corset. I am sure they thought I was insane to attempt the climb and until we reached our destination I agreed with them. However my physical agony was obliterated by the thrill of seeing the ruins of that ancient city, unknown to the modern world until this century. How many other ancient wonders are still lost to us?

Tomorrow we leave for Buenos Aires; then on to Montevideo and Rio de Janeiro.

Please express my condolences to Mrs. Perkins, and, when you call on her again, take some of the roses from the garden. I have never known them to bloom in such profusion.

Much love,<br>Bess

JUNE 28 1955<br>RIO DE JANEIRO

MR SAM GARNER
2364 DREXEL DRIVE
DALLAS   TEXAS
PLEASE ARRANGE TO HAVE WHEELCHAIR WAITING AT AIRPORT
FOR MY ARRIVAL MONDAY AND BOOK HOSPITAL ROOM   AM SUF-

FERING FROM SEVERE CASE OF DYSENTERY BUT FORTUNATELY
MISSED ONLY ONE DAY OF SIGHTSEEING

HASTA LA VISTA

BESS

July 4, 1956
Dallas

Dear Mavis,

I am celebrating Independence Day with added fervor after a year of seeing so many women my age declare their dependence upon society.

At her daughter's insistence Lydia sold the spacious home in Denton where she and Manning lived so happily and moved to San Antonio. She hopes to find an apartment of her own but for the moment she is staying with Marian and her family and I for one doubt that she will ever leave. Unfortunately her small pension from the university can hardly support an independent life style and her family advised her to invest the money she made from the sale of her house in something with a potential for long-range profit.

My neighbor, Mrs. Perkins, has also sold her home, and, rather than burden her children with the problems a place of her own would involve, has elected to move into a retirement hotel where all her decisions will be made for her.

I find both alternatives equally abhorrent and am determined to live out my days under my own roof. Not necessarily this roof, however. With the grandchildren going off in different directions and family gatherings turning into an ordeal for everyone but me, there is no longer any need for a house this large.

However, Sam becomes like a man possessed at the slightest mention of selling it and swears he will never set foot in an apartment no matter how comfortable or convenient it would be for me. You would think he owned this house instead of just paying board all these years. Unfortunately under Texas law, I cannot sell it without his signature, so for now we will continue as we are.

It seems strange to be spending the summer in Texas. Usually by now I am far away. However, I have had so much trouble with my back since my return from South America, I am afraid my traveling days are over.

Betsy leaves for college in September, and knowing my namesake is abroad in the land will perhaps keep me content at home. She has chosen Hollins College in Virginia, primarily because of the year-abroad program offered there, beginning in the second term of the sophomore year. It is the only program of its kind open to someone who has never studied French, and I am embarrassed to admit my first grandchild falls into this category. Against my advice her parents urged her to study Spanish in high school, thinking the proximity of Mexico made this a more practical choice. Happily she has finally realized that in spirit we are closer to France than to any country in the world—and she can hardly restrain her impatience to get to Paris.

I spend most of my time now comfortably enthroned in the hospital bed I bought last summer. The telephone is on one side of my bed and my new television set with remote controls on the other. I find that television seldom engages the mind as fully as it does the eye so I keep my radio and record player within easy reach.

I spend every Saturday afternoon doubly entertained, watching a sports event on television and listening to the opera on the radio. If the opera is not being broadcast, I stack my record player with symphonies. It occurred to me recently that by buying two copies of each album I could have the complete experience of a piece of music without interruption to reverse the record. The salesman had difficulty understanding my order at first, but when I finally succeeded in explaining it to him, he said he was going to suggest it to all his customers.

I grow increasingly impatient with my friends who mourn the past and decry the present. I am thrilled with every technological advance I have lived to enjoy.

I only wish Sam could enjoy the life and health he still has, instead of lamenting what he has lost. His eyesight is very bad now but he would still be trying to drive if the children had not sold his car. He threatened suicide that day but I said anyone who allowed him to drive would be an accomplice to murder—at least if he committed suicide, he would only be taking one life.

To try to lift his spirits, I called the Lighthouse for the Blind and requested a volunteer to come to the house two days a week and read to him. I pointed out to them that I had made substantial contributions to their cause over the years and now felt entitled to derive some personal benefit from my philanthropy.

They sent a very personable young man who listened sympathetically while Sam poured out his tale of woe. I had gathered a stack of reading material for him, but at the end of the afternoon it was still untouched. However I suppose Sam needs a listener more than a reader. The next time he came Sam made a separate financial arrangement with him to cover the use of his car and they now spend their afternoons together driving around town.

The first stop on their route is usually the steel company, but yesterday I had a call from the president, asking me as politely as possible to try to keep Sam away from the office. Of course as chairman of the board he is entitled to see any of the company records on demand, but it is naturally very disrupting when he appears without warning and demands an accounting of all recent expenditures.

The company has prospered since his retirement but he insists that appearances are deceiving and that in fact the company is going down the drain without him. Despite the sizable salary he still receives, he laments to anyone who will listen that he is going to die in the poorhouse. His Christmas checks to the children last year were accompanied by such a list of financial grievances that Eleanor threatened to return hers to him uncashed. Fortunately the rest of us prevailed upon her to accept the check with all the grace he lacked in giving it.

It is very sad to see how little is left for a man who has devoted his life to making money when that motive is removed. He still sets his alarm for seven every morning, showers and shaves, then reads the morning newspaper while devouring a hearty breakfast. During that hour he is a happy man, but at 8 A.M. his day is over, and he has no appetite at all by dinner. No wonder women outlive men. We have had to be responsible for the shape of our lives from the beginning. Even women with jobs face a full work load every day at home. Every woman knows that making a living is just the first step. But for too many men it is the entire trip.

I must close now and get dressed for the party the children are giving for Sam and me. Today is our thirty-fourth wedding anniversary. However, frankly, I have never considered longevity alone a cause for celebration.

I think of you so often in your home in Honey Grove, living just as you have always lived. Even though you were married to my father, more and more I think of you as a sister—and often feel closer to you living at a distance than to the friends and family I see every day.

My love,

Bess

le 10 mai 1958
Dallas

Mlle. Betsy Burton
aux bons soins de Madame la Comtesse d'Orville
25 rue Coquillière
Paris 1er, France

Ma chère petite fille,

J'étais vraiment éblouie par ta lettre du 7 avril. Quand je pense que tu es arrivée en France avec le vocabulaire d'un enfant naissant —c'est-à-dire pas un seul mot—alors, je sais comment tu as étudié pendant les mois passés.

C'est bon de lire *Le Monde* tous les jours (je ne connais pas *Le Canard Enchaîné*—peut-être tu m'enverras une copie) mais n'oublie pas de jeter un coup d'oeuil de temps en temps au Paris édition du *New York Herald Tribune* que j'ai commandé pour toi. Malgré ta nouvelle affection pour la France, tu es après tout Américaine et tu y resteras toute ta vie. Il ne faut pas perdre de vue ton propre pays cette année.

La situation politique en France à ce moment me paraît assez grave, mais, si j'ai permis à ma fille de voyager dans l'Allemagne d'Hitler, je n'ai aucun lieu de me tourmenter pour toi dans la France du Général de Gaulle. Nous avons eu des années bien agréables sous nôtre propre général. Je souhaite le même pour nôtre voisin à l'autre côté de l'Atlantique.

Amuse-toi bien—et surtout fais attention à tout ce qui se passe. Tu as de la chance d'être témoin à une page très intéressante dans la longue histoire de France.

Je t'embrasse de tout mon coeur,

Nana

Ma petite Betsy,

Though you went back to college last week, I look at your picture smiling at me from the Sunday paper and imagine you are still sitting across from me, planning your future.

I have been accepting congratulations all morning from friends who just read your engagement announcement. I have been in constant communication with your father ever since you announced your intentions to the family, planning an appropriate wedding present—and have decided on a sizable cash settlement which I am trying to persuade your grandfather to match.

To my dismay he grows more reluctant every year to acknowledge his responsibility to the only children and grandchildren he will ever have, and getting him to part with anything in cash requires unrelenting argument. However he has tentatively agreed to turn over to you one hundred shares of stock in an Australian oil company which he assures me will be worth at least twice as much as my wedding present within a decade. I certainly hope so, but since in the meantime it is worth quite a bit less, I am trying to convince him to give you a check for the balance so that, in the beginning at least, our gifts will be equal.

Now that I am approaching my seventieth birthday, your father has advised me to begin dividing my estate to avoid inheritance taxes. I am meeting him at his office tomorrow to sign the papers necessary to convert my estate into a "living trust."

He gave the same advice to Sam but needless to say it has gone unheeded. Sam is determined to remain financially independent to the end of his days—a worthy goal and one I share completely—but unfortunately he has a very distorted idea of how much he will need in relation to how much I am convinced he has. For the next few years I will be giving away as much as the law allows in advance of death, and I am certain Sam could afford to do likewise. However no amount of argument can convince him he is not going to die a pauper.

I trust my heirs will continue to abide by the unwritten law that has always guided financial activity in our family: capital is to be invested, only income should be spent. Of course my first investment on receiving a substantial inheritance from my mother was in my husband's future and the returns from that investment provided the basis for the financial security I still enjoy.

Your future husband has chosen a field of endeavor where the risks are as high as the potential rewards. Be prepared to offer him any support necessary to achieve his goals; only then will you have earned the right to share in his success.

I appreciate your desire for a quiet wedding, but I trust you will allow me to have a rehearsal dinner for you here at home. Though in recent years I have longed to be rid of all these rooms, I am glad now that I am still here. Your wedding will provide an excuse for one more party. I expect it will be the last one I will ever give.

Please let me know the kind of food your young man prefers so that I may plan a menu to his liking. I noticed when I took the two of you to dinner at L'Auberge last week, he left several things on his plate untouched. I trust he did not feel excluded by the lively conversation you and I shared in French with the waiter. I have not seen a man look so helpless since your father encountered his first artichoke at my dinner table. However, your father now eats artichokes regularly, and I trust in time your husband will come to appreciate and hopefully to share your love of all things French— food as well as language.

For a marriage to succeed, each partner should be excited by the abilities of the other and not feel threatened by an interest that is not shared. You must not begin your marriage by denying all that you are or you will never develop into all that you can be. There is no challenge in the world like the loving presence of someone who believes the best of you, and I trust your marriage will lead to great accomplishments for you both. I am happy to say I met my match —once—and I hope you have met yours.

My love,

Nana

June 26, 1960

Dallas

Dearest Totsie and Dwight,

How gala to celebrate a golden wedding anniversary when the two of you have spent less than half of the past fifty years legally joined in wedlock—but that may be the secret of marital longevity. I wish I could have been there to share in the festivities with you, but I was busy with a wedding here. Betsy was married in Dallas and will be moving to New Haven in the fall where her new husband will continue his graduate studies at Yale. I will be sad to see them go, but true intimacy often thrives on separation—as our friendship and indeed your own marriage have proved.

I am determined not to repeat with my grandchildren the mistake I made with my children—using every means of coercion at my command, emotional as well as financial, to keep them close to me. Ever since Andrew came home from the war, I have had both children at my beck and call. I try to take comfort in the duty visits they pay once a week, but in my heart I am bereft. Polite strangers have taken the place of the two precious allies I sought to keep at my side forever. No mother was ever more terrified of being abandoned in her old age than I—and no mother ever did more to make it happen by doing so much to prevent it.

But at least as consolation for the loss of my children, I have had the good fortune to become my grandchildren's best friend. When September comes, I am determined to bid my namesake bon voyage without a tear as she sets out on a marital adventure that will take her everywhere but back to Texas to live. I wonder where her mother would be today if I had not kept begging her to return home.

One life is simply not enough for all the lessons there are to learn. Thank God for grandchildren! I would like my epitaph to read, "To be continued."

Je vous embrasse,<br>Bess


March 1, 1963<br>Dallas

Dear Marian,

I was so distressed to learn of Lydia's fall and loss of consciousness. I pray she will recover, but in the event of her death, I think the more practical course is to bury her there and avoid the expense of bringing the body back to the family plot in Honey Grove. I am sure it is her wish to remain as close to you in death as she has in life—

and to put you to as little trouble as possible. Let me know if you need help of any kind.

Your loving aunt,<br>Bess

March 15, 1963<br>Dallas

Dearest Lydia,

I am delighted to hear of your amazing recovery—and sorry if you were offended by the suggestions I offered your daughter in advance of her bereavement. But I felt it was my responsibility to indicate a few guidelines to follow in the event of your death, since you had failed to make your thoughts on the subject known to her. Please be assured that no one could be happier than I that my advice was premature.

However, I would suggest you put into written form immediately all your wishes concerning the future disposition of your person and property. This is a step I took some time ago—soon after my return from South America when I had to face the brutal fact that I was not going to live forever. Naturally any such document can be amended to accommodate changing circumstances. I meet with Walter at least once a year to revise my will.

I know many people our age who refuse to discuss or even to consider the possibility of their death. But I deem it an act of the utmost irresponsibility to place the burden of one's demise on one's survivors. Whatever regrets I take with me to my grave, they will not include one at having left *anything* unsaid.

This past December I made new arrangements with the mausoleum which has been my second home since I brought Rob and Robin back to Dallas. I decided to purchase a family corner consisting of six crypts in addition to the two I already own. In lieu of my usual Christmas checks, I gave crypts to Eleanor and Walter and Andrew and Nell. They were visibly stunned but I assured them they would be grateful later. Sam and I will of course occupy the two remaining crypts and I have an option on an adjoining one for any grandchild who chooses not to marry. Though a person may cherish independence in life, no one should be alone in death.

I have visited all the leading morticians in this area to compare prices and services and have already made my selection, along with a sizable down payment. My children will undoubtedly be too overcome by grief on the day of my death to consider cutting corners, so I have done it for them.

I have also discussed with Dean O'Brien at the Cathedral the service I envision for my funeral. However, I am keeping an open letter with my will, reiterating my wishes in the event he should precede me in death, leaving my last rites to a stranger. My children refuse to listen when I try to discuss funeral arrangements with them, finding the topic unbearably grim, so unless I put it in writing I am afraid no one will remember that my favorite hymn is "The Battle Hymn of the Republic."

Forgive me for dwelling at such length on a subject that may be as abhorrent to you as it appears to be to everyone else I know. Sam flies into a rage if I attempt to question him about his final wishes and berates me till bedtime for assuming I will outlive him. Sometimes it is hard for me to remember what a gentle, sweet-tempered man he was when I married him. His doctor insists the change in his personality has nothing to do with me but results from the hardening of the arteries that so often accompanies old age. I cling desperately to this consoling thought as I struggle to keep from drowning in the ocean of his abuse.

And yet for all his bitterness at being deprived of his sight and robust health, I never saw a man less ready to die. His stubborn insistence on continuing to live every day just as he always has and at the same time refusing to enjoy a minute of it causes me more pain than my own considerable infirmities. When I am with him, I am ready to die whether he is or not. This may sound like heresy but you do not know how fortunate you were to lose your husband while you still loved him. Life can be as cruel a thief as death, stripping a person of all the qualities that once inspired love and leaving only a hate-provoking shell.

I am so happy to think of you recovering your strength and remaining as alert as ever in mind and spirit. Even though we no longer see each other, I am stronger just knowing you are there.

Devotedly,

Bess

May 15, 1963
Dallas

Dear Dwight and Totsie,

I have been feeling very old since the death last month of my stepmother, who was actually younger than I. However, the enclosed clipping from *The New York Times* makes me happy I am still alive. It is the first time that august journal has ever taken notice of anyone in my family, though I have subscribed to it faithfully for over forty years. And now not just an article—but a photograph as well. It was a happy day for me, loving the theater as I do, when my oldest granddaughter married an aspiring playwright, but I am thrilled to have the drama critics confirm my high opinion of his talent with an award of excellence—even though it was for what is known as an Off-Broadway production.

When I called to offer congratulations, I was greeted with more good news, though nothing worthy of *The Times'* attention: my first great-grandchild will arrive with the new year. Suddenly seventy-two does not seem old at all. I even feel like getting down my suitcases. Now that I have family living in New York again, I am overwhelmed with the desire to make one last round of the theaters.

And after that I may appear on your doorstep. What fun it would be to spend time with the only other two people my age who are as young as I.

A bientôt—j'espère,

Bess

May 16, 1963
Dallas

Ma petite Betsy,

Much as I adore being the first to know about anything, I would have gladly relinquished the honor this morning. Your premature announcement to me has caused your dear mother immense pain.

When you told me yesterday that I was about to become a great-grandmother, I assumed you had already shared the glad tidings with your parents. I immediately made an appointment with your father to revise my will. We were discussing inheritance taxes in his office when your mother stopped by, hoping to find him free for lunch. She was stunned to learn of your impending motherhood from me and not from you. Your father was equally shocked, having assumed we were discussing great-grandchildren in general and not realizing the occasion for our meeting had been provided by the imminent arrival of a particular great-grandchild. Like many lawyers, I am afraid that, in looking for the forest, he too often misses the trees.

Under ordinary circumstances your mother would never allow me to see her disappointment—in anything—but this time it was too new to hide, and she let me take her in my arms to comfort her for the first time since 1936 when she found her poet lover living with a man. How ironic that it took a slight from her daughter to return my daughter to my waiting arms—if only for a moment.

Your father, clearly feeling that so much emotion was out of place in the office of a prominent attorney, especially when the tears were streaming from the faces of his immediate family, was enormously relieved when I invited your mother to have lunch with me. He went as far as the elevator with us, then hurried off to a Community Chest luncheon for which we had already made him several minutes late.

I was quite flattered when your mother decided to cancel her afternoon sculpture class at the Art Museum and spend the rest of the day with me. We did some shopping at Neiman-Marcus (though hardly a sales clerk there these days remembers my name—and I feel the merchandise is slipping a bit, too) but mostly we just talked, saying things to each other we have left unsaid for the past quarter century. I cannot tell you how sad I was when she finally had to leave me for her own family.

I have never spoken to you of the estrangement that has existed between your mother and me since she left my house for hers. Instead I concentrated my attention on you in silence, trying to conceal my disappointment in my daughter by my devotion to her daughter. But even in my silence I must be to blame for your miscalculation in making me the first to know about the baby. If so, I apologize for allowing you to see my neglect and thereby encouraging you to accord me the respect you owe your mother. I am speaking to you now not as a grandmother but as the mother of your mother—the daughter I adore—when I beg you to call home tonight and share your good news with someone who loves you even more than I do.

But I also beg you not to allow this reprimand to reflect in any way on my joy at the thought of seeing another generation come to life before I die. Though I am not free to discuss the terms of my will with you at this time, be assured I am doing everything in my power to see that my estate provides for the needs of your children and hopefully for their children as well. I trust my immediate survivors will not take offense at my decision to delay the division of my estate and the ensuing distribution of principal for as long as possible under law. Your father, who is one of those immediate survivors, of course, made no attempt to talk me out of it. Perhaps by now he considers it a useless exercise to try to talk me out of anything, but I would prefer to believe he agrees with my feeling that I will have done enough for my children and grandchildren during my lifetime. Those who have profited from my life should not expect to derive further profit from my death. Your children and grandchildren, on the other hand, will know me only as the name on a check that arrives quarterly, but I hope in time they will come to understand that the name belonged to someone who loved them sight unseen.

I cannot wait to be with you until you come home for Christmas, so I have decided to fly to New York for a quick visit. I have made reservations at the Algonquin so that I can get to the theater on my own every night. (At my age it is unwise to depend on the kindness of taxi drivers.) I am reserving an adjoining room for you (and your husband if he cares to join us), so that we can see as much of each other as possible during my stay.

I will be arriving at Idlewild at 5:30 P.M. on Braniff Flight 76. Trust you will be there to meet me. Please make dinner reservations at the Rainbow Room. Don't tell me it is no longer chic—I have already heard—but there is no more beautiful view in all of New York City. And how I love to dine looking down on a city.

A bientôt,
Nana


June 21, 1963
Dallas

Dear Totsie and Dwight,

I had a wonderful trip to New York. Betsy and her husband rented a limousine to meet me at the airport, a magnificent gesture in view of their limited resources. I repaid their generous welcome by taking them to the theater every night and then to dinner afterwards. They declined my offer of an adjoining room at the Algonquin, preferring the privacy of their Greenwich Village apartment. They never go to sleep before four in the morning so I did not count on their company until after lunch each day.

This left my mornings free to relocate the landmarks of my past. At the Metropolitan Museum I became so completely immersed in memories of my last visit there with Eleanor that I called a stranger by her name. When she turned around in surprise and I saw that she was no one I knew, I suddenly grew faint and confused. I was so dizzy I could hardly walk so she very kindly guided me to the front entrance and helped me down those endless stairs into a taxi.

I did not mention the incident to my grandchildren, who were waiting for me at the hotel. Though they are more inclined than their parents to treat me as an equal, I did not want their solicitude to inhibit our fun. That night at their insistence we saw the play that has caused such a stir, *Who's Afraid of Virginia Woolf?* I did not care for the playwright's message, but reveled in his language. After the theater we enjoyed a steak dinner at the Hickory House to the accompaniment of a jazz piano.

However, now that I am safely home, I do not plan to leave again —at least for awhile. Aside from that moment of dislocation in time and space while staring at El Greco's *Storm Over Toledo,* I have been in good health, but on my return I found Sam wandering around the house in a state of extreme confusion. He kept asking me where I had been. My explanation would satisfy him momentarily and then he would ask again. According to the doctor, he suffered a mild stroke in my absence and I cannot risk leaving again.

So I am afraid I will not be seeing you after all—certainly not this summer and maybe never. But perhaps it is better not to meet again —just to remember each other as we were. Please write as often as you can—it will keep me from missing you so much.

Je vous embrasse,

Bess

November 23, 1963
Dallas
4 A.M.

Dear Mrs. Kennedy,

I hope you will not allow the postmark on this letter to prevent you from reading it. Though I realize I am only one of millions who share your grief, I cannot help feeling a special kinship with you tonight.

You see, like yourself, I lost my husband when I was still young with children to raise, so I know how alone and abandoned you must feel at this moment. But unlike you, I could not direct my anger at an assassin—or at the city that harbored him.

I moved to Dallas as a new bride soon after the turn of the century and watched with pride as it welcomed people from all parts of the world, of every religious persuasion and political conviction. However, only yesterday did I realize we had also become a metropolis large enough to shelter a madman.

Today is my seventy-third birthday. Until now I have regarded every year added to my allotted three score and ten as a personal triumph. But tonight keeping vigil with my radio and television and reliving the horror of the last twelve hours, I feel for the first time that I may have lived too long.

I feel too close to you tonight to call you Mrs. Kennedy—and you are so much more a person than that title implies. Today the nation sees you only as the widow of our fallen leader, but in the weeks and months to come, you must remember what a remarkable woman you can and shall be in your own right.

Courage, ma chère Jacqueline. Je vous embrasse de tout mon coeur.

Elizabeth Steed Garner


Christmas Eve, 1963
Dallas

Dearest Lydia,

This is the last Christmas I will spend in this house, and I have insisted that the family gather here for the day. In the past I have spent the morning with Eleanor and Walter in their home and the evening with Andrew and Nell at theirs. But this year I want to be surrounded by my family in my own home.

In recent years I have given only cursory attention to Christmas decorating, leaving to the children the task of transforming their homes with trees and wreaths and candles. But today I bought the tallest fir I could find and decorated it with all the trinkets that have been stored in the attic for the last twenty years.

Sam continues in the convalescent home where he has been since he suffered a second stroke on Thanksgiving Day. I visit him every day and though he always smiles when he sees me, his conversation is usually incoherent. I have the feeling he is asking about going home and I tell him we must wait until he is well. However, the doctor holds little hope for any improvement in his condition and feels he should have constant medical supervision.

Under these circumstances there is nothing to prevent me from selling the house, since Sam's confused mental state obviates the need for his signature on the deed. And I am anxious to oversee personally the distribution of all my worldly possessions. I will require very little in the apartment to which I am planning to move and would like to see the rest properly placed with my heirs.

For the past month I have devoted the time I do not spend with Sam to compiling an extensive inventory of my personal effects and their approximate market value so that I can divide them fairly. The older grandchildren have indicated an interest in certain items and I am doing my best to accommodate them—even at the expense of my new apartment. I would much rather see my grandchildren happy than reserve the items of their choice for my own use. The younger grandchildren who are still in school have shown no interest in anything I own, but I am putting aside a representative selection for each of them so that they will not have cause later to chide me for my neglect.

The house will go on the market after the holidays, and the real estate agent assures me it will be sold within a month. I plan to leave the Christmas tree standing in the front hallway and let the children and grandchildren strip it of its decorations, taking the ones they want to keep. Any sorrow accompanying my move should soon be assuaged by the greatly anticipated arrival of my first great-grandchild.

Joyeux Noël,<br>Bess

Elizabeth Steed Garner, prominent resident of Dallas since 1909, died today at her home, a luxury apartment overlooking Turtle Creek.

She was born in 1890 in the little town of Honey Grove, 100 miles north of Dallas, which her father, Andrew Alcott, helped to found. She attended Mary Baldwin College in Virginia but left without a diploma to marry her grade-school sweetheart, Robert Randolph Steed, son of a leading Texas educator.

The young couple arrived in Dallas for their honeymoon. With the support of his wife, Mr. Steed became a leader in the burgeoning real-estate business that saw the population of Dallas grow from 90,000 to 150,000 in the nine years he lived here.

The young couple and their three children moved to St. Louis to accommodate Mr. Steed's growing involvement in the field of insurance, and in 1918 he became president of Midwestern Life Insurance Company. However, exhausted by his unstinting efforts in the final war-bond campaign of World War I, he succumbed to the influenza that reached epidemic proportions after the war and died in 1919.

His widow moved back to Dallas, though she continued to travel extensively until confined to her home by failing health. In 1922 she married a young engineer, Samson Arlington Garner, who had moved to Texas from Pennsylvania. She watched with pride as he rose through the ranks to become president of Daltex Steel Company, and when he became chairman of the board in 1960, she was a major stockholder in the company.

A member of the Dallas Shakespeare Club and charter subscriber to the civic music series and the Dallas Symphony Orchestra, Mrs. Garner devoted herself to the cultural life of the city. Her will provides for the donation of all her works of art to the Dallas Museum of Fine Arts.

In lieu of flowers, friends are asked to contribute to the memorial fund established by the Shakespeare Club in her name for the encouragement of contemporary playwrights.

Mrs. Garner is a member of St. Matthew's Episcopal Cathedral where the funeral service will be held. Burial will be in Hillcrest Mausoleum.

She is survived by a daughter, Eleanor Elizabeth Burton, and a son, Andrew Alcott Steed, both of Dallas; six grandchildren and one great-grandchild.

June 15, 1966
Dallas

City Editor
*The Dallas Morning News*
Dallas, Texas

Dear Sir:

I am enclosing an obituary notice I have composed in advance of my death for you to keep on file in your morgue. If I have omitted any essential details—beyond the cause and time of death—or if you have any further questions, please feel free to call me. I would like to spare my family any intrusion on their grief on the day of my death —and there are undoubtedly many details in my life about which they would be understandably vague.

I am also enclosing a portrait photograph which I would like for you to copy and return to me as promptly as possible. It is not the most recent photograph I possess but it is easily the most flattering, so I trust you will indulge this final vanity on my part and see that it accompanies my obituary notice in the newspaper. Surely it is my right to choose the way I would like to be remembered.

I know that *The New York Times* prepares obituaries in advance on prominent people and usually calls the subject for a personal interview. I assume *The Dallas News* does not follow this policy since I am seventy-five years old and no one has called. If there is any doubt about the prominent position I have occupied in this community, along with both my husbands, you have only to check with your editor, whose father was my neighbor and finally even my friend.

I realize of course that the obituary notice may not be printed exactly as I composed it; however, I would be very interested in seeing any edited version. Perhaps you would be kind enough to submit one for my approval when you return the photograph.

Sincerely,
Bess Steed Garner

P.S. I have also drafted my husband's obituary notice, which I am enclosing. In view of his failing health, you would be well advised to place it in a more current file than you do mine.

August 10, 1967
Dallas

Dear Dwight and Totsie,

There was a time when I wanted desperately to move to New York. But the children were young and Sam asked me to marry him and so it is only now, over forty years later, that I am experiencing the exhilaration of an independent life in a high-rise apartment of my own. Of course I am looking down on Turtle Creek, not Central Park, but at night all I see are the bright lights and I could be in any big city in the world.

Many of my friends have expressed a wish to return to the little towns where they were born to spend their twilight years but to me there is nothing to match sunset in the city. I take great comfort in the thought of all the strangers living above and below me in this building—of all the lives I have not touched going on around me. I exult in the size of this city and the rate at which it continues to grow. And living in the midst of it, I no longer feel I have been deprived of anything. I am sorry Lydia died without having had her own apartment. She went from her parents to her husband to her daughter without ever living a life that was completely her own.

My devoted housekeeper, who has shared my life longer than either of my husbands, is enjoying our present life style as much as I am. Fortunately she is a decade younger than I am, and still capable of driving an automobile with impunity. When I sold my house, I bought a new Oldsmobile Cutlass and registered it in her name, though I am responsible for its maintenance until I die. Every after- noon we set out on our rounds and drive till sundown when we pause to see Sam.

He has finally stopped asking about going home and yesterday I understood why. He and our former neighbor, Mrs. Perkins, were seated side by side on the sun porch when I arrived for my afternoon visit, sharing the contented silence of two people who have long since said everything they have to say. Then to my amazement I saw that they were holding hands. They greeted me politely but with no recognition of any earlier role I had played in either of their lives.

From previous conversation I assumed my neighbor still had some grasp of reality. She questioned me extensively at the time I sold my house and seemed quite concerned at what she clearly considered my final abandonment of my husband. She always took pity on him when I left town on an extended trip and during my absences he was a frequent dinner guest in her home. Yesterday I could almost suspect that her seeming indifference to my presence was caused more by her solicitude for Sam than by any reduction in her mental capacity.

When Sam finally spoke, he asked if I saw the family of redbirds nesting outside the window. I did not have to look to know that he was talking about a window he had not seen in almost four years. I realized then that he was back in our breakfast room on Drexel Drive and the hand he thought he was holding was mine. Whatever her motive, I could only be grateful to my former neighbor for providing the illusion of my constant presence and allowing me the freedom of an independent life.

Betsy and her husband have been here with the baby all summer. It is such a miracle to see another generation coming to consciousness. I would be quite content to spend every day in their company but I try to limit my visits to twice a week. I take the whole family out to dinner whenever I can in an attempt to repay the delight my great-grandchild has given me.

She talks all the time and I cannot tell you the thrill it gives me to hear a new little voice saying, "Nana." I telephone every night just before her bedtime and talk to her until her mother takes the phone away. She never says very much but her mother assures me she listens enthralled, and I love telling her how much she has meant to me, whether she understands what I am saying or not. I have always enjoyed the telephone but the members of my family never seem to have time for the leisurely conversations I prefer. I suppose my great-granddaughter will soon be too busy for me too, but I am thankful that at the age of three she is still fascinated by everything I have to say.

The only other person who will listen as long as I care to talk is Sam. Every night after dinner I retire to my bed and from there I call to tell him good night. One night I was attending the theater with my friends the Townsends and forgot to call, and the next day the nurse told me Sam would not allow her to turn off his bedside light that night. He made her understand that he wanted to be able to see the telephone so he could answer it when it rang. She tried to tell him that the switchboard had closed but he just kept shaking his head and shouting if she got near the light. He finally fell asleep with the light shining in his face.

Since that night, no matter where I am, I have never forgotten to call and say good night. He does not have much more to say on the other end than my great-grandbaby and while her vocabulary grows daily, his diminishes. But I know he is listening and if I ask a question often enough, he will finally make some sort of sound in reply. Of course I have no idea what he is saying but then I never ask a question without already knowing the answer.

Betsy is encouraging me to fly to Los Angeles this fall for the premiere of her husband's new play at the theater complex that has just opened there, and I am very tempted to accept. Why don't the two of you meet me there and you can see what my family has produced in the way of plays and progeny? Both levels of production fill me with pride and I love being included in their lives. I do worry about leaving Sam, though I would of course call him every night long distance. I wonder if he would miss my visits every afternoon. Unfortunately there is no way to be sure.

I cannot get the thought of the trip out of my mind. We have maintained our friendship by letter for too long. And now, with so many of my dearest friends and relatives beyond my reach forever, I want nothing more than to put my arms around you both.

I remember in French class freshman year when we learned the expression "j'ai le coeur gros" to denote a heart swollen with emotion. At the time it seemed like a rather vulgar expression to me but that was before I knew how crude and vulgar life can be at the end as, one by one, we lose everyone we love. Everything in me aches and throbs to be with you. "J'ai le coeur gros" when I think of you and my longing will not be satisfied until the two of you are once again in my embrace.

Je vous embrasse,

Bess

November 23, 1967
Dallas

Dearest Totsie and Dwight,

My suitcase was packed for a morning flight to Los Angeles when the call came that Sam had died peacefully in his sleep. I had seen him in the afternoon and told him good night by telephone and I am so grateful I was here. I canceled my reservations and very much doubt now that I will ever leave Dallas again.

I look around at how few of my friends are left. We are like the survivors of some terrible storm. The quality of life can no longer concern us. For the moment it is enough just to exist. And so we must go about the business of burying our dead and try not to think beyond the simple tasks that each day presents.

When I called Betsy to tell her about Sam, she told me the news she had been saving for my visit to California: another great-grand-child is on the way. So how can I despair when my announcement of death is met with the promise of new life? It is extremely danger-ous to fly during the early months of pregnancy so I insisted she stay safely in Los Angeles and not consider coming home for the funeral.

I am very tired. I look at the suitcases standing empty beside my closet and wonder how I could have contemplated such a long trip.

It is getting late now. I will eat dinner and then I must not forget to call Sam—


November 24, 1967

Mrs. Garner suffered a massive stroke last night. The doctor said it would have been fatal for anyone else her age but apparently she has the constitution of someone much younger. When I was packing her suitcase to take to the hospital, I found this letter beside her bed. I know how strongly she feels about leaving letters unanswered, so I am sending it on to you, even though it appears to be unfinished.
Sincerely,
Marthareen Jenkins
Housekeeper to Mrs. Garner

June 19, 1968
Dallas

Dear Betsy,

It is hard for me but I want you to know. Baby is beautiful. Like child of Cloud Fairy. I want to hold. Not just pictures. When will we see? You can go and leave baby here. I will hold tight to her hand when car comes. Trust me. Soon baby will walk, thinking I am always behind. Not to be afraid. All you have to teach.

Guests coming soon. Eleanor, too. And still no flowers on the table. I must go into the garden. Nothing blooms here and where did redbirds go? I want to go far away. Another country. So many places I never saw.

This is a strange land. Sun never stops shining. I am so tired. I want to sleep but light in my eyes. Must call Sam so he to bed. Then I can sail. Dining with Captain tonight. Write me. I want letters waiting.

A Dieu,
Nana